BEWARE
THE WOLF

PARANORMAL INVESTIGATIONS TEAM

BOOK 1

Prologue

Ash

"Ashlyn Kyria Caitlyn Doyle." Ash kept her gaze front and centre as Caitlyn whirled in her direction, and the Fates kept on speaking, this time in perfect unison.

"You have meddled with the hands of fate when you should not have. You have divulged destinies that you should not have. You have changed the course of the future when you were ordered not to. For that, you cannot go unpunished."

"No. Leave her alone."

Zach was on his knees a heartbeat later, gasping for air and clutching at his throat. Everyone tried to move around her, yet they were somehow frozen. Zach's face turned red, and Ash pushed past everyone to stand in front of Zach.

"He has done nothing wrong. I have. I accept that I must be punished, but please—I will bear whatever punishment if you leave him unharmed."

The three sisters shared a look, then they nodded, and Zach was suddenly gone, vanished as if he had not been gasping for air a mere moment ago.

"He has been returned from whence he came. Unharmed. We will allow you a moment to say farewell, then we will administer punishment."

Ash spun as her parents engulfed her in a tight embrace. "I love you both so, so much."

Her dad gripped her face in his hands, eyes wolf amber. "I am *so very proud of you, my beautiful girl. I will love you until my last breath."*

Ash was crying now as Derek stepped aside to let Ever embrace her. Ash had to hope that her mom was strong enough to defeat Odin. "Thank you for coming back. For making me see. For letting me love you. I love you."

"Kick his ass for me, Mom. Kick his ass."

Ash nodded to Caitlyn, Melanie, and Erika, then lifted her hammer and strode over to where the Fates stood. She jerked her chin up and felt the steel of her family at her back as she inclined her head to the Fates.

"I'm ready to go home."

Skuld pursed her lips as if pondering Ash's punishment. "Since your birth, we have wondered if the considerable amount of power in you would influence the path of destiny, and it has. You are cocky, unapologetic, reckless, and under the false belief that you are invincible."

Urðr looked at the hammer tattoo on her forearm. "Thor was an adult when he inherited the power of Mjölnir, and he took his responsibilities seriously. You consider it a birthright. We will ensure you learn from that misconception."

Verðandi grabbed her arm, and Ash thought she was being burnt alive as she screamed, the tattoo on her flesh searing and bubbling as the Fate singed it from her skin. She dropped Mjölnir, her beloved hammer vanishing before her eyes, and Ash cried, for it was like losing a limb.

Her body jerked, the movement taking with it the strength and magic that made her worthy of wielding Thor's hammer. She sagged to the ground, her wolf in her eyes as she searched for the part of her that made her a goddess.

She did not find it.

"You have been stripped of the magic that allowed you to be chosen by Thor. You are still wolf, and you are still Valkyrie.

Should you earn the right to be made worthy once again, then Mjölnir will be returned to you. Let us see if destiny is all."

Oh gods, she was dying. This pain, this loss was immense as she staggered to her feet, unable to turn to face the people she loved the most as Skuld clicked her fingers, and suddenly she was standing in the apartment she shared with Zach.

Her legs gave out, too much loss to deal with, as strong arms went around her and kept her from falling to the ground.

"It's okay. I've got you. I've always got you."

She let Zach hold her, tears staining her face, soaking his tee as he reassured her that she was okay, that everything would be okay.

"I am so very proud of you, my beautiful girl. I will love you until my last breath."

Her dad's words played out in her head again, and Ash knew that losing her hammer now didn't mean she had lost it forever. She might know what happened in the past, but the future was still unwritten. Her story was not over yet, and she would be the one to wield the pen and write her own chapters.

When she was done wallowing in her sadness, Ash swept the tears from her eyes, remembering that she was not helpless. She was the daughter of Derek Doyle and Ever Chace, and she would work twice as hard to prove she was worthy.

The door to the apartment swung open, and eyes of dark brown swept over her. "Still alive, then?"

"Fuck off, brat. I can't deal with you right now."

Her baby brother stepped aside as Derek Doyle loomed in the doorway, his eyes a shock of amber, his hair speckled with a little grey around the ears as he glared at Ash with that alpha stare of his.

Ash waved at him, ignoring Gideon as he stuck out his tongue at her while her dad stepped closer. She took a step back as the full force of his wolf bore down on hers, and she knew he was seething with anger right about now.

"Hey, Daddy. Miss me?"

Chapter One

Ash

FIVE YEARS LATER

"Watch your six, Ash!"

Her best friend and partner's voice sounded in her earpiece a single second before the supe she had been tracking managed to sneak up behind her and would have shredded her with wicked claws had she not jerked to the right, slamming into the stone brick hard.

Her hand instinctively rose to summon her beloved hammer, Mjölnir, and then that ache in her chest when she remembered that Mjölnir was lost to her, like a phantom limb that still called out to her. Five years had passed since her little trip into the past had cost her Mjölnir, but the pain of that never got easier.

Ash pushed off the wall and took off after the goblin. The goblin had been linked to several wolves that had been murdered and Ash was determined to find out exactly what the goblin knew. If she'd had Mjölnir then she could have swung her hammer and knocked the idiot on his ass instead of having to chase after him.

But Ash was still a wolf who enjoyed the thrill of the hunt.

Pumping her arms, Ash ducked and weaved through the people on Cork's North Main Street, shouting that she was P.I.T. as she ran. Everyone knew to get out of the damned way when one of the agents of the Paranormal Investigations Team was chasing down an unsub.

Her dad had been one of the founding members of P.I.T., along with her aunt Caitlyn, and now, her dad was the head of the entire department. There were units all over Ireland and even some European countries were beginning to use the Irish model to police the supernaturals in their country.

Ash herself had only been barely sixteen when she had become an agent in the same class as her best friend. It might have seemed young, but the fact that she wielded her hammer was one of the reasons why she had been allowed to apply so early. And working with Zach meant she always had someone she trusted watching her six.

Zachary Moore was older than her by five years, but from the moment that Ash had been born, the two of them had been inseparable. He was a cat shifter, and a warlock, who had been raised by his dad, Ricky, her dad's best friend, and Melanie, his stepmom. Zach's biological mom had died when he was five and Uncle Ricky hadn't even known he had a son.

But Ricky and Melanie had raised Zach, and he was one of the smartest people she knew.

Their lives sounded very soap opera when you tried to explain it to anyone who had not grown up with them. Ash had travelled to the past when she was nearly seventeen to stop her mother from going through with her original decision to not have her, and in doing so, Ash had revealed too much, changed too much in the future, and was still being punished for her actions.

And that's not even considering her sociopath of a mate who Ash hadn't seen in a while.

Ash caught sight of the goblin as he darted down a side lane, then heard Zach's voice in her ear. "I got the front; you block him from escaping back the way he came."

She went down after the goblin, her eyes adjusting to the

darkness with an ease that was all wolf. She inhaled as she ran, Zach's unique scent alerting her that her best friend was exactly where she needed him to be. Ash heard him shout at the goblin to stop, and then Ash could see the creature scurrying back the way he had come, heading straight toward her.

Ash flattened herself against the wall, knowing that the goblin's eyesight wasn't as good as hers in the darkness and they had a shit sense of smell. She waited until he was a few feet from her location, then stuck her foot out. The goblin shrieked as he fell over her foot, landed on the ground with a thud, and Ash put her booted foot down on his back and growled.

The goblin went still at the sound of it.

Zach jogged up the lane, a grin curving his lips as he took out a set of cuffs and then put them on the goblin's wrists. Hauling him up once Ash took her boot off his back, Zach had one hand on the scruff of his neck and the other on one of his arms.

"Dude, that was stupid. You know better than to turn rabbit and run when all we wanted to do was talk to ya."

The goblin shook his head. "I know nothing about nothing."

Ash rolled her eyes, then jerked her head toward the top of the lane and she and Zach started to move. "Sure you don't. You can try and convince us of that back at the station."

The goblin tried to kick her in the shin, but Zach shoved him forward. When they got to the end of the alleyway, Ash saw that Zach's car was idling on the street. The idiot probably left the keys in it too. Zach opened the back door and shoved the goblin in, then turned to face Ash.

There was no denying that Zach was handsome. Black hair that was slicked back and sometimes reached down to his shoulders. Green eyes that sparkled with mischief. He had taken to wearing a bit more scuff than usual the last year, and now that he had invented a pair of contacts that he could wear to avoid the thick rimmed glasses he'd used to need there was no denying why her bestie was never short of the offer of a lover.

Zach was tall too, a little taller than her, with broad shoulders, and a body that was honed with muscle and agility, part of it being his shifter physiology and part of it the training they had done to get to where they were and continued to do.

"Why are you looking at me like that?" Zach asked her as he leaned against the car and arched a brow.

Ash grinned, giving him a deadpan look as she replied. "I was just thinking that you are a handsome bastard."

Zach rolled his eyes. "I know. But when you've stopped admiring me for the perfect specimen that I am, maybe we can take the detainee back to the station and finish this shift?"

"Hot date?" Ash asked as she shoved him out of the way to get into the passenger side of the car.

Zach chuckled, walking round to his side and leaned on the roof of the car. "I wish. Your dad asked me to give mom a hand with the new recruits with the technical stuff."

It made sense that her dad would ask Zach. Melanie had taught him all she knew about technology and her dad would have kept him out of the field and staying in the lab if he hadn't of needed someone out there with Ash.

And besides, her uncle Arik was just as good as Zach with the techy stuff. Though Arik was younger than her by just over a year, he was her mother's brother, and the son of her grandmother Freya, and Zach's uncle Killian. Everyone, including Freya, had been surprised when she had fallen in love with Ricky's brother, and then pregnant with Arik after everything that had happened to her grandmother with Odin. Freya had been forced to pretend to be hard and cruel, and her pregnancy with Ever had not been a joyous one.

And while her pregnancy had been an easy, happy event, when Arik was born, Freya realized that her son had inherited the powers of her late brother Freyr, and the infant had the ability to make anyone fall in love with him. So in order to stop a riot, Arik stayed in Ops and only hung out with his family and friends, people who already loved him, so as not to influence them with his power.

Leaning back in her seat, Ash sighed, and fiddled with the star chain around her neck. "Don't go easy on the bratlets. Just cause they are family doesn't mean they get an easy time of it. We certainly didn't."

Zach laughed, shaking his head. "I think after all the shit we've put them through, Gideon and Lyra will be grand. You know Gideon feels like he has something to prove since your dad only just let him join up."

Her younger brother, Gideon, had been born with no other powers than the ability to shift into a wolf. Their parents had waited for some godlike powers to manifest and when they didn't, her dad decided that Gideon would have to wait until he was at least eighteen to join up. And then to give him an extra year, they had sent both Gideon and Lyra, Erika and Loki's daughter, off to Valhalla to train with the Valkyrie.

It was weird to think of Gideon as an agent of P.I.T., and she worried about him. She had always been a little bit of an asshole about the fact she was worthy of the powers of Thor, and her brother was just normal, but now that she was just a wolf with added Valkyrie, Ash hated how she had treated Gideon.

They drove to the station in relative silence, Zach tapping his fingers on the steering wheel in time with the music playing. Thunder rumbled overhead and Ash pressed her face to the window, then watched as lightning streaked through the sky. The ache in her chest felt like a boulder in her chest.

"Should you earn the right to be made worthy once again, then Mjölnir will be returned to you."

Ash had been trying since the day she returned from the past to be worthy of Mjölnir, and she had not heard a damn word from the Fates. You would think that having played her part in stopping the world from ending would give the Fates a dose of happy endorphins and give her back the piece of her that was missing.

Ash felt a hand land on her thigh, looked over to see that Zach had placed his hand on her leg to steady her. He knew that the sound of thunder always made her feel this wave of sadness, and he was trying to show her that he was there for her without saying a word.

When they arrived at the station, they handed the goblin over to the supes at the desk to be processed and they headed to the break room to grab something to eat before they went and interviewed the goblin. Ash was suddenly starving as she pushed open the door and almost groaned when she caught sight of the takeout on the side. Heading straight over to the box of chicken nuggets, Ash tossed one into her mouth.

"As sophisticated as always, A.K."

Ash flipped Zach off as he grabbed a sandwich and flopped down on the couch, letting out a sigh. The room was empty at the moment, but it was normally full of other members of the team. Killian Moore was their section leader, his partner Chrissy Canty just under him. Kenzie Blake was also part of their team when she wasn't on special assignment. Then there was her and Zach, Arik, and the newest member of their team, Torin McNamara.

Torin had been brought in by her dad almost six months ago and Ash still knew very little about the vampire other than his ability meant that he could be standing in a room full of people and not a single person would realize he was there.

Ash walked over to the couch, lifted Zach's legs up and then sat down, letting go of his legs letting them rest across her lap. He wiggled his fingers, and she tossed him a nugget, then ate two more in quick succession. They stayed in the break room for like ten minutes before the door opened and Arik came in.

"Alright cuz." Zach said in greeting and Arik smiled, his shoulders relaxing.

Ash wondered what it would feel like to be compelled by Arik's powers to love him. When Ash had been old enough to understand what Arik's powers could do, she had gone to him and asked if there was any way his power could kill a mating bond. Arik had looked so grief stricken as he shook his head, but Ash had just hugged him, telling him she would find a way to break it...

And yet, five years later, she wasn't any closer to finding a way to make it happen.

Just before she had gone into the past, Ash had been driven to follow this thread inside her that lead her to her mate. Her mate turned out to be Fenrir, the monstrous wolf of Norse lore and Ash had no choice when the bond snapped into being.

Fenrir, or Grey, as Ash called him, had followed her to the past and when she had returned, minus her beloved hammer, Ash had been in so much pain, so much anguish that she had taken it out on Grey. She'd sworn to him that she would find a way to end the bond between them and she hated him, despised seeing him all the time.

Grey had simply stood there and taken the abuse that Ash hurled at him, then vanished. Zach had been the one to offer her comfort as she broke down. That had been over four years ago, and she only felt or saw Grey from a distance. Ash flexed inside her mind, reaching for the mating bond but she only got static. The line that had once been open and clear was now shut off and Ash had no clue what had happened to it.

Ash blinked out of her thoughts as Zach sat up and Arik leaned in the doorway. He wore a long-sleeved shirt buttoned at the wrist, and a waistcoat over it. He wore a tie, and his dress slacks were black. Arik had high cheekbones, and a face that showed that he was descendant of gods. His brownish blonde hair was gelled back to reveal ice blue eyes.

"The boss has called everyone to the training centre. There's been more wolf killings."

Ash and Zach exchanged a look. The killer was escalating. What had started out as one kill a week had quickly turned to one kill every second day. Ash had never been on a case of a killer who had increased their kills so rapidly.

"How many?"

Arik shifted, running a hand down his tie. "I think Caitlyn said there were five bodies. Same MO."

Shit…this was bad…this was really bad.

Both Ash and Zach got to their feet, and Zach headed out first, leaving Ash to link her arm through Arik's. She knew her uncle was nervous in crowded rooms and usually her and Zach kept an eye on him to make sure that his anxiety didn't spike and cause him to leak his power. The last time that had happened, a lion shifter had started to pull off Arik's clothes, completely under the spell and Killian had set the shifter on fire to protect his son.

Arik had not come in to work for a week after that incident.

Ash strode into the training centre, walking right over to where Killian and Chrissy stood. Killian nudged his son on the shoulder and grinned, and Arik rolled his eyes. Zach slotted himself in to stand beside Ash, as she glanced around. She spotted all of the original members of P.I.T. and her family standing over at the side.

Zach's parents were standing at the top of the room, talking, as were Caitlyn Hardi and Donnie O'Carroll. Erika Sands, Loki's mate and Lyra's mom was leaning against the wall, her eyes closed but there was no doubt the Valkyrie general, and goddess of war, was fully aware of everything going on around her.

Ash's gaze fell on the new recruits, and to the stoney expression of her younger brother. As if he felt her eyes on him, Gideon lifted his amber eyes to hers, gave her a look, and Ash lifted her middle finger to give him a little sibling greeting. Gideon bared his teeth, knowing that there was no way he could retaliate with everyone watching the new recruits so closely.

"Anyone have any idea what this gathering is all about?"

Ash jumped at the sound of Torin's voice, the vampire there in the blink of an eye. Punching him in the shoulder, the vampire just laughed, his brown eyes dancing. Ash also noted how Arik had stiffened at the sound of Torin's voice, and Torin was also acutely aware of it.

"Arik."

"Torin."

The clipped tone from her uncle made Torin grin.

Ash turned so that she faced the team. "I'm getting you a bell."

"Oh a collar. Kinky."

Zach barked out a laugh as Ash shook her head, but she could see her uncle's cheeks pinken at what Torin had said. When Torin stepped into the spot Ash had vacated, Arik shifted further toward his father like he was afraid to touch Torin.

If the vampire noted Arik's unease, he didn't show it.

Torin was still a mystery to them all. He had shown up with her dad six months ago and been inserted into the team. Ash had tried to pry some information from the vampire, who was older than his Ben Barnes good looks gave off, but without much success. Ash and Zach had both tried to involve him in things and sometimes Torin showed up, and other times, he didn't.

Ash looked at Killian. "You have any more ideas about why we are all here?"

Killian shrugged, then Ash saw him frown making her look at Zach. Her best friend's eyes were wide, his lips parted, and it was then that Ash felt a familiar aura that made her whirl round, a snarl on her lips.

Her dad was standing beside the rest of his team, his lips pressed firmly together, his eyes searching for her and when they did, his expression softened. But Ash's attention was on the creature standing beside her father.

Gone was the inky black hair that she had run her fingers through, it was now cut tight to his skull in a way that Ash knew would feel sharp against her palms. He had a dark stubble and a beard that seemed to make him even more goddamn attractive. Black eyes that looked unfeeling and dead starred into the crowd. His body, clad in all black, looked even more toned in the time since she had seen him. Her wolf howled inside her head and Ash took an involuntary step toward the man who had yet to look at her, her mate, the man she loved to hate...

What the fuck was Grey doing with her dad?

Chapter Two

Fenrir

THE URGE TO GO TO HIS MATE ALMOST THREATENED TO BE HIS undoing. Fenrir had made a point of not seeking Ashlyn out the moment he had stepped into the room with her father. Not that he did not know exactly where she was standing. Her scent was a lure to him, her aura like a siren's song that he had been devoid of for too long.

Fenrir forced his features to remain impassive, as his hold on the mating bond threatened to slip from his grasp. When Ashlyn had sent him away with the promise of severing the bond, Fenrir had found a way to stop his thoughts from filtering down the bond to Ashlyn. However it had left him open to all of her feelings, her thoughts, and there were times when his mind was so full of things that he did not understand, that he felt like he was going mad.

He had been...surprised...when Ashlyn's father had come to him and asked for his help on this case. When Fenrir had snorted and said to Derek Doyle that he was most certainly the wrong person for this type of job, the alpha wolf had told Fenrir that he needed a wolf whose mind worked differently to those on his teams so they could catch this killer.

Fenrir had agreed to partake in this hunt purely because it served his own desire to be closer to Ashlyn. He cared not for a killer who was murdering wolves. Joining in on the hunt simply gave him access to his mate, and he had less of a chance of her being angry with him if it was her father who was responsible for their proximity.

A murmur of voices sounded amongst those gathered and he heard his name. Shifting his gaze ever so slightly, his youngest sister, Lyra waved at him. Fenrir inclined his head. Lyra had never treated him like he was something other than her brother, and as much as he was able to, he felt a sort of kinship with her. Lyra was like him; an anomaly, the daughter of a god, and he was curious to see what that would entail for her.

Their other sister, Hel was the goddess of death, and Fenrir humoured her when she visited him because she was one of the few creatures who might in fact be able to kill him. He did not think Lyra would be able to do that, however he wasn't 100% certain because after all her mother was the daughter of the god of war.

Derek cleared his throat and held up his hand to silence the crowd. Fenrir admired the way in which the wolf had power over a variety of different supernatural creatures. All of their attention was on their boss, though some kept glancing at him, trying to figure out who and what he was.

"Listen up," Derek started, folding his arms across his chest. Fenrir watched his gestures, his stance, looking for a weakness, even though he wasn't planning on killing the other wolf. Not when killing Ashlyn's father would give her even more reason to be angry with him.

"Five more wolves were killed last night. That's a massive escalation. We are almost absolutely certain that the killer is another wolf. Every resource we have will now be focused on this case and this case alone. Senior agents Hardi and O'Carroll will be handing out assignments. All leave is cancelled until further notice. We need everyone on board to catch this bastard."

Derek glanced over his shoulder at Fenrir, then back to

his agents. "I have called in every available agent to help us hunt down the killer. I've also brought in an expert on abnormal wolves who will be working closely on this with us. If you have any questions for Agent Grey Wulfe, then please come to one of us or the senior agents."

Fenrir heard Ashlyn snort at the name, even though he could still feel her annoyance through the bond. It had taken him time to learn what each emotion meant, and to filter them though it was now harder with the pathway from him to Ashlyn being closed off.

"You have an hour to eat, sleep or whatever the hell you want, but then you will report to your team lead for assignments." Derek shifted his gaze to Killian Moore, the uncle of Ashlyn's cat. "Agent Moore hold your team back a moment please."

Fenrir kept his eyes on the crowd, assessing for any threats, was unprepared when Lyra came over and grinned at him. "You never said you were gonna be working with us when you came by last week."

Fenrir looked at his sister. "I did not know then. Derek only came to me a few hours ago."

Lyra put her hand on Fenrir's arm, and he had to tell himself that this was normal amongst siblings. "Maybe we could spar some day when things die down? Or we could have dinner?"

Fenrir tried to see how doing either of those things might benefit him, however he could not see a way in which they would. He remembered the advice his father had given him, the words he had written in the journal his father had given him as a gift, that sometimes people did things for others that was of no benefit to them, especially for family.

He still could not see the point in that if he was being honest.

Lyra blinked, her shoulders sagging when Fenrir still had

not answered her, and it occurred to him that making Lyra happy would please her parents, and since he needed Loki to give him advice on the ways of being human, Fenrir needed to keep Loki onside.

"I'm sure we could find time to spar."

Lyra grinned and gave his arm a squeeze. "That's gonna be awesome. Thanks bro."

"Agent Sands, go find your team leader and see what tasks you are gonna be assigned." His stepmother had come over, her eyes watching Fenrir with a wariness that had not dissipated in the years he had known her.

Lyra's cheeks heated but then she was gone, hurrying off to do what her mother had told her to do. Erika came to stand in front of him, glaring at him and Fenrir just tilted his head. "Hello mother."

"I wish to fuck you would stop calling me that." She grumbled, shaking her head.

Fenrir chuckled, then said. "Lyra has asked me to spar with her. I said yes. Just so you know."

Erika had no chance to answer him because Derek called him over. Fenrir strolled over to where Derek stood and inclined his head to Ricky and Donnie. He had met the two vampires when they had freed him from the chains that Tyr had bound him in. Both Donnie and Erika had the ability to bind him once more in the chains, and Ricky was a physic vampire, who could syphon the power from his veins.

He kept them on the list of people that it made sense to have on his side.

The people in the room were still filtering out as he heard Ashlyn growl. "Are you fucking kidding me? Like a heads up that you were bringing him here would have been goddamn nice."

Fenrir turned in his mate's direction. Her anger was so palpable, Fenrir could almost feel it radiating from her skin.

He wanted to bury his nose in the crook of her neck and breathe in the scent of her rage. Her eyes burned with the force of it, and it took everything in Fenrir not to shiver at the hint of violence in them.

Fenrir did not like many things, but he did like violence. He had not known he liked violence before the mating bond snapped into place. Through the bond, and his observations of Ashlyn, he realized that the emotions she felt when she was happy, or enjoyed something, was akin to what he felt on a successful kill.

Derek arched a brow at his daughter. "I do not have to explain my actions to you, Agent Doyle. If you have a problem with working with him, then I have no problem benching you. In case you forgot, we have a devolving killer on the loose killing wolves."

Ashlyn threw her hands in the air. "So you brought in a killer to catch a killer? For fuck sake, dad, I don't want him here."

Derek growled, his nostrils flaring. Fenrir could see that the pair were about to have a massive argument, however Ashlyn's cat came over and yanked her away. A muscle ticked in Fenrir's jaw. He knew that the emotion that he was feeling was jealously and he hated it. He would have killed the cat many years ago, but doing so would not endear him to Ashlyn, for she loved that cat as much if not more than her blooded brother.

Zach must have said something to Ashlyn too low for him to hear, his hands on her shoulders, and she shoved him away, then snarled. "I don't care, Z. That psychopath is not what I need right now."

His mate knew calling him a psychopath was factually incorrect. His father had told him that the humans would categorize him as more of a sociopath since he did not understand most emotions, though the mating bond had forced him to try and make sense of the emotions Ashlyn felt. And being that he was a wolf and not human at all, his thirst for violence or his like of the hunt, was abnormal for a run of the mill sociopath.

Not that Fenrir cared how others tried to define him...he was who he was and the only person whose opinion mattered to him was Ashlyn's. He needed her to accept him and to stop with the nonsense quest of hers to break the mating bond between them.

When Ashlyn had gone to the past, the bond had suddenly gone silent and in his head, nothing had made sense. The calmness that came with being bonded to Ashlyn had vanished and all that was left of him was the animal he was underneath the human form he had taken to walk among society.

In his desperate search for her, Fenrir had almost killed Zach until he had a moment of clarity that the cat was his only way to get to Ashlyn and halt the confusion in his mind. He did not understand why she despised him, even though he knew that she was attracted to him. It reminded him of the moment his mate had appeared before him, and he had chased her through the woods.

Fenrir chased the wolf through the forest. Her scent was in his nose now, the hunt in his bones. Every single instinct in him told Fenrir that he needed to catch her, though he did not know why. When she had appeared in the mouth of the cave, a cat shifter beside her, something altered inside him.

To prevent the pair from stumbling upon Odin in the cave, Fenrir had grabbed the cat by the throat, ready to snap his neck, but the she-wolf had shouted at him not to hurt her brother. They did not smell like they were related, but he knew that his own father claimed a Valkyrie as his sister though they shared no patronage.

As Fenrir chased her, he caught the scent of her blood, knew she must have hurt herself in some way. It made it easier for Fenrir to track her, however, he found that he disliked the thought of her being hurt.

He heard her snarl of frustration as she ran deeper and deeper into the forest and if he did not get to her, she may just become lost to the magic of the woods, never to emerge.

He could see her up ahead, watched as her hood slipped from over her head and Fenrir was almost struck by how beautiful she was, her hair ash blonde and her features, they were pleasing to him. The she-wolf ground to a halt, released a breath as she frowned, and that made Fenrir chuckle softly. He knew she had heard him because she shuddered.

Ash skipped to a stop and blew out a shaky breath. His deep masculine chuckle sent shivers crawling up her spine and her wolf tilted her head in interest. He stepped beside her, inhaled the scent of her, then said. "Little wolf, little wolf. Little red hood. I do love a good chase."

Fenrir could tell that she was fighting to urge to take off once more. He watched as she withdrew a dagger from under her cape and held it against her own stomach, as if she thought he might not sense it.

"Do you know who I am, little wolf? Do you know what I am?"

"Don't know, don't care. You hurt my friend and now, I'm going to repay the favour."

Lightning quick, the she-wolf struck, sinking the blade into the curve of his neck. Fenrir hissed as the she-wolf stumbled back, as the darkness shifted suddenly, as it tended to do, and doused them in light. As Fenrir drank in the beauty of her, this she-wolf, and she glanced over her shoulder for a means to escape before she turned her attention back to him.

Her eyes widened as she looked at him, and Fenrir wondered if she liked what she saw.

Fenrir curved his lips into a smile as he stepped closer, the thrill of the hunt igniting in his veins once more with every step that she retreated as he advanced. There came a searing pain in his mind, as the she-wolf sucked in a breath.

Her thoughts, her feelings, they all filtered through this soul deep bond that Fenrir had only heard about and believed him incapable of obtaining due to his lack of emotions.

"Mine." Fenrir growled, understanding that the she-wolf was his mate.

She snorted. "I don't think so. I need to have a word with my wolf and convince her we need to make better choices. So, why don't you stay there, and I'll go have a word."

He found that he was not opposed to her feistiness.

"What is your name, little wolf?"

His mate was stubborn as she refused to answer him. He asked her again, then again, and when she refused, and Fenrir could hear her think of running. He was in front of her between one breath and the next, one hand around her throat. He could scent her arousal; knew she craved him as much as he seemed to crave her.

Fenrir pushed a little bit more power into his words. "What is your name, little wolf? I will not ask you again."

His mate rebelled against his demand, though she finally said through clenched teeth. "Ashlyn. Ash, my friends call me Ash."

Ashlyn...his mate was called Ashlyn.

Fenrir gave a little squeeze at her throat, then said. "Hello, my Ashlyn. My name is Fenrir, and I have been waiting for you for an eternity."

"Zach, I need you and Arik to get the newbies up to speed with the way you run things from the coms room. They are too green to be out in the field just yet."

"Yes sir."

Ashlyn had her arms now crossed against her chest in a defensive pose, but it did not slip Fenrir's notice that it simply pushed her breasts upward and made his palms itch to touch her. It had been an age since he had been close enough to touch her, only coming to be near her when he could no longer stand being away from her.

She did not know how much of the madness being near her chased away.

"Please don't say it. Please don't fucking say it."

Fenrir remained still as Derek turned to look at his daughter. "You will work with Fenrir. You will behave in a professional manner, or so help me Agent Doyle, I will kick your ass back into training until you stop behaving like a child."

Ashlyn looked hurt by her father's words and Fenrir had to close his eyes and reign in the urge to harm the other wolf for hurting his mate. Loki had been trying to teach him to think before he reacted in violence, though it seemed for the most part like a waste of time. However, in moments like this he had to acknowledge that Loki may have a point.

Ashlyn's emotions were so strong through the bond that Fenrir had to bite down on the inside of his mouth to not hiss out at the surge of them. He heard Donnie swear, and glared over at the mind reader, who just shook his head, as if clearing the dust from his mind.

Interesting. Fenrir made a note to himself that he would need to shield more carefully.

"If Ash wants to work with someone else, I can work with Fenrir." The cat offered, and it made Fenrir's claws want to slice through flesh and bone.

His mate looked relieved at the prospect of not having to work with him and Fenrir had to swallow down the rage inside his chest. He had given her the space she had wanted and yet still she wanted nothing to do with him.

Derek looked over his shoulder at Fenrir, and he simply lifted his shoulders like he did not care who he worked with. He finally gave into the urge to look directly at Ashlyn, and he wanted to howl and sink his teeth into her flesh, to mark her skin so everyone would know that she belonged to him and him alone.

Whatever Ashlyn saw in his eyes, she sighed, her shoulders slumping in defeat as she ground out. "I'll do it. I'll work with him. But I want my objection noted. When this goes tits up, and let me be very clear, I 100% believe that is what's going to happen, I don't want any blame for the shit he might do assigned to me."

"Noted." Came her father's gruff response and then his mate was walking toward him.

She stopped mere inches from him, her amber eyes held his brazenly. "Grey Wulfe? That's a stupid alias."

Fenrir shrugged, his eyebrow arching. "It seemed fitting at the time. Shall we get started?"

Ashlyn stood there, looking at him, and Fenrir tried and failed not to reach out and touch her. He made to tuck her hair behind her ear, a gesture he had seen men do with their mates before. Ashlyn jerked back, her amber eyes flaring.

"Don't fucking touch me. I don't belong to you."

He felt the sting of her words through the mating bond, and he growled, leaning forward so that their noses almost touched. "That is where you are wrong, Ashlyn. You are mine. We both know it." He let his lips curve into a smile. "Let us begin the hunt. I have a sudden urge to spill blood."

Chapter Three

Ash

ASH WAS FUMING AS SHE STORMED OUT OF THE TRAINING centre, feeling the heart of Grey's eyes on her. She was mad at him for agreeing to this farce, and livid at the fact that her dad had given her a dressing down in front of her entire team. Her father had not spoken to her in that tone since the day she had arrived back from the past and he had totally lost his shit with her. Then something changed in him, like the new memories slipped into place and he understood.

Right now she hated how her body reacted to Fenrir, hated how the urge to touch him was so overwhelming that Ash wanted to rub herself against him, skin to skin. Stomping down hallway she made her way to the break room when a vampire stepped into her path.

Caitlyn Hardi was one of the most beautiful women Ash had ever laid eyes on. She looked like a runway model, with shoulder length black hair, grey eyes, and a face that had once captured the attention of a vampire who became so obsessed with her that he'd killed Caitlyn's entire family in order to have her.

When Ash had gone to the past, she had finally understood what Zach had been telling her for years about how Caitlyn often smelt sad. Ash had seen it for herself, and because of that, and all that Caitlyn had done since to not succumb to the darkness, Ash respected the hell out of her even more than she originally had.

Caitlyn halted just before the door to the break room, her grey eyes lifting to Fenrir, and Ash was surprised when she gave him a warm smile. "It is good to see you, Fenrir."

There was a slight pause that told Ash that Grey was trying to figure out a response to Caitlyn's warm welcome, but the god who was her mate replied. "Lady Caitlyn."

She would have snorted at his forced tone, but that would give Grey the impression he had done something wrong, and the last thing Ash wanted to do was spend her free hour explaining social norms. She might not want to be his mate, but yet, she didn't want to ridicule him for something that he just couldn't help.

Caitlyn shifted her gaze back to Ash. "Might I have a word?"

Ash glanced over her shoulder at Fenrir. "Can you be trusted to go in there and not eat anyone?"

"I ate a rather large god for breakfast. I am not feeling hungry just yet."

Ash rolled her eyes, pushed open the door, and stepped back to let Fenrir walk into the room. There was no one in there just yet, but she knew the rest of her team would come round the back way and while Zach had some interactions with Fenrir, Torin and Arik, Killian and Chrissy had not.

Ash leaned against the wall and folded her arms across her chest. "If you are about to chew me out like my dad just did, can you save it for tomorrow? I think I've had my quota of being talked down to by my favourite people today."

Caitlyn offered her a sad smile. "You father received some awful news with the latest batch of victims that has made him a little bad tempered. When we had a meeting after the news came in, he asked us what we thought of involving your

Fenrir, and as this case has now taken a personal turn, we decided that we need to use every advantage we have."

"He's not my Fenrir, but whatever," Ash mumbled, heaving out a sigh as she heard Zach's voice from inside, and hoped that no one ended up bloody. "What's happened that forced ye all to bring in the monstrous wolf?"

Caitlyn paused while one of the uniformed gardaí strode by, inclining his head to them both before disappearing around a corner. The queen of the vampires ran a hand through her hair and she gave Ash a small smile before she spoke.

"The family of wolves that was killed yesterday was one we all knew. The victims your dad had gone personally to the scene to check out was the family of Arthur De Valera."

Ash sucked in a breath. Her dad and Arthur went way back to when he had been a lone wolf not wanting to join Arthur's pack, however after the events where her grandfather Odin had tried to remake the world, he and Arthur had actually become friends.

She had also heard that when her mom first appeared on that scene, Arthur had flirted with Ever, and that had riled her dad up even more. Not long before Ash had been born, Arthur had taken a mate, and their first pup was born when Ash was one.

"We're sure it's the same killer?"

"Oui. Their throats were clawed out and the hearts were devoured. There is hope that the killer glutted themselves on the hearts and now will remain dormant long enough for us to gather more evidence."

Ash shook her head. "All the family is dead? His youngest just graduated from UCC."

Caitlyn shifted her weight and glanced down the hall. "Oui. They were in Cork to celebrate her graduation and had rented a place in the city to stay for a few days. They were murdered there."

Shit…

Ash knew that her dad would be blaming himself for not finding the killer before Arthur and his family were killed, and now she understood why he must have been desperate to bring in Fenrir. She had seen Fenrir kill before, seen how much he had enjoyed it, and if Ash was trying to bring someone who might think like the killer they were hunting, he was the obvious choice.

"He could have just told me before the meeting. I would have understood." Ash said quietly, as Caitlyn closed the distance between them and rested a hand on her shoulder.

"He is not thinking rationally, is mon loup. And he knows how adverse you are to being in Fenrir's company. If I am being honest, I also think his fatherly instincts might have played a part in his decision because with wolves being murdered, who would dare come to harm you with the threat of Fenrir in the way."

Ash felt the simmer of anger course through her veins, hurt that her dad felt like she couldn't protect herself, and Caitlyn laughed, shaking her head. "Daughters and fathers. I saw it with my own Jessamine and Sebastian. You might be a badass, but you are and will always be his little girl. Take it easy on him. He is also missing your mother."

Her mom, Ever Chace, or well, Ever Doyle now, was away in Valhalla, the realm of the Valkyries this week and her dad hated being separated from his mate. Usually, when his cases allowed, her dad went with her mom, but with this horrible case ongoing, there was no chance of her dad getting a break to visit his mate.

Ash should have been able to see the strain in her dad's features, because even though the mating bond with Fenrir was all out of whack, it was still there, and her wolf missed him when he wasn't around.

"Has Mateo had any luck finding what I asked?"

Mateo De Silva was a Spanish vampire who had been made by Caitlyn's oldest friend Marcel, and he was very good at finding things. Ash had asked Caitlyn to ask Mateo to look for some magical weapon that could break the bond between her and Fenrir, but the frustrated vampire had yet to come across anything that might do the job.

"He is still looking."

Ash let loose a sigh, heard laughter in the break room. "I'd better go make sure that Grey doesn't snap and use someone's rib as a toothpick."

Caitlyn gave her shoulder a squeeze before she let go, "Try and go easy with Fenrir, mon petit loup. From what Derek has told me, Fenrir refused to come at first because it might upset you. He might not know too much about emotions, and yet, he knows what your hate of him feels like."

Ash wanted to argue with Caitlyn that she didn't hate Fenrir, far from it and that scared the fuck out of her. She didn't know how much of her wanting him was down to the bond, or what she really felt herself. Caitlyn patted her cheek and strode away, and Ash closed her eyes and let out an exasperated sigh.

"You shouldn't frown so much darling, you'll get wrinkles."

Ash's eyes snapped open to see Torin grinning at her. She wanted to understand his trick of not being seen until he wanted to be seen, but every time Ash asked him how he did it, Torin tapped his nose and just vanished. It was so bloody annoying.

"I had heard that you had a mate and yet, I was not expecting all the broody deliciousness."

Ash snorted, rolling her eyes. "You can have him if you want."

"I'm a sucker for a psycho with guy liner." Torin teased, winking at Ash as she shook her head.

The vampire opened the door to the break room and held it for her. "After you, Ash. I'd also prefer not to have one of my ribs used as a toothpick."

Ash turned walking backwards as she pointed at the dark-haired vampire. "It's rude to eavesdrop on private conversations."

Torin flashed her a toothy grin as he drawled. "If it was a private conversation, then you should have had it in a sound-proof room, darling, and not within earshot of a dozen different supernaturals."

Ash barked out a laugh and without thinking, shoved Torin by placing her palms on his chest. It was then she felt the presence at her back, the entire room falling silent. There was a dart of jealousy through the bond before all Ash got was static again. Torin's eyes widened before he stepped back and held his hands up.

"As I was just telling Ash, I would much rather you didn't use my ribs as a toothpick."

"I don't like the taste of vampire. Reminds me of spoiled meat."

If it had been anyone but Grey making that statement, Ash would have thought that he was making a joke, and while he might possess the capacity to make a flippant state-ment or even tease, it was mostly directed at Ash, so she wasn't too sure if Fenrir was just being honest about the taste of vampire.

Torin chuckled and shook his head. "I don't know whether to be relieved or insulted by that. I meant no offense, Fenrir."

A throat cleared and Ash glanced over at Killian, who was standing with some files. Stepping out from in between Fenrir and Torin, Ash went over and took one of the files before she hoisted herself up on to the counter beside Zach. She ignored her best friend as he nudged her shoulder, and opened the file, wincing as took in the initial crime scene photos.

Like the other murders, there was no denying that the mauling of the throats was done with werewolf claws. At the first kill sites, there had been multiple testing and while the claws seemed to be larger than an average wolf, there was no denying it was a wolf.

You could see the indentation of claws at the chest, where the killer had ripped the heart from the victim's chest and eaten it. They knew this because at the first crime scene there had been a little piece of the heart left over that had fang marks in it.

The next crime scene there had been no leftovers.

Ash was a wolf, so she understood eating a piece of the kill after a hunt. However, that was when she was in her wolf self and she had never ever felt the desire to eat the flesh of a human or supernatural in her human form even if she was the one who had killed them. Her dad had explained to her when she was younger that the wolf ate the kill to honour the animal who had died so they could hunt.

Zach didn't understand that aspect of being a hunter because while he hunted in his cat form, he was more likely to eat rabbit or mouse than say a deer. And more often than not, like a cat, he liked to give the animals he killed as gifts.

Ash lifted her head and looked at the only other wolf on the team, Chrissy. Older than Ash by over a decade, Chrissy had joined the team because she had once been the victim of a human who was killing supernaturals and eating pieces of them hoping to absorb their power. She had fought back and according to Killian; Ash's dad had made such an impression that from that moment on she only ever wanted to be an agent of P.I.T. This must bring up some memories for Chrissy, but if it did, it wasn't showing on her teammate's face.

"I know I'm missing something here," Zach began, reaching around Ash to grab a biscuit which he broke and gave half to Ash without stopping his question. "Why eat the heart? That's gotta be tough as hell even for a werewolf's teeth."

"When Donnelly took me, he wanted to drain my bone marrow. He hoped digesting the marrow would fuse with his DNA and make him supernatural." Chrissy said, walking back and forth as she studied her own file. "He truly was mad because if he'd just checked out the science of it, there's no way to eat part of a supernatural creature and become one yourself."

"Then what does he hope to achieve by consuming the hearts?" Torin asked from the far corner of the room where he had gone to stand.

Ash glanced over to the wall that Fenrir leaned against, his eyes closed, his hands in the pockets of his black jeans. To anyone looking at him now, well any non-supernatural creature, he just looked like any other handsome bad boy. The possessive part of Ash that she blamed on her wolf, wanted everyone to know that he was hers...

As if he sensed her eyes on him, Fenrir opened his own, the black irises looked fathomless. Ash thought she saw a flash of red before he simply closed his eyes again and started speaking. "The slashing of the throat is to prove that a simple tear, claws against flesh can end their lives. The eating of the heart is about claiming power over the kill. They may not enjoy the physical act of eating the heart because the meat would be too gamey. It is all about acknowledging the power they feel over claiming the kills."

In that exact moment, Ash knew why her dad wanted Fenrir on the case. As much as she hated to admit it, Fenrir had a better insight than anyone in this room. His thought process was different because he was different. His incapacity for most emotions meant that while the thought of consuming victim's hearts was unthinkable to Ash, Grey would have no qualms about it.

"Is that why you ate Tyr's hand? You wanted to have power over him." Torin asked Fenrir, and Ash wanted to strangle the vampire.

Fenrir just shrugged his shoulders, not bothering to open his eyes. "I was too young to think like a predator then. I simply did not wish to be bound. I did like the sound of the snap as I crunched his bones though."

Torin let out a strangled sound as Zach laughed and Ash rolled her eyes. "Too much information, Grey."

When nothing came in the way of an apology, Ash rubbed her temple. Zach's watch beeped, and he checked the messages, then nudged Ash again with his shoulder before pushing off the counter. "That's Arik. I gotta go and get the newbies set up."

Torin perked up at the mention of Arik. "I'll come with you. I have time before I meet with a contact of mine."

Zach grinned, knowing full well that Torin was trying to get under Arik's skin, and he headed toward the door Ash had come in, then paused as he pulled open the door. "Fenrir."

"Cat."

With a snort, Zach looked over his shoulder and raised a brow. After all the years they had been best friends, it was as if they had a secret way of talking. That quirk of his brows was him asking Ash if she was gonna be okay. Ash held up both hands to indicate five by five and Zach headed out. They had both been a little obsessed with Buffy the Vampire Slayer growing up.

Torin tipped his imaginary hat at them and ducked out after Zach. Killian looked from her to Fenrir, then back at Ash. "We're heading to the scene to get the low down. I'll call ya later if we get anything substantial."

Killian and Chrissy headed out too, but not before Killian paused to tell Fenrir that he would pass on the information about the kills to Derek. Fenrir nodded in acknowledgement, and when they were gone, it left just Ash alone in the room with him.

Fenrir stayed where he was, unmoving, and Ash wasn't sure if she should say something and bring up the last time they had been this close to one another, or just let it lie. It was definitely a bigger discussion than they really had time for. But Grey being here didn't exactly give her a clear head.

"I can go if you do not want me here. It does not benefit me to have you angry at me for agreeing to your father's request."

Loathe as she was to admit it, they needed Fenrir. He was their advantage, the factor no one saw coming. And much like he had been instrumental in the fall of Odin, he might just be the thing that helped them solve this case.

"You can stay," Ash said softly, pushing off the counter. "That thing you said was good to know. I know my dad wouldn't have brought you in unless he thought you could swing this in our favour. I have to go meet a contact, so I guess you get to tag along."

Grey opened his eyes and looked at her. "Tell me the location and I'll flash there."

Ash's cheeks heated. "I can't flash anymore, remember? You'll have to come in the car with me."

Ash waited for him to offer to flash them both, knew she

couldn't take being that up close and personal with him, however all he did was shove away from the wall, open the door, and look at her in a way that made her heart skip a goddamn beat.

"Shall we?"

The Killer

THE KILLER CLOSED THEIR EYES AND INHALED A BREATH; THE newfound power in their veins both foreign and familiar at the same time. Full...they felt full, like they could not even take a sip of water in fear they might explode. They had glutted themselves on the kill and yet, the satisfaction in their veins made them smile. Reaching out, they put a hand against the cold of the mirror in the bathroom and reached for the magic in their veins, connecting one world to another.

Their legs trembled at the weight of the gaze of the god who looked them dead in the eyes.

"You have doled out more justice I see."

"The wicked and the liars have suffered for their crimes."

The god tilted his head and tapped his chin. "Do not forget that once you have served justice on those who have wronged you that you fulfil our bargain. There is justice that I require to be delivered too. Or have you forgotten?"

A chill raced along the killer's spine. "I have not. I still have work to do before I can enact your vengeance. I will deliver what it is that you have asked. I will not renege on our bargain. And once I do, you will grant me what I asked for?"

The god smiled; however, it was not warm, or friendly, it was cold as ice. "A bargain stuck is a bargain fulfilled. My blood will be your blood and you will spend the rest of your immortal life dolling out justice."

The killer removed their hand from the mirror, severing the connection.

They had been reborn, the magic of the gods now in their veins and they no longer answer to the name given to them at birth for they were now called Justice, and justice would be theirs.

Chapter Four

Zach

ZACH WANTED TO GO BACK AND BE THERE FOR ASH AS SHE dealt with Fenrir, but as he told himself many times before, not his circus, not his monkeys. While Ash was his best friend, Fenrir was her mate whether she wanted him to be or not. He'd grown up seeing how fiercely mates cared for one another and he sure as shit wasn't getting in the middle of the two of them.

Besides, he and Fenrir had an understanding, after a conversation where Fenrir had almost killed him, and had only stopped because he needed Zach to get to the past and get to Ash. Fenrir had been in a haze of anger and had tossed Zach around like he was a ragdoll before almost strangling him.

Lifting his hand to his throat, Zach couldn't help but remember the conversation.

Fenrir's eyes blazed red, his grip tightening around Zach's throat as he used his godly strength and lifted Zach off the ground so that his feet dangled in the air. Fenrir's inhuman growl filled the room as he leaned in and bared his teeth.

"Where is my mate, cat?"

Zach tried to answer the god, but all that came out was a squeak. Fenrir must have realized that Zach couldn't answer him with a hand around his throat, so he let go, and Zach had to use his cat reflexes to land on his feet.

He rubbed at his throat and lifted his gaze to Fenrir's. Zach had seen the god appear human but, in this moment, there was no mistaking that there was nothing human about the Norse deity before him who had murder in his eyes.

"She went to the past to ensure her future. Something happened that meant she was ceasing to exist. Ash will come back when she has achieved what she went back to do."

Fenrir's gaze narrowed. "Ashlyn does not have the power to traverse through time and space. How did she go back, cat?"

Zach made to move toward his computer and Fenrir snarled, his fingers curling into fists like he was actively trying not to harm Zach. Reaching for one of the broken shards of the Bifrost, Zach handed one to Fenrir, then backed away from the rabid wolf.

"I used magic to tweak the already magical properties of the Bifrost to take Ash not to Asgard, but to the past. All she had to do was hold it and think of the time and place she wanted to go and in theory, it should do it."

Fenrir looked at the shard of glass in his hand, then lifted those red eyes to Zach. "Clever cat. Answer me truthfully or I will withstand any of Ashlyn's rage and tear out your innards. Did it work?"

Zach blew out a breath and ran a hand through his hair. "I think so. If it didn't then I wouldn't remember Ash because she wouldn't exist. I have to have faith that she got where she needed to go, and she will come back home soon."

Fenrir tilted his head when his voice cracked, like he was trying to make sense of Zach's reaction. "You cannot have her. Ashlyn is mine."

Ah, so Fenrir was confused, and of course he was... he did not understand platonic love.

"I don't want Ash like that, Fenrir. She has been my sister for as long as I can remember. I would take a bullet for her, and she would me. I know she is your mate, and I have no reason to get in the way of that. But Ash is my best friend, and I love her. If you *want any advice, I'd get used to having me around. If Ash thinks we get along, she might soften toward you."*

The god blinked slowly, a frown on his lips. "Why would you offer me this information when it has no benefit to you?"

"Because any mate we take will have to accept that we are in each other's lives and that won't change. It might be a foreign thing to you, but family is important to Ash, and she wouldn't deal with not being around us all."

Fenrir was quiet for the longest time and Zach wondered if he was considering what Zach had told him or considering the upshot of actually killing him. In the end, Fenrir inclined his head, and replied. "I do not think I will kill you just yet. As you said, it would not serve me well where Ashlyn is concerned."

Curling his hands around the shard of Bifrost, Fenrir smirked then vanished into the ether just like Ash had. Zach slumped down in his seat and prayed to the gods that Ash was where she had planned to go, or Fenrir was gonna come back and tear him apart limb from limb.

After worrying for a couple of days, and after a sudden visit from the Fates, Zach had gone back to the past for a flying visit. It had been a trip to say the least, and Zach had spent the last five years wondering if the shards of the Bifrost that he had magically hidden could be used again.

He told himself that he was more level-headed than Ash, and that if he went to the past, then he could refrain from interfering too much. Zach hadn't told anyone about what he had been thinking, though he suspected that Donnie had gleaned the snippet from his mind, when the mind-reading vampire had pulled him aside and told him the past was best left well alone.

He'd also encouraged Zach to talk to his parents about what was going on in his head, but Zach hadn't wanted to upset them if they knew the reason he wanted to go back into the past was because his biological mother had been on his mind a lot.

Zach had been five when his mom had been killed, and his uncle, Fionn, who had moved up the country so he and Zach only spoke once in a while, had dropped him off at his dad's house. He'd not understood then that his dad hadn't known he existed, but he had stepped in and shown up when Zach needed him.

And then there was his mom. Melanie Newton-Moore had been the only mom he really remembered. Sadie was a distant memory and while his parents never shied away from talking about her, even though Zach knew she had hurt his dad, Zach couldn't help but think that he was missing something.

Fuck, he really wasn't thinking straight because it was starting to sound like he was complaining. He wasn't, far from it. Zach had grown up surrounded by love and family. He'd been allowed to grow and follow his own path, was never left alone to deal with anything in his life.

Maybe he should just ask someone to take the shards of the Bifrost far away and remove the temptation from his hands. After all, the Fates had punished Ash for defying them and had taken away the parts of her that made her the goddess of thunder and it had almost killed Ash.

Still fucking did.

"You seem lost in thoughts, Zach?"

Zach snorted and glanced over at the vampire walking beside him. "I was just thinking how much fun it would have been to see how Fenrir would have acted if you had been the one to put hands on Ash instead of it being the other way round."

Torin laughed, shaking his head. "That is one scary son of a bitch."

They walked into the control room, and Zach felt his lips

curve into a smile. He had worked in here with his mom, who had taught him all he knew about computers. His mom had been a hacker before she had joined P.I.T. and had continued to gain knowledge even after becoming a vampire and gaining the ability to garner lies and truths, and force someone to tell the truth.

Zach had only felt the full extent of her power once, when she had been mad at him for something he didn't really remember and she had demanded that he tell her the truth, and he had cried before spilling his guts and his mom had been so horrified by her slip in control that she had taken herself across the field to stay with Caitlyn and Donnie for a few days.

His dad had explained to Zach that she wasn't mad at him for misbehaving, and just upset that she had used her power on him and made him cry. After almost a week of not seeing her, Zach had snuck out and climbed into her old bedroom in his cat form and refused to go home without her.

As if she could sense his thoughts, or she just picked up on his scent, his mom looked away from the screen she was currently sat behind and gave him this megawatt smile. She looked like she always had looked to Zach, this insanely strong woman with ginger hair and green eyes that sparkled with life and love.

"Zach, come here a sec. I can't get your program to sync up. What am I missing here?"

Torin slipped in after him and watched Arik, who seemed oblivious to the vampire's attention. It sucked that the kid always had his guard up, afraid that one slip of emotion would lead to another incident like the many times one or more of them had foiled a kidnap attempt. Zach himself had shifted once and clawed a woman who tried to take Arik when he was a baby.

He walked over to his mom, heard her mutter "Stupid

thing" as she growled at the computer. Zach nudged her out of the way and keyed in a few things and it loaded fully. His mom gave him a little bit of side eye, and that made Zach laugh, giving her a hug,

"You need to tell me how you did that. I'm not so rusty that being out in the field means you have surpassed me in the techy skills."

"Nah, mom. I just have added code in there so that I have control over the entire network. It ensures that I can never get fired." Zach remarked with a cheeky grin.

"Now you sound just like your dad." His mom grumbled, though her tone was light, teasing. One of the newbies called Melanie over and she gave his arm a squeeze before she rushed over. Zach went over to his corner of the room that was right next to Arik's own workstation. The son of the goddess Freya didn't flinch around him like he used to, because Zach loved him like a little brother even though they were cousins so he couldn't be influenced by his power.

Although, Freya had once explained that his power might still affect those who already loved him, making them fiercely protective but Zach was okay with that. Having grown up around family who were fiercely protective, Zach as the oldest was happy to watch over the rest of their little pack. Even the two newest members of P.I.T.

He glanced over to where Gideon, Ash's brother was trying to show Lyra, Erika and Loki's daughter, how to work the program that shifted through every camera in Cork. Lyra was too busy looking at the youngest Doyle to take note of what Gideon was trying to show her. She tried to sweep her hair from off her shoulder and knocked over a glass of water all over the keyboard and it crackled and shorted.

Her mother might be the goddess of war and her dad the god of mischief, but Lyra was the goddess of clumsiness and that was why her parents had put off having her join P.I.T.

for as long as possible, hoping she would grow out of her accident-prone tendencies.

Her co-ordination had improved but she was still a magnet for accidents.

Lyra looked all flustered as Gideon swept the keyboard away from the goddess without a word, moved the glass, and put a towel down on the water before he calmly went back to showing her how to switch screens to see more camera views as if nothing had happened.

Zach logged into his own computers and immediately went to the camera screen outside the station. He watched as Ash walked out, Fenrir right behind her, before she walked over to her own car and unlocked it. She said something to Fenrir, and he just gave her this look that made Zach want to laugh out loud.

Then the wolf god looked the camera dead in the eye like he knew Zach was watching them and Zach swiped his screen to open another angle to watch as Ash's car was driving out of the carpark, and he let out a sigh of relief.

The door to the communication room opened, and Derek Doyle came striding in. Zach had been in awe of the captain of the entire paranormal division of the garda since he was a boy, and he knew that everyone that Derek worked with respected the hell out of him for all he achieved.

The door closed behind him and Derek's eyes slid to where Torin was standing in the corner and inclined his head to the vampire. He walked up to Derek, and they exchanged a few words before Torin just seemed to dissipate.

Derek said his mom's name, and Zach listened as he told her that he needed to go question a couple of witnesses and had need of her skillset. His mom nodded, then glanced over her shoulder. "Okay newbies, I'm gonna leave you in Agent Moore's capable hands. You listen to him as you would me, okay?"

There was a round of yes Ma'ams and then they were gone. Zach gave the trainees their orders, then went back to his own work, keeping an ear out in case they needed any help. Most seemed to have adapted to the training, the technical stuff as much a part as the physical training. Zach made sure that he kept his mind and his body sharp.

The panther that was another part of him stretched lazily inside his mind as Zach realized it had been a while since he had shifted and just enjoyed being in his cat form. The techy stuff he did with his mom, the warlock stuff with his dad, but since his bio mom had been murdered by her clan, Zach never even thought of going to them to see if it felt different running with cats than it did with the wolves.

"The cameras around the rental property were interfered with." Arik said suddenly, dragging Zach from his thoughts.

"How so?"

Arik sent Zach the file and then he pointed to the screen. "Just around the estimated time of the first death, the cameras go all shaky, like there is an interference. Three hours later and they suddenly come alive."

"Can you check back on the other victims and see if the same thing happened? It could mean that either the killer knows enough technical stuff to mess with the system, or their supernatural frequency is so out of whack that it interferes with the technology."

Arik's gaze narrowed like he wasn't understanding so Zach explained it to him. "Every supernatural has an aura or frequency. Sometimes, a supernatural frequency is so out there that it messes with the tech. My dad for example can't use an android system because his frequency fucks with the components. That's why he always bitches about having to use an iPhone."

The other man smiled. "That makes sense. My mom can't

use a microwave. The last time she tried it caught fire. It must be because her frequency is different."

Zach knew Arik was uneasy about others touching him, though Zach learned that it was okay with people he knew. Reaching out, Zach clasped him on the shoulder, ignoring the way his friend stiffened out of habit. "Exactly. You'll see it at times with family photos if too many of the descendants of gods or gods themselves are in the photo. The frequency makes a clear shot impossible."

"I'll bring up the other CCTV from the other murders that I can, but I do know that some of the victims killed were in places that had little or no CCTV."

Zach knew that of course, considering that up until Arthur De Valera was killed, the victims of this particular killer had been all scumbags, it wasn't really surprising. The first victim had been a trafficker in the sex trade. The next one a wolf who had a taste for the young, and the victims just got progressively worse as the murders had gone on. Up until Arthur, Zach wasn't the only one who thought this vigilante wolf was doing something they all wished they could do, even if it was the wrong way to go about it. Still, Derek had been right when he said they had to treat this like any other, and now failing to catch them had resulted in the loss of innocent lives.

What Zach couldn't figure out in his head was why just wolves? Why not target other supernaturals or humans doing sketchy shit and take them out? The killer obviously had a bias against themselves and other wolves. But why?

Zach scrubbed a hand down his face. Man, he was tired. The whole team had been running on caffeine and stubbornness for the last couple of weeks. He'd give anything for a break in the case, to find the killer, and have a few days to do nothing. Maybe have a drink, or five.

What the team needed now was one of those massive

family barbeques they had every couple of months and just let loose and have fun. None of that would be happening if they didn't find this killer and put the case to bed.

There would always be another monster lurking in the shadows, waiting to pounce, and even though his family had put to bed the revolt of gods and monsters, and Zach wasn't blessed with visions of the future, he couldn't help but think this case altered something fundamental that would change them all.

Or maybe he was just full of nonsense and needed a good night sleep?

He heard a crash and looked over to see that Lyra had managed to get wrapped up in some cables and taken out a whole monitor in the process of turning round. She was still wrapped in all the wires, though how she had managed to do that when Zach himself had made sure the wires were all tucked away, Zach would never know.

Poor Lyra looked embarrassed, and Gideon was trying not to laugh.

It was gonna be a long night and day.

Ya, Zach could really do with a drink right now.

Chapter Five

Ash

ASH COULDN'T HELP BUT KEEP LOOKING AT FENRIR AS HE SAT beside her in the car. Most wolves would have an issue with relinquishing control especially alpha wolves and there was no doubt that Fenrir was on another level of alphaness. But he just stayed silent, looking out the window into the night and for some reason it irritated Ash.

Tightening her grip on the steering wheel, she headed for the city centre, specifically North Main Street which was the supernatural quarter of the city. The main stretch of the street was bright and touristy, luring humans who wanted a look at the creatures in a natural habitat, whereas Ash knew that once you went off the main street and dared to traipse down the many side streets, the chances of you coming back out alive got way slimmer.

Even though the radio was on a low level, Ash was finding the silence almost unbearable. Her wolf was going bloody crazy inside her being this close to Fenrir and not touching him. Ash was stubborn as hell though and refused to give in to the temptation to reach for him.

It made her think again about the fight they had when Fenrir had shown up at a club she was at with Zach, and a shifter got handsy and Fenrir had snapped. Ash had gone out to get blind drunk to forget about losing her hammer and missing the people she had left in the past, knowing full well it made no sense considering they were here in the present. She had been in so much pain that she needed an outlet for her anger and pain and that had been Fenrir.

The music was pumping so loudly that Ash could feel the vibrations from the speakers in the floor, pulsing up into her body. She swayed to the music, twirling, and laughing as she spotted Zach making out with a witch in a corner of the dance floor.

Sweat slicked her skin as Ash knocked back her drink, then set the empty shot glass down on the nearest ledge before making her way to the centre of the dance floor. The buzz of alcohol felt like lightning in her veins and just thinking that brought with it another wave of sorrow.

Warm hands landed on her waist and moved her with the music. Ash closed her eyes and leaned her head back against a solid hard chest. Hot, wet, lips pressed against the side of her neck and inside her head, her wolf howled in protest.

Not. Our. Mate.

Ash wanted to snap that that was the whole fucking point of this. Not to think about the wolf who had been putting pressure on her to acknowledge him as her mate like she had promised. No matter how many times that she told him that she had only promised to try, and she had tried. But she still had no desire to be mated to Fenrir.

She could feel how eager the man behind her was and she angled her head just a bit. The man groaned and it was then that Ash felt the kiss of teeth on her flesh and knew she had been riling up a vampire who wanted a taste of her. Maybe it was recklessness on her part, but Ash craved the oblivion that came from the supposed high from a vampire bite. Most vampires could make the experience a pleasurable one, though Ash knew some didn't bother and just let it hurt.

Tonight, Ash wasn't sure which option she wanted.

Teeth grazed her skin and Ash shuddered, closing her eyes and waiting for the sting of pain. She didn't know what to expect since she had never been bitten before and her heart started to race inside her chest in anticipation.

Every hair on her body stood to attention at the animalistic growl that filled the dance floor, then Ash felt the vampire's body being hauled away from her. Eyes darting open, Ash whirled round to see Fenrir beating seven kinds of hell out of the vampire. His claws were fully out, the hew of red of his eyes like a beacon.

Ash hadn't even known that her mate was nearby, her senses and the bond muted by the alcohol. Zach had abandoned his date to come over to Ash. The music halted, and everyone was just standing by and watching as Fenrir punched the vampire repeatedly in the face. Blood and flesh and maybe a tooth or two ended up in the middle of the dance floor and Ash didn't know what to do.

Fenrir snarled and lifted his clawed hand ready to rip out the vampire's heart when Ash shouted at him to stop. He glanced over his shoulder at Ash, and she swallowed at the hardened expression on his face. She had never seen him so angry.

"Please, Grey. Stop."

Instead of ripping out the vampire's heart, Fenrir slashed the vampire's throat, blood gushing out and splattering Fenrir as he slowly got to his feet, turned toward Ash and then grabbed her arm, yanking her with him as he made to stalk out of the nightclub.

Zach made to follow out, but Fenrir daggered him with blood-red eyes. "Stay, cat."

Fenrir didn't let go of her until the cold night air hit her in a sobering smack, then she found herself against a wall. A bottle of water appeared in Fenrir's hand, and he slapped it into Ash's hand. "Wash the fucking scent of the vampire off your skin."

Ash unscrewed the bottle and instead of doing what Fenrir had asked, she took a drink of the water and then poured the rest of it out on the ground. Her mate looked like he might spontaneously combust, and she was here for it.

Fenrir crossed his arms across his chest. "Explain." He demanded.

"Go to Hell, Grey. I don't owe you shit."

His restraint snapped and Ash found herself pressed against the wall; a hand wrapped around her throat. His nostrils flared and he growled. "If you want to be bitten then I will bite you, not some undead parasite. Me. Your mate."

Ash shoved at his chest, but there was no moving the wolf god. "I don't want to be bitten by you. I don't want your hands on me, Grey. I don't want you. Get that into your thick skull. I, Ashlyn, don't want you."

Fenrir tilted his head in a wolflike way and Ash continued, her voice rising. "Do you understand, Fenrir? I don't want you. I want to find away to cut the bond and be done with you. I hate being mated to you. I despise seeing you all the time no matter what the wolf wants. Me, the girl, I can't fucking stand being mated to you."

Ash had never heard herself sound so cruel, so hard, so venomous. Fenrir blinked slowly, the red receding and leaving just the onyx black of his eyes that sometimes, looked like galaxies were trapped in there. Ash's chest was heaving and for a split second, she felt something akin to pain coming down the bond before Fenrir closed his eyes and the feeling was gone.

The hand wrapped around her throat slowly loosened its hold, and Fenrir stepped back. She could almost see him trying to make sense of what she had said, to understand it, however he had just held her gaze for a moment more, then vanished.

Ash had burst into tears, her knees buckling, and it was Zach who had appeared and wrapped his arms around her, the wolf inside her howling for its mate...

"Concentrate on the road, Ashlyn."

The sound of Fenrir's voice dragged her from her thoughts, and she glared at him only to find that he wasn't even looking at her, he was still gazing out the window. She snorted, dismissing his chastising tone and kept driving on. After another stretch of silence, Ash couldn't help but try and get some of her questions answered.

"Where have you been?"

Fenrir didn't ask her to elaborate on her question, he just simply said. "I went back to acting as Odin's guard dog."

Ash felt like a total bitch then. She had rejected him, and he had gone back to the cave where he had been held captive for eons. Four years he had stayed in the realm that Ash had first found him, because she had sent him away.

"But you didn't stay there, right?"

"No. I did not. However, I stayed away like you wanted." Fenrir said as he finally turned to look at her.

Four years had done nothing to stop the appeal of him. When Ash had first met Fenrir, he had looked like a teen heartthrob, a bad boy, and Ash was attracted to him. Now, he had aged himself up and he still had that bad boy thing going for him. There was no denying he was handsome...that wasn't the issue with being his mate.

Ash pulled into an empty spot outside Chester's bar, knowing full well that this spot was reserved for the vampire himself, however Ash had been pissing Chester off for years parking here and he could come bitch and moan at her all he wanted.

Fenrir got out of the car, and she saw him cast a steely eye around the street. Ash noticed a few admiring glances toward the wolf god, and jealousy prickled at her senses before she swallowed it down. Fenrir turned to look at her and arched a brow, a slight smile curving his lips before he blinked, and the smile was gone.

Before she had screamed at him in the alleyway, Ash had been able to pick up on thoughts and that from the mating bond. But now, as she tried to get a feel for what Grey was thinking, she got nothing. Though it seemed like Fenrir was getting some feedback from her.

Ash inclined her head for Fenrir to follow her, as she ducked down one of the side alleys. She could feel the menacing presence of Fenrir at her back, and it was strangely comforting. She wound her way through the network of alleys and lanes, then as she came to the location her CI had agreed to meet, she turned to Fenrir.

"I have been cultivating this CI for years so please don't do anything to scare the bastard. He somehow has the best information in Cork City and for some reason, he likes me."

Fenrir roamed his eyes over Ash, and she barely contained the shiver that danced along her spine. "I bet he does."

Ash rolled her eyes and just carried on, not wanting to go near that comment with a ten-foot pole. The streetlight flickered like a strobe light as Ash stepped out and her CI was sitting on a keg. Two barely legal humans were standing by him, handing over money as her CI handed over a little baggy and Ash put two fingers into her mouth and gave a shrill whistle.

All three men looked over at Ash she cleared her throat and pointed to the badge on the loop of her jeans. The two humans almost fell over one another scrambling to get away. Fenrir chuckled beside her, and Ash felt a smile curve her own lips.

"Aw come on, Doyle. That's gonna stop me from selling any more product tonight."

Ash shrugged her shoulders, then walked toward the rat shifter. Twitch had been one of Ash's earliest collars, and when the rat had given Ash some info that had led to a massive arrest, Ash had decided to offer the low-level dealer a choice; a spell on Spike Island or give Ash information. He'd taken the CI route rather than spend a day on the prison island used for supernatural prisoners.

"You know the deal, Twitch. Pedal your shit to supes and we don't have an issue. But those two were all human. That's not behaving yourself."

Short and round, Twitch's face, well twitched, like his whiskers were moving and his eyes flashed pink. He sniffed the air, then looked beyond Ash to where Fenrir was standing off to the side trying not to look menacing.

Fat chance of that.

"No cat tonight?"

Ash shook her head. "Nope. Whatcha got for me?"

Twitch shook his head and leaned back against the wall. "Nah, I've got nothing for ya tonight, Doyle. Unless you want to double my fee. Those two humans fucked off with my product and my money. A rat's gotta eat too, yano."

"I hear they have nice meals on Spike Island. And I'm sure both Chester and the vampires would be keen to know that the rats are selling to humans on their turf. Don't think they'd want to drain ya dry, rat, but killing ya might keep them amused...for maybe a minute."

The rat hissed at Ash, however she just laughed. "Come on, Twitch, you know you always end up doing what I want in the end. Then you can scurry back to whatever sewer you crawled out of and curse my name to the gods. Since I'm related to most of them, I'm not sure anyone would listen though."

"Fucking she-wolves. Goddamn bitches." Twitch mumbled.

"Woof, woof." Ash replied with a grin, then she growled in her chest, making Twitch jump.

Ash laughed then, rolling her eyes. She was having too much fun playing with the rat. She watched as he reached inside his jacket and pulled out a gun, his hand shaking as he pointed it at Ash. She put her hand up to call Mjolnir and the pain of the loss hit her so suddenly, she froze.

Fenrir, on the other hand, had no reservations.

Ash stood and watched as Fenrir *moved* knocking the gun from Twitch's hand and had the rat pinned against the wall, one hand wrapped around his throat. It was almost comical that the short rat was kicking his little legs as if that would free him from Fenrir's grasp.

"Come on, Doyle." Twitch squeaked. "Tell the brute to let me go."

Ash strolled over to where Fenrir had the rat pinned. "You gonna give me my information?"

"I don't have anything to give you!"

Fenrir growled, Twitch's eyes widening. "Oh fuck...the rumours are goddamn true."

Ash wasn't sure what rumours Twitch was referring to, but she could scent how terrified the rat was of Fenrir, and Ash was enjoying it a little bit more than she should. A healthy dose of fear never did anyone any harm.

"Come on, Grey, you can't kill him."

Her mate turned his head to look over his shoulder at her, arching a dark brow as if to say I most certainly could. Ash wasn't sure if this was one of those situations where you had to be literal with what you said or if Grey was playing along to frighten the bejaysus out of the rat.

Ash sighed, making a point to rub her temple as Twitch watched her. "I mean you *could* kill him. I know you could, but I meant that you *shouldn't*. He really hasn't done anything wrong."

Fenrir turned back to the rat. "He pulled a gun on my mate. I *should* kill him for that alone. And he sells drugs to humans who don't know any better. I *could* snap his neck and leave him for the birds to peck at his flesh."

The scent of urine filled the alley and Ash had to bite the inside of her mouth to stop from laughing as Fenrir stepped back from the rat, still holding him at the throat.

Ash strode closer and leaned against Fenrir, felt him shudder and his jaw clenched. She ignored the sense of calmness that seeped into her bones at the barest touch and arched her brows at Twitch.

"Tell me."

"Okay, okay." Twitch said, then Ash nudged Fenrir in the ribs, and he sat the rat back down on his keg not so softly. He unwrapped his hand from the rat's throat and stayed next to Ash. The rat glanced at the gun that had been knocked to the ground, then back at Fenrir.

"The wolf killing the wolves. The word on the street is that before the alpha and his family were killed, all the victims were part of the same network who traded young supes. The kills were low level grunts. But the higher ups are nervous. They've been moving the product round and themselves. Trying to stay out of the usual places. That's all I got."

Fenrir snarled, letting red flood his eyes, because Ash could see it reflected in the dark.

"Shit, okay but this is the last thing I know. This ring or whatever you wanna call it, they've been around for years, and they have politicians and cops and wealthy backers keeping the thing hidden. The killer knows too much to not have been either part of it, or one of the traded."

Ash's blood was boiling. As much as she hated the vigilante shit, she found she couldn't blame the wolf for killing as those vile werewolves. There was a special place in Hell for monsters who harmed kids, harmed innocents. But what about Arthur? There was no way he was any part of that. No matter what way she looked at this, he just didn't fit, but it was obvious that she wasn't going to get those answers here.

"Scurry along, rat. I'm suddenly feeling peckish."

Twitch looked to Ash. "My money?"

Ash made a point of looking to the gun, then back at the rat. "Call this a gesture of goodwill for pulling a gun on me. You do that again and you and me are done. Got it."

Twitch clambered up the keg and onto the roof before he even bothered to answer Ash, as Fenrir walked away from her and picked up the gun. She watched as he popped out the magazine, then the bullet in the chamber and then the gun vanished.

"Where did you learn to do that?" Ash heard herself asking, knowing that guns weren't exactly a god's weapon of choice.

Fenrir shrugged. "I had time to spare. And an adequate teacher."

Ash wanted to press him for more information when her phone chimed, and she pulled it out. "Shit, Zach said we need to head back to the station for a briefing. Let's go."

Fenrir nodded, motioning for her to go ahead of him, and it was only when Ash was walking up the alley back to her chair that she realized she missed the feel of Fenrir against her. She had been the one to initiate the contact, and Fenrir had restrained himself.

What the hell was she supposed to do with that?

Chapter Six

Fenrir

"WERE YOU REALLY GOING TO KILL TWITCH?"

Those were the first words Ashlyn had spoken to him since they had driven from the city centre, and Fenrir didn't know if it was best in this instance to be honest with Ashlyn or to skirt around the truth so that she did not have an excuse to despise him even more.

Ashlyn parked the car in the spot that was just in front of the station and unbuckled her seatbelt. It was torture to be locked inside the metal vehicle, trapped with that woody scent of hers that made him want to press his nose into the curve of her neck and drink her in until he was drunk on her. Fenrir had almost lost his control when she had leaned into him, and Fenrir knew he had been delusional in his thinking that the distance had muted the need he had for her.

It had not.

"Grey?"

Angling his body so that he could look at his mate, Fenrir decided that Ashlyn had always been more receptive to him when he had been honest with her, and through the bond, he knew this, not because Ashlyn had told him. She had no idea what Fenrir had done to minimize the flow of the mating bond, and what it cost him in return.

"He drew a gun on you. I was not lying when I said I

should kill him for that slight. I know you asked me not to frighten the rat, however, should you need him again, my actions will make him think twice about doing something so foolish again."

Ashlyn frowned and Fenrir felt her...confusion ...yes that was it.

"I can take care of myself, Grey."

"I know this. I would not have accepted a weak mate. I find it very satisfying when you act feral and vicious. You might not like to hear that, but it is the truth."

Ashlyn let loose a startled laugh and Fenrir soaked it in, committed it to memory. "Jesus, Grey, from you, that almost sounded romantic."

Fenrir frowned, narrowing his gaze. "Is that what you want, Ashlyn? Romantic gestures?"

Ashlyn opened her mouth, closed it, then sighed. "I don't know, Grey. I don't know."

Well, that wasn't very helpful to him.

His mate got out of the car and Fenrir breathed in deeply, taking in as much of her scent as he could before he followed her and got out of the car. He watched as she greeted other agents, smiling and laughing, and at ease with those she worked with. The bond between them shimmered with joy, a feeling Fenrir did not truly understand. Ashlyn felt even more of this when she was with the cat, with her family, and her friends.

The only time Ashlyn did not have this emotion was when she was with him.

Fenrir stopped walking and closed his eyes, trying to deal with the sudden onslaught of emotions from Ashlyn. That night that she had almost let the vampire bite her and had made her feelings abundantly clear, Fenrir had somehow known how to stem the flow of feedback from him through the bond. It prevented Ashlyn from learning more about him that could make her despise him more.

However, doing so opened the feedback from Ashlyn to him wide and Fenrir was unable to prevent the feedback without loosening his control on the flow from him to Ashlyn. He could not tell her how maddening it was for him to have stayed away the last four years when he could *feel* how much better her life was without him.

And he would never tell her how on occasions like this very moment, when her emotions were so pure and so heavy, Fenrir who did not understand the emotions suffered what he had learned was close to a panic attack for a human.

Apparently, it was not good for a sociopath to panic as it often led to bloodshed.

"Grey?"

He heard Ashlyn's voice and he growled. He was rooted to the spot, and he knew he must appear weak, and Ashlyn was not a weak mate, she did not deserve a weak mate. When he felt like he was about to lose control of it all, he felt her hand rest on his chest where his heart raced, and it calmed him.

"You wanna tell me what's going on in that head of yours?"

"No." He ground out, leaning forward to rest his forehead against hers. It was the closest skin to skin contact he could risk forcing upon her without her running from him.

In the state he was in, Fenrir would chase her and no good would come from that.

He heard his Ashlyn sigh, as she rested her other hand on his chest too, then hummed a song that had been on the radio on the drive back. It was not much; however, it was enough for him to shove away the panic, forcing out her emotions and then he opened his eyes to see her amber ones looking at him.

"You okay now?"

"Yes." Fenrir answered after a couple of seconds because he found he did not want to break this contact with his mate.

He knew Ashlyn was about to pull away, her hands came off his chest, and Fenrir wanted to tangle his fingers into her golden locks and yank her forward, capture her lips with his and feel her melt against him. It was the only time when she did not despise him and despised herself more.

"Come on, Grey. We need to update the team on what Twitch told us."

Fenrir had no choice but to follow Ashlyn into the station. It did not slip his notice that lots of the supernatural creatures gave him a wide berth, even when they were friendly with his Ashlyn. It did not bother Fenrir, for he was a predator, and they should fear him.

They made their way into a briefing room that was already quite full when they arrived. Fenrir stayed back, letting Ashlyn weave her way through the crowd to stand beside her cat. Zach glanced over his shoulder at him, then turned back to where Ashlyn's father was standing with the other members of P.I.T., including his stepmother. Her gaze landed on him, then Erika stepped forward and said something to Ashlyn, his mate shaking her head and Erika stepped back.

Fenrir had known since the moment he was free of the chains of Gleipnir and had made his appearance back in this world that his stepmother would have no reservations in killing him if she had to, even if it hurt his father. She was written in his journal as one of the people who might actively try to kill him, and while Fenrir could not kill the Valkyrie general and goddess of war, he could be on his guard around her.

Derek cleared his throat and the entire room fell silent. "As you all know by now, last night, the killer we are hunting deviated from their pattern to kill a good man, a good wolf. Arthur De Valera held the Munster pack for more than three decades and having previously determined that the reasoning behind the killer's motives was justice, the killing of Arthur and his family wasn't justice."

Derek looked at his daughter. "You get anything from your CI?"

He watched as Ashlyn straightened. "Yes sir. Twitch was certain that the wolves killed before last night were all part of a decades old trafficking ring. Low level scum but the killings have the higher ups in a spin. Twitch told me they've been moving the "product" and themselves around."

That made the agents all snarl and growl, and in theory Fenrir knew he should react in an appropriate manner, however he also believed that the agents should not be surprised at the evil in this world. In any world.

"He also said that the ring has stayed under the radar because they have wealthy backers, politicians, and even cops working to keep it hidden. Twitch eventually confessed that the ring think that the killer was either part of it once upon a time or was one of the traded who escaped."

Ashlyn's father nodded, then it was the cat's father who asked. "You get anything else? Names? Locations?"

Ashlyn shook her head. "Nope. I think that was all he had and then Grey made Twitch piss himself so I knew I was getting nothing else from him."

Every single agent turned to look at him, but it was Derek who spoke to him. "Why did you make him piss himself?"

"He was stupid enough to pull a gun on Ashlyn. Now, he will not do it ever again."

Derek's eyes darted to his daughter, and she sighed. "I'm fine. It was fine. I don't even think he knew how to pull the trigger let alone had the balls to do it. It was grand."

Derek inclined his head at Fenrir, and it reminded him of

a conversation they had had in the past, where he had approved of Fenrir's words and that had pissed off his mate.

Derek stepped up to Fenrir and the had to admire his bravery. "You might be tied to her but that also ties you to us. You hurt her, and she has me, her mother, and a whole pack of aunts and uncles who will gut you if you harm a hair on her head."

Giving the other wolf a feral grin, Fenrir stated. "Ashlyn is my mate. I would never harm her. She may think me a little, psychotic, as she puts it, and perhaps I am. But I would rather be restrained again against my will than harm her. Though I would love to go toe to toe with any of her so-called aunts and uncles. See how long they last."

Fenrir had been taken aback when Derek had simply laughed before saying. "Ash is right, you are psychotic."

Ashlyn yanked her hand out of Fenrir's, her anger like a pulse inside of him as she growled and stormed out.

Derek looked at him, then sighed. "She'll be okay. Let me talk to her."

Fenrir tilted his head, curious. "Why would you encourage the mating when you know what I am?"

Derek had reached out then, clasping a hand on Fenrir's shoulder. "I have enemies, her mom has enemies, and those enemies are less likely to come for her to get to us if they know that her mate is Fenrisúlfr."

There was a discussion happening about possible locations of the ring, and Fenrir closed his eyes and drowned out most of the discussion, just listening to the bare minimum. It mattered not to him what places they suspected until they were certain of a whereabouts.

Then he would hunt.

He heard Derek tell most of them to take the day to rest and he would call them if they needed to be back on shift. He knew Ashlyn and her team would stay behind, so he waited with them until the only supernaturals in the room were Ashlyn's team and the original members of P.I.T..

"Right, Zach tell me what you and Arik figured out."

Fenrir opened his eyes and looked over at Freya's son. He too was standing off to the side, his eyes downward as he mumbled. "It was mostly, Zach."

The cat nudged his cousin. "Team effort. Arik noted that some of the footage of the rental property was sketchy at the times of the murders, and then it was working perfectly again. Like there was an interference."

"Someone messed with the CCTV?" The vampire who was the grandson of Tyr asked.

The cat shook his head. "We don't think so. I think that whoever is killing the wolves has a supernatural frequency that messes with technology."

"Like Ricky with android phones?" Melanie Newton-Moore asked her son.

The cat grinned, making his dad swear. "Exactly. The more power a supe has the more chance they have an alternative frequency. Freya can't use a microwave. Dad can't use android phones. Since Odin's power was distributed to some of you, it altered your frequency and affects some of you using certain tech."

Caitlyn looked at her mate. "That would explain why you shorted the electric vehicle just last week."

Donnie snorted, rolling his eyes. "Told ya we didn't need a remote-controlled car. Now we defo know we can't get one."

It was only when everyone laughed did Fenrir realized the vampire had been making a joke. It made him want to reach into his pocket and take out his journal and make note of this. Jesting and sarcasm were things that sometimes were lost on him.

"I'm gonna work on a device that can test the frequency of supes. If we can nail down what frequency the killer is omitting, then we might be able to single them out and use that to pinpoint their location."

Derek walked over and poured himself a coffee. "Do you think that each supe has a frequency unique to them? Like a fingerprint?"

Zach gave a nonchalant shrug of his shoulders. "That's the working theory, ya. Once I get stuck into making the device, I'll test the theory on you guys, and Fenrir, if he doesn't mind."

The cat turned to look at him, and Fenrir gave a brief nod of his head after weighing up his options. If the cat was able to manufacture a device that could track a supernatural creature based on their aura, then he was not sure he wanted the cat to have that power over him.

Having decided that if Fenrir had been reluctant to do what Zach wanted him to do, then it might have made the other supernaturals in this room mad at him, and that would make Ashlyn mad at him so for now, he had agreed to what it was the cat asked of him. There was always the chance Zach could not make the device and Fenrir would have refused for nothing.

"Okay, Zach, you and Arik work on that, make it a priority. Ash, give it a few nights then track down Twitch again and see if he's heard anything else. Cait, you get in touch with Chester and see if he has heard anything. But with what Ash said, just keep in mind that Chester likes to collect the unusual, so he could be a part of this."

Caitlyn frowned and folded her arms across her chest. Fenrir noted that people tended to do this when they were defensive or angered. Ashlyn did it when she was being defensive, or she was annoyed. Fenrir had that noted in his journal.

"Chester may have his, appetites, however I do not think he is stupid enough or depraved enough to partake in something that could take away all the creature comforts that he enjoys so much."

Donnie wrapped an arm around his mate's waist, and she leaned into him, resting her head on his broad shoulder. He had seen other mated pairs do something similar and just under an hour ago, Ashlyn had leaned into him...

His confusion was aggravating.

"Is that what you want, Ashlyn? Romantic gestures?"

"I don't know, Grey. I don't know."

Fenrir felt a sort of shiver in the air, a tiny taste of magic, and when he glanced to his right, the vampire Torin had suddenly appeared in the room. He grinned at Fenrir, who growled in response and bared his teeth. Torin held up his hands in apology.

"Right, noted. No sneaking up on the wolf with the red eyes. Lesson learned."

Fenrir tilted his head at the vampire. "That will not happen again. The sneaking. I know what to sense now before you show yourself. Next time I might have my claws out."

The vampire didn't seem in the least bit scared of him. "If it was anyone else, I'd think you were flirting with me. I kinda like it."

This was part of the bantering that Fenrir had a hard time working out but somehow, he knew that this Torin was teasing him, so Fenrir decided to try and see if he had judged the situation correctly.

"Sorry to disappoint, vampire. But you aren't my type."

"What is your type then, handsome?"

"Alive." Fenrir said deadpanned and the vampire let loose a chortle of laughter before he sobered, and reigned himself in when his boss said his name.

"Right," Torin started, "So one of my sources claimed not to know anything about any murders, but I tracked him and listened to a phone call where he was told that the product had been moved to three locations on the outskirts of the county. They said that they were gonna lie low for a few days and see if the killer was caught. Didn't get any locations because he hung up and then got way too up close and personal with a troll for my delicate eyes."

Arik snorted, then flushed a shade of red that darkened his skin from the neck up, making the vampire grin, and only made the red stand out more. Fenrir didn't think the young god was angry, so he must be embarrassed. He quickly left the room when Derek dismissed them, and Fenrir waited to see what Ashlynn was going to do.

"You need me to stick around and start work on the device?" Zach asked his team leader, Killian.

The warlock shook his head. "Nah, head home, eat, and sleep. And for god's sake, shower folks, you are smelling a little ripe."

Fenrir frowned because he didn't think they smelled ripe, but then they laughed, and he realized it must be another form of a joke. He didn't understand how telling someone they smelled when they did not was funny at all.

Torin was already gone as Zach slung his arm around Ashlyn's shoulder. "I'm starving. You want to stop at that twenty-four-hour Chinese take away you like and take some food home before we crash?"

As if to answer, Ashlyn's stomach grumbled. "Oh hell ya. A full belly and my bed sounds like heaven right now. You're buying."

The cat laughed and then turned to come toward him, and Ashlyn's face fell.

"Hey Fenrir, you wanna come eat with us?" Zach asked and something told Fenrir that his invite was genuine.

Fenrir looked at his mate, and even if he had been unable to read her expression, he felt through the bond that she wanted him to decline. Ashlyn wanted away from him. And it almost destroyed him.

Without another word, Fenrir flashed away from his mate.

The Killer

HANDS TREMBLING, THEY LOOKED OVER AT THE WOLF SLUMPED against their kitchen counter. Blood dripped from the head wound. The other wolf had not moved in a while, but they could hear his heartbeat. It was strong, the sound of the thump thump but it made them feel sickened.

They had not expected for his scent to trigger memories of what had been done to them. Flashbacks of pain, and terror, made their body shake and bile to lodge in their throat.

This wolf deserved to die.

They deserved to die for all the pain that they had inflicted on others like them.

As unwell as they felt, the thought of eating the heart made them want to vomit.

But the god had told them that eating the hearts would prepare them for the power now in their veins. It would help cement it in their person, so they would never be a victim again. They would be a power, a god, and justice would be theirs to dole out.

They could not leave this wolf alive.

The wolf in question stirred, groaned, and pried his eyes open. Cold blue eyes looked up at them, and his gaze narrowed as he seemed to recognise them. The hairs on their arms stood up as the wolf put his hand to his bleeding head.

"I know you."

"Not anymore." They replied, letting a smile curve their lips. "I am here to serve you justice for all the children you harmed."

The wolf had the audacity to laugh at them and it snapped the control any semblance of control they had. Their body rippled, the change not hurting them like it had when they were a mere were-wolf. Bigger now too.

Steam dripped from their mouth as the other wolf screamed and tried to scramble away.

They might not be able to eat the heart, but they could certainly inflict as much pain on the other wolf as possible before death came to claim him. He tried to run, he tried to escape, and they gave them that moment of hope before they pounced and tore the wolf's flesh from his bones.

Chapter Seven

Ash

ASH HAD ALMOST LOST HER APPETITE THE MOMENT SHE HAD seen the destroyed expression on Grey's face at her obvious rejection. He hadn't said anything, just disappeared and made her feel like a right bitch. There was no doubt that she was struggling with having Fenrir back in her life and he had been nothing but stoic.

Apart from the little blind panic Ash had felt outside the station. She was so used to the static in the bond that when the flare of panic had slipped through, that she didn't realize it was coming from Grey until she had turned and seen him rooted to the spot.

Zach hadn't commented on the interaction, or asked Ash any questions and she was grateful for that. She needed time to sort things out in her head and couldn't help but think if she was confused, then Fenrir must be even more so.

After gorging herself on Chinese food and a quick shower, Ash had crawled into bed to try and get some sleep. Sleep evaded her though and she spent an hour or so tossing and turning before deciding that she was just gonna get up and stop thinking so hard.

She could hear Zach snoring in his room as she padded her way out to the living area of their apartment. She made herself a hot cup of Ribena since caffeine was a bad idea when she was already wired, then grabbed a cosy blanket and settled down on the couch to watch one of her shows.

Ash was half a season in and almost through her second cup of Ribena and half a packet of chocolate digestives when she heard the door of Zach's bedroom open. He sauntered out of his room, dressed in sleep shorts and nothing else, his shoulder length hair loose and hanging in waves.

He grumbled at her, then made him and her a Ribena before he flopped down on the couch beside her, stretched and yawned. "Couldn't sleep?"

"Nope."

Ash went back to watching one of her fave shows. She could tell that Zach was trying to get her to talk about stuff, but all Ash wanted to do was watch her show, and not talk about serious shit that had already kept her awake.

"What are you doing, Ash?" Zach asked, pulling at her braid when she didn't immediately answer him.

Pinching him on the arm, Ash didn't bother glancing away from the TV to answer Zach. "I'm comfort watching."

"You're comfort watching a show about serial killers?"

"Yup." Ash replied before taking a sip from her mug and grabbing the last biscuit.

"You're comfort watching a show about a cult of serial killers?"

Ash wasn't sure where this conversation was going or why Zach was interrupting her comfort watch, and while she was going to ignore him, like most cats, he'd pester her until she did what he wanted and gave her an answer. "Yup."

"But why?"

Reaching for the remote, Ash paused the episode just as her boy Joe was about to kill the lawyer in his car with his nemesis Ryan Hardy on the phone because she didn't want to miss anything because Zach chose to be a chatty Cathy when he should be asleep.

Rolling her eyes as she released a sigh, Ash told Zach. "Joe Carroll deserved better and maybe if I rewatch it the gods might get sick of watching me watch it and change his fate."

Zach was silent for a moment, then he replied in that big brother tone of his. "Ash, buddy, it's just a TV show."

Ash's mouth dropped open as she glared at Zach, just realizing the fatal flaw her best friend had. How fucking dare he diss Joe like that.

"You can go now," she said, picking up the remote to press play again. "I don't need your negativity in my life."

Ash felt the weight of Zach's gaze on her, then huffed out an exaggerated breath before looking back at him. "What?"

Zack was still staring at Ash, then his smile curved into a smug one that made Ash want to punch him as he said, "Aha... I get it now. It makes complete sense."

"Get what now?"

Zach looked to the TV then back at Ash. "Why you have it bad for Fenrir. ...you're attracted to serial killers."

Ash was too shocked by the comparison to toss back a retort at him and when she did, it kinda fell flat. "Have you seen your last two girlfriends? Total bunny boilers? One of them literally wanted to know if we had a pot big enough to cook rabbit ...you like crazy."

"Right back at ya, A.K., right back at ya."

Ash grabbed a pillow and smacked Zach with it, but he was laughing so hard it hardly made the impact that she wanted. Suddenly not wanting to watch her fave serial killer show anymore, Ash got up and stalked to the window, watching the rain falling down below.

"Hey, I was only teasing. I'm sure the fact your comfort show is about a cult of serial killers says more about you than the fact that you are mated to the literal Norse monstrous god."

Ash threw her hands up in the air as she turned round to

face Zach. "Ugh, I wish someone had written a book about this!"

Zach chuckled, hugging the pillow Ash had thrown at him. "What kinda book, Ash?"

"Rules for dating your psychopathic mate."

"Technically, he's a sociopath not a psychopath. Different psychopathy." Zach informed like she didn't already know that since they were in the same abnormal offender's class.

"That doesn't help me."

Zach shrugged, giving her a soft smile. "I know but it's all I've got."

Ash was suddenly so fucking exhausted. "Can I sleep with you tonight? Since there's no bunny boilers in there?"

Zach shook his head with added vigour. "Hell no. You think that I want to explain to your very reactive mate that your skin smells like me more strongly than usually because we slept in the same bed? I don't have a death wish, Ash."

Ash wasn't sure how to respond to that, but it annoyed the fuck out of her. Thankfully, a knock sounded at the door, and both she and Zach looked at it. Zach checked his watch, then got up to go answer it.

"If that's the fucking asshole wolf who thinks he's my mate, you can tell him to fuck off!" Ash shouted loud enough for whoever was beyond the door to hear her.

Zach gave her this sort of what the fuck kind of look before he opened the door to see her dad standing outside. Ash almost laughed when Zach straightened and almost stumbled over his words. "Sir, uh Derek. Come in."

Stepping aside so her dad could come into the apartment, Zach closed the door and excused himself to go back to bed, ignoring Ash as she called him a coward. Her dad came in and sat on one of the armchairs, then leaned forward and rested his elbows on his knees and his chin on his fist.

"I hope you don't mind me stropping by, but I felt we needed to clear the air."

Ash came over and flopped down on the couch, pulling her blanket over her legs. "It's okay, dad. Aunty Caity told me that it was Arthur, and I knew why you brought Grey in to help. I was just shocked to see him after so long."

"How long has it been?"

"Bout four years," Ash told her dad and he blinked in surprise. "I mean, there's been times when I think I've seen him or when I can like feel him nearby. But actually spoken to him, ya, it's been about four years."

"I can send him away if his presence makes you uncomfortable." Her dad offered, and when Ash looked at him, she could see that he looked exhausted.

"It's okay. He's given us some good insight so no point sending him away when it would be quite obvious you did so not to solve the case and catch a killer, but to make me feel better."

"You, your brother, and your mom are my number one priority, Ash."

His tone was fierce, absolute and Ash gave him a smile. "I know dad, I know."

Her dad didn't say anything just got up and made himself a coffee and then came back over to sit down. He looked like he hadn't slept in days, and he probably hadn't. He scrubbed a hand down his face, then looked at her.

Having sent them all home to get some sleep, Ash wondered why he had come over now to talk when he could have waited to see her back at the station in a couple of hours. Her face must have given away her question because her dad took a sip of his coffee before speaking.

"I was headed out to go home when I heard noise from the gym. Donnie and Fenrir were sparring, with Ricky and

Caitlyn watching. I went in and sat next to Caitlyn, and she asked me if I had cleared the air with you."

Since when did Donnie and Grey spar with each other?

"I told Caitlyn I hadn't the chance yet, and Fenrir kicked Donnie's legs from underneath him then looked at me and told me that you had not slept yet and were still awake."

By the gods, could Grey get that from her through the bond?

What else could he get?

Her dad saw the confused look on her face. "Your bond isn't working like it should, is it?"

Ash shook her head, picked at her blanket. "I think it's my fault. I've rejected him and the distance must have damaged it. But then how can he still know when I'm asleep or not? It doesn't make sense."

Her dad drank more of his coffee, then set the mug down. "When your mom realized what she was and the danger she had brought to our door, she bolted. The distance and the fact that she was the more powerful of the two of us, meant she could mute the bond somehow. And she wasn't fully into her power yet, but I think Fenrir had influenced the bond somehow."

Ash's mind was spinning. How the hell could he do that? What the fuck did it all mean?

"What do you feel from the bond?"

"Mostly static. Sometimes like tonight, I get something and then it's gone. With mom in Valhalla, is that not what your bond feels like?"

Her dad smiled, and it make him seem younger. "No. Right now, your mom is happy. She misses us but being in Valhalla, with the other Valkyrie, it's in her blood and the sand, the sun, the ocean, it all calls to her. If I concentrate hard enough or she wants me to see, images can come through the bond as well."

That kind of bond sounded amazing. It sounded like a thing of love, and she didn't have that with Grey. She wasn't sure he was capable of being in love...maybe that was the problem.

"Listen, Ash, I'm not telling you this to betray a confidence or to influence you in any way. But I do think you should know that I spoke to Loki. He said that a mating bond is like a two-way street, back and forth between mates. It is a thing of magic and while it is possible to stop the traffic in one direction, to do it both ways is almost impossible."

Ash mulled over her dad's words, trying to make sense of his analogy. So the static that she was hearing was because Fenrir had stopped the flow from him to Ash, but what did that mean about the flow from Ash to him?

"Fenrir kicked Donnie's legs from underneath him then looked at me and told me that you had not slept yet and were still awake."

Her lips parted as air whooshed out of her lungs. No...all this time...

"He blocked me from the force of the mating bond and left himself wide open to what I was giving off. Why would he do that? Why would he do that, dad?"

Her dad got up and came to sit beside her, and Ash let him pull her to him. He kissed the top of her head. "I don't know, sweetheart. Loki and me think that he logically believed that you were averse to him being your mate because of his lack of emotions, so he cut off the part that allowed you to see him for who he is. But that left him wide open to all of your emotions, which must be hard considering he doesn't comprehend them like we do."

Ash's brain was starting to hurt as she leaned away from her dad. "I'm confused."

Her dad scratched at his stubble. "Okay. So think of emotions like a language. If someone is speaking in a language you understand, then you can follow the conversation and even join in. Then if someone started speaking in a language you didn't know, it might be confusing for you."

"And because Grey is working so hard to stop me from getting feedback from him, he's stuck with all of my emotions, my feelings, and sometimes it overloads him?"

Now his sudden reaction at the station earlier made sense. Something she was feeling or doing must have given him a sort of overload and it wasn't until she had touched him that Fenrir had been able to pull himself out of it.

Her dad nodded. "Loki and I believe so. He saw something similar when Lyra hugged him suddenly and Fenrir hugged her back. It was like reflex and then he looked at Loki like he didn't understand what he was doing or why he was doing it."

"Does it hurt him?"

Her dad tilted his head. "You know the answer to that. The only thing I can say is that being away from your mom even for a week hurts me. If I didn't have the bond, then I dunno if I would be mentally capable of functioning. It might be different for you two since you are actively resisting the mate bond. Though Fenrir has far stronger will power if he managed to stay out of your way for four years when it would have been torture for him to know that you were getting on with your life."

Emotion clogged her throat. "Don't say that, dad. I might not want to have had the mating bond forced on me, but I don't want him to be suffering. I'm not a monster."

Her dad reached out and cupped her cheek. "I know you're not, Ash. What you were was an almost seventeen-year-old girl who found out that her mate was a wolf from Norse mythology, then had to deal with the fact that she might have ceased to exist. It's a lot to deal with and I think, five years later, so that you don't put any blame on me or mom, you have transferred it all to the monster who came into your life."

Ash was suddenly on the defensive. "I don't think he's a monster, dad. He's just misunderstood."

Her dad grinned, as he gave her cheek a little pat. "Spoken like a mate defending her own mate. And I don't think he's a monster either, Ash. He was nothing more than a child when Odin had the only person who Fenrir trusted trick him into being chained for an eternity. Who knows if Fenrir might have adjusted more normally surrounded by the love and support you kids all got."

Fuck, but her dad was right. She had defended him and then her dad had spoken something that Ash had wondered since that night in the forest after she had stumbled upon Fenrir guarding her grandfather. If Grey had been one of them from the very start, would she feel as indifferent as she did about the mating bond?

Ash had been so lost in her own head that she looked over and saw that her dad had fallen asleep beside her, his hand dropping to his own lap. She dragged the blanket up over him and curled up beside him, then turned back on her murdery show so she wouldn't have to think too hard about what she and her dad had discussed about Fenrir.

Sometime between the lawyer's murder and the next episode, Ash herself must have fallen asleep, only to be woken by the sound of her dad's phone going off. She sat up as her dad pulled his phone out of his pocket and pressed the answer on it.

"Donnie? What's up?"

Ash's ears perked up as she heard the vampire she used to have a childhood crush on tell her dad there had been another murder, though it was sloppy and looked like the killer had lost the control they had on previous kills. That this victim might have a personal connection.

"I'm at Ash and Zach's. I'll bring them with me. Can you get hold of Fenrir? His eyes might be good here."

"Sure, he's still at the station. He whopped my ass and then Caitlyn started talking to him in French and now they are talking, and I have no clue what's going on. She feels happy though, so I know he's not planning on murdering me."

Her dad laughed and hung up the phone as Ash got to her feet and headed toward her bedroom to throw on some clothes and to wake Zach when her dad called her name.

"Take the time to think about what we talked about. Ask yourself is it worth losing your mate because you're scared. You might be immortal but even immortals can die. Fenrir can die. This destiny and future thing is not set in stone, sweetheart."

Ash stared at her dad for another couple of heartbeats before she pivoted, banging on Zach's door as she walked past. "Rise and shine, kitty cat. We got a fresh body to check out."

Zach swore and Ash heard him get out of bed, then trip over something that made him let loose a string of curses that had her dad chuckling from the living room, and Ash smiled despite the tornado going on in her head as she went to get dressed.

Chapter Eight

Ash

Ash sat in the passenger seat of her dad's car, with Zach in the back. It reminded Ash of times when she was younger, and her dad used to take her and Zach out to learn the ins and outs of the city. It might seem like a strange thing to do with kids; however, Ash and Zach had trained with Valkyrie and the others on the Paranormal Investigations Team from an early age. It was just a normal part of their upbringing.

Her dad pulled into a spot just outside an apartment complex to see Ricky coming toward the car with a grim expression on his face. Ash got out and heard a retching sound and looked over to see Donnie vomiting into the bushes.

Ricky clapped his son on the back, and then tracked Ash's eyes. "He's grand. Never did like being flashed places. Fenrir didn't want to wait to drive over, so he just grabbed Donnie and then they were here."

Ash's heart stuttered. She should have known to expect Grey to be here, but after her conversation with her dad, Ash didn't know if she was ready to confront some truths. She had little time to contemplate things as Donnie came over and Derek reached into his car and tossed the vampire a bottle of water.

"Why were you with Fenrir?" Ash blurted out, and Donnie turned to look at her and she started to sing some nineties pop song over and over in her mind so he couldn't read her mind.

Donnie gave her a warm smile. "He was in the gym by himself, and I asked if he needed a sparring partner. I actually got the feeling he didn't have anywhere else to be until another body dropped. Kinda felt sorry for the kid."

Ash snorted at Donnie calling Fenrir a kid. Considering that her mate was eons older than anyone here, it was hard to imagine him as a child. Although it didn't stop her from feeling bad that Fenrir just stayed at the station waiting for another murder because she hadn't wanted him to come for dinner.

"Can you see inside his head?" she asked quietly, worrying at her bottom lip.

Donnie held her gaze, then tucked a strand of hair behind her ear. "Sometimes. But I'm not gonna tell ya what I hear, Ash. The kid is entitled to his privacy. You get to hear his thoughts through the bond though, right?"

Ash flushed with embarrassment and when Donnie looked at Derek, her dad shook his head and no more was said about it. Zach nudged her shoulder and then asked his dad where the body was. They all headed in together, up to the top floor and into the penthouse suite. The apartment was double the size of the place she shared with Zach and was all white marble countertops and tiled flooring.

Stepping inside the apartment, Ash had to navigate around the bloody paw prints. They were bigger than the average werewolf, which aligned with their conclusion about the clawed throats being done by a bigger wolf. Blood was splattered around the place and there were spots on the walls leading into the expansive kitchen living area. It looked like the blood streaked could be from a wolf brushing its fur along the wall and the blood had come off in the process.

Once they had all gathered in the kitchen area, Ash could

see the victim's leg and nothing else was on the counter, like it had been haphazardly tossed there. The entire apartment looked like something from a slasher movie. Blood, gore, and various body parts were littered around the room but there was no sign of the torso so far.

Awareness pickled on her senses as Fenrir stepped out of the bedroom and their eyes clashed.

He was wearing black jeans, a black tee, and a black peacoat that came down to his knees. On his feet were battered trainers, which looked strange on the wolf god, and it made Ash want to smile. Fenrir tilted his head, as if trying to figure out what was going on in Ash's head, then he shook his head and continued to walk around the room.

Ash and Zach exchanged a look as Fenrir inhaled deeply, then opened his mouth as if to say something, but decided against it and clamped it shut. He shifted his gaze to her dad, and he inclined his head.

"It's okay, Grey. Tell us what you see."

His gaze went to Ash, and then back to her dad.

Did he not want to talk with her in the room?

Fenrir started to walk around the room again, and when he did eventually start to speak, Ash found herself entranced by him.

"This kill is unlike the other crime scenes. It's rushed. Sloppy. The heart was only bitten and not devoured. There could be a lot of mitigating factors in this. For example, the killer was still too full from eating the other family's hearts and they could not complete the ritual."

Ash took in the state of the room, and she had to agree with Fenrir on the sloppiness of the kills. The killer had never torn his victims apart like this before. Were they devolving quicker than the team had anticipated?

"There was no sexual element to the kill but for some reason, this kill aroused the killer. You can scent it in the air.

I was not at the other crime scenes so I cannot be certain they didn't get off on the other kills too. I can scent anger too, for that emotion is one of the most potent and has a bite to it. I think if the killer was angry and near me, I might know them."

Fenrir pushed up the sleeves on his coat and Ash sucked in a breath. That was her bracelet on his wrist. It was one she had made years ago with Lyra, and it was on her dresser in a box. It consisted of beads and her name, Ash, spelled out on it.

If Fenrir noted her shock, he didn't say anything because he was too busy looking at the destroyed furniture and the upturned sofa. He inhaled again then looked over at her dad. "This is the most personal kill to our murderer. They trashed the apartment as another way to assert dominance. The wolf marked its territory. Every room carries a scent of urine."

Fenrir stepped around one of the crime scene techs, then his eyes darted back and forth. "They had a connection to this victim. I do not think the killer knew that when they arrived, but from the anger, I assume if the killer was a victim of the trafficking ring, then this wolf harmed them in some way. The clawed off penis in the bedroom would support my conclusion."

Almost every man in the room winced and Ash rolled her eyes. Her dad stepped further into the room, and then asked Fenrir where the torso was. Fenrir inclined his head, then they all followed him into the bedroom. The bedroom was as big as the living and kitchen area, with white carpet that was soaked in blood.

"I think the leg was ripped off as the murder victim tried to run away, because there is a safe room in the walk-in wardrobe. They would not have gotten far because of the blood loss. The shock alone would have killed them."

They all stood looking at the torso. The arms looked like

they had been torn off, there was jagged marks on the shoulders that would indicate bite marks. The other leg was across the room by the window and the throat was slashed like the other murders, but the head was missing.

The heart was sitting on the dresser, a single bite taken out of it, though the bite marks seemed smaller than ones on the torso. Ash drifted over to where the heart was and leaned over to look at it as she took out a pair of gloves from her pocket.

"It's like they tried to eat it in human form. Nibbled on it and then just couldn't." Ash offered, then turned back to the rest of the team.

"You get the most potent scents from this room. It lingers outside also, but fades. Like after the kill, they tried to eat the heart, couldn't, and then they were so angry at not completing their ritual that they vented all their frustration on the apartment, and then pissed on the furniture." Fenrir said, crouching down to take in the torso.

Her dad partially shifted his hand, his wolf claws on display. He was bigger in wolf form than an average wolf, but there was no way her dad's claws could have made those marks on the torso. Her dad tried to follow the pattern, but his claws were too small.

Her dad straightened, then looked at Fenrir and some unspoken conversation happened between them, and Ash was still confused when Fenrir said. "Ashlyn must leave first."

"Hey what did I do? What's going on?" she demanded, first looking at her dad, then at Fenrir, but it was Fenrir who gave her the explanation.

"Having you see me as the monster I am does not benefit me in any way. I would not have you look at me with further disdain and add it to the list you have of my faults. Therefore, I will not take my true form with you in the room."

That made her heart feel sad, and Fenrir growled and turned away to look out the window.

"Grey, I've seen you in wolf form before. At least you can't talk back to me then. I promise I won't hold it against you. *Please?*"

There was no pomp and pageantry in Fenrir's change. His body rippled and thankfully the bedroom was nearly the size of a field because Grey in wolf form was massive. He seemed to know that he would not fit, and Ash watched as he shook his limbs out, and became a monstrous gray wolf smaller in size than Ash knew he really was. Saliva dripped from his mouth, the droplets hissing as they landed on the ground.

The wolf was still huge, and its sword like claws clacked as Fenrir slowly made his way to the torso. His red eyes looked to Ash for a split second, then he lifted a massive paw and made a slashing movement above the claw marks. He then opened his mouth, the insane-sized teeth making Ash shudder, as Fenrir mimicked biting the arm off at the shoulder and tossing it aside.

Donnie and Ricky both swore when Fenrir mimicked the claws at the victim's crotch.

"So too small for a normal werewolf but smaller than Fenrir in his full wolf form. Thanks Fenrir, you can change back again. That was a great help."

The wolf huffed out a breath then glanced over at Ash. She made her way over and ran her hand over the wolf's muzzle when Fenrir lowered it to her. His eyes closed and Ash noted how content she felt being so close to Fenrir.

He bopped her hand when she stopped rubbing him, and Ash laughed. "That's enough petting, Grey. We still have work to do."

In the blink of an eye, Fenrir shifted back into his human form, and Ash made to step back. Fenrir snapped out his hand and wrapped his fingers around her wrist. She met his eyes, held them and he bared his teeth. Ash bared hers back, and that made Fenrir grin before he let go of her wrist and turned back to the others.

"The killer took the head with them when they left but as the deceased could be traced by their scent, I assume they tossed it somewhere near the building."

"There's some bins out front. Shit, I think the maintenance guy said that the garbage pickup was today." Donnie said before he and Ricky bolted out of the room, and her dad and Fenrir followed them out.

Ash and Zach took one last look around the room, then followed everyone down to search for the head. Donnie and Ricky were already in the bins, and Grey was walking around the courtyard, like he was tracking a scent.

"I hate to say it, but that was impressive. It's fucking fascinating watching his thought process." Zach said as he leaned against the wall and folded his arms across his chest. "I found it interesting that he knew what anger smelt like. I know there are certain ones he does get, but hell, you can't deny that's interesting."

Ash mimicked Zach's stance and huffed out a breath that made her best friend look at her. "What's eating you? You've been unusually quiet since your dad rocked up at our place."

Her eyes darted over to where Fenrir had come to stand by the bins. "My dad said that he and Loki were talking about Fenrir and the mating bond. Dad explained that his one with my mom goes both ways, that he can feel her emotions, and she his. That sometimes they can send images and locations and stuff."

"And you don't have that with Fenrir?"

Ash shook her head. "When we first mated, I did. But after the nightclub incident and me basically telling Grey that I hated him and the bond, and I wanted him to fuck off, all I get is static most of the time. I didn't understand why I still sometimes get things, but not all the time, but then dad explained what he and Loki think."

She laid it all out for Zach, trying her best to explain it to him like her dad did and her best friend listened, nodded in places, and then when she told him that Fenrir must be getting everything from her and because he was blocking the feedback to her, he couldn't block her feedback to him.

"Do you think he's trying to protect you in his own way?"

Ash shrugged, playing with the chain around her neck. "That's what my dad thinks. That he thinks blocking me will stop me from hating him so much. I remember what he said to me when he came into the past to find me. The pain when he spoke in my mind and said, *You left me.* I did leave him without a second thought to myself about how it would affect him."

"Ash, you were scared and confused. You can't blame yourself for that."

Ash peered over at Zach. "He was so overwhelmed by the sudden loss that he almost killed you. I'd never have forgiven myself if my selfishness cost me you."

Zach nudged her shoulder. "Hey, I'm still here. And so is he. And for someone who doesn't have the capacity to form bonds, Fenrir is trying really hard to play nice with your family and friends. Your dad's language analogy is spot on. Maybe cut him and yourself some slack."

Ash didn't get a chance to respond because Killian and Chrissy came out of the building and headed straight for them. Her team leader and his partner looked a little pale, but Ash noted that Chrissy looked a little green. Reaching out, she touched her hand to Chrissy's.

"It's hard to compartmentalize a scene like that. You okay?"

Chrissy gave Ash a tight smile. "I'm grand, thanks."

"I've got it!" Shouted Ricky as he appeared out of the bin like a jack in the box, carrying the severed head like a trophy.

Zach groaned, rolling his eyes with a smile on his face. "It would be less embarrassing if he wasn't grinning like he had won the lotto."

"If you think that's embarrassing, just remember the time you and me walked into the squad room and caught your parents in a compromising position."

Zach shoved at her. "Fuck off, A.K. Mom was only feeding."

Ash laughed as she bounced out of his way. "Oh ya, then why did your dad have his pants around his ankles?"

Zach growled stalking toward her. "I hate you. I fucking hate you."

"No, you don't you love me." Ash blew Zach a kiss and laughed as he gave her the finger. It felt good to laugh even though they were in the middle of a horrendous crime scene.

Having looked at the head and obviously not spotting anything of interest, Fenrir had walked out into the carpark. She saw his nose twitch and then he was walking further away from the crime scene. She caught her dad's eye and he nodded, knowing that Ash was going after him.

Fenrir kept walking as Ash tried to stay downwind of whatever he was tracking, and she knew damn well not to get in the way of a wolf on the hunt. When he stopped suddenly, and crouched down, his hand reached and when he lifted it, there was blood.

"Come, Ashlyn, tell me what you scent."

Ash crouched down beside him and inhaled. She got the scent of blood, a citrusy sort of bitter scent but that was it. She didn't get the scent of anger like Fenrir did, or maybe she didn't associate it like he did.

"I can smell the victim's blood and a bitter sort of scent. Is that what anger smells like to you?"

Fenrir shrugged, keeping his eyes out into the darkness. "It can differ. Your anger smells like your scent, and fire, but that is because I am attuned to you. Stranger's scents are just that. I know what it smells like, even if I do not understand it sometimes."

Ash opened her mouth to speak but Fenrir was already rising. "The blood and the scents end here. The killer must have got in a vehicle. There are no cameras here, but as your cat said, the killer's frequency may have interfered with it anyway. Your father is calling us. We should go."

By the time Ash scrambled to her feet, Fenrir was already a couple of strides ahead of her and she came up to them after Fenrir had given him the added information. Her dad told Fenrir they were all heading back to the station and to come with them.

Fenrir glanced at her, and Ash gave him a smile before Fenrir vanished.

The wolf inside her howled at his absence.

"Oh thank fuck," Donnie mumbled, coming to stand with them. "I don't think my stomach could deal with the trip back."

The Killer

THE WOLF GOD SAW TOO MUCH.

The wolf god knew to look for their scent, their anger.

They should not have left the heart. They should have taken it and kept it to eat at a later stage but the thought of eating again made them want to vomit. They had tried to purge the bloated feeling from their person to no avail. They were starting to think that it was because of the god power in their veins that they were starting to lose the things that made them human.

Though they had never been human to begin with.

They needed to take a beat...make the team think that they had stopped their killing spree. Let the power settle into their bones, and then, when they were all rested then they could strike again.

It had occurred to them that the god who had come to them and offered the bargain was making them ill so that their end of the bargain could be fulfilled. They knew that the power promised to them wouldn't truly be theirs until Donnie O'Carroll removed the chains that bound him.

Leaning against the sink, they lifted one hand and placed it on the mirror and the connection shimmered into being. The god sat in the cave he was being held and lifted his eyes to meet theirs in the mirror.

"Do you have the grandson of Tyr?"

"Not yet. The monstrous wolf sees things unlike the others. He might find out who I am."

Odin tapped his chin, his eyes gleaming. "Then make them think that it is the son of Loki that they hunt for. Steer them in his direction and whilst they look to Fenrir, bring me the vampire. Then the power that eats at you will be yours, absolutely."

A wave of pain rippled through their body and the connection to Odin severed.

They could kill again and put the blame of the wolf god.

And then once they delivered Donnie to Odin, the power would be theirs.

Chapter Nine

Fenrir

FENRIR WAS PERPLEXED THAT ASHLYN HAD SEEMED MORE AT ease with his wolf form then of him in his human form. There was none of the trepidation that she felt when he was in human skin, and he could not make sense of it. When he had flashed back to the station, Fenrir had taken out his journal and written down the scenario so that he could ask his father when they next saw one another.

Loki had been very accommodating with Fenrir and never made him feel abnormal for asking question that a normal supernatural would already have understood. He had not expected his father to be, well fatherly, like he observed the other parents be, however Fenrir was appreciative of his advice.

As Fenrir walked through the station, he still garnered attention, though it was less than when he first arrived. He did not like too much attention on him, unless it was Ashlyn who was giving it, though her attention since that night she sent him away had been dwindling.

Fenrir heard voices from inside the coms room, and he paused as he heard Freya's son say to the vampire. "You shouldn't come too close. I don't want my power to influence you."

"Why won't you believe me when I tell you it won't? You

could come out with me one night and I'll show you how unaffected I am by it."

It was the vampire Fenrir did not like. The pretty one that Ashlyn was always laughing with. He had overheard his mate talking to the cat when the vampire had first joined the team, when he had been spying on her, and she had said that she found him pretty.

Fenrir was not pretty. He was rough around the edges. He would never be pretty like the vampire who made her laugh, and it made him want to kill this vampire. He was an obstacle in his way and if it would not have upset Ashlyn, he would already have killed him.

"I know absolutely nothing about you." Arik muttered, and then the pretty vampire chuckled.

"Come out with me and get to know me."

"No. Now please let me get back to work."

Fenrir thought back on a conversation that he had with Loki, where Loki explained that if a person says no, and they sound like they are in distress, it was their duty to step in and protect them. Ashlyn would step in but Fenrir could not figure out if Ashlyn's uncle was actually in distress.

He didn't scent like he was afraid.

Fenrir stayed where he was just in case, then heard the vampire sigh. "I like to wear blue socks."

"I'm sorry, what? Blue socks?"

The vampire chuckled and Fenrir thought it sounded like when Ashlyn's cat was …flirting with a woman. "I wear dark clothes all the time and the blue socks are cheerful. It's like a secret and now you know something about me that no one else does. So now you'll come out with me?"

"No. I will not. Please leave me alone."

Fenrir heard the scrape of a chair, and he flashed outside, not wanting the young god to know that he had been snooping, as

Lyra called it. It was apparently rude to listen in to other people's conversations. Fenrir didn't understand how it was rude. If they wanted to have a private conversation, then it should be had where someone didn't have the opportunity to listen in.

The night had fully settled in while they were at the crime scene, the moon peeking out through a blanket of clouds, and Fenrir could scent rain in the air. He sat on top of one of the tables, his feet on the bench and lifted his face to the sky. He…enjoyed…yes, that was the feeling. He enjoyed being outside. For too long, Fenrir had only been able to see the outside of the cave where he had resided, the outside world there, but out of his grasp.

It was why he now tried not to linger inside if he could avoid it.

Loki had asked him once if he could pinpoint when or if he ever had emotions. Fenrir had shrugged, stating that he had always found it hard to understand the emotions of others, however, Tyr's trickery had done something else to him on a fundamental level. Loki believed it was the years of isolation, of not having any companionship, that made him the sociopath.

Fenrir did not argue with him because he knew Loki felt guilty about not having found him sooner. And as Loki was helping him, Fenrir had told Loki that if he had been freed before Donnie and Ricky came to him, then it might not have been good for Midgard and the only way he was here and not mindless was because of his tie to Ashlyn.

The door opened behind him and he heard Arik swearing under his breath and he kicked something that clattered along the concrete. Fenrir kept his gaze adverted, but he felt the young god come further down and then he spotted Fenrir.

Fenrir wondered if he would retreat inside, but Fenrir could hear his heart beating as he came round, and Arik's gaze landed on him. His scrutiny made Fenrir want to snarl, though that might scare the other man, and in return make Ashlyn mad.

Turning his head so that he was looking at Ashlyn's uncle, the man swallowed hard, then glanced at the door like he wanted to run. Fenrir snorted, then looked back up at the moon.

"Have you a question, little god? Ask it and I may answer."

Arik hesitated, then said. "May I sit?"

Fenrir didn't like having people that close to him, especially ones with the power to possibly make him feel love for someone other than Ashlyn. He nodded however, and Arik climbed up to sit beside him on the table. They sat in relative silence for a time, and Fenrir found that he was not annoyed by Arik's presence.

"What's it like not to feel?" Arik asked quietly.

Fenrir glanced at the other man. "Is this because of the pretty vampire?"

Arik choked out a laugh, though Fenrir hadn't been trying to make a joke or be amusing.

"Do you think Torin is pretty?" Arik asked him, a smile on his face.

Fenrir snorted. "I do not. Ashlyn called him pretty once. I am trying to understand if others think he is pretty too."

By the way Arik's cheeks pinked, he obviously did think the vampire was pretty like Ashlyn did.

"You don't have to worry about Ash thinking Torin is pretty. She's never been attracted to pretty guys. I mean she had this massive crush on Donnie for years and the-"

Fenrir growled. This was new information to him. Donnie was mated and should not be what Ashlyn was looking at. She should be looking at him.

"Shit, I'm sorry. Like she was a kid. She grew out of it. She doesn't like Donnie in that way anymore. Okay?"

Fenrir had yet to decide if he needed to have a word with Tyr's grandson or not.

"Anyways, you don't have to answer me. I was just curious."

Fenrir shifted to look at the young god, then he shrugged. "It is all I have ever known. There are some emotions that I understand, anger, jealously, but too many that are foreign to me. I...understand is the wrong word, but I know through the bond that Ashlyn loves you. I don't understand why even though I know you are family. That is the only way I can explain it."

"That actually makes sense."

Fenrir was surprised that he had managed to explain it in a way that Arik could understand.

"I would ask you a question in return."

Arik grinned and leaned his chin on his hand that rested on his knee. "Shoot. I'll try and answer it as well as you did mine."

Fenrir did not know why Arik was praising him when it was of no benefit to the young god, Fenrir had already answered his question.

"How does it make you feel to know that with your power, it would be almost impossible to understand if someone loved you in truth?" Arik looked away and Fenrir wondered if he had upset him, and Loki had told him that it was important to acknowledge when you upset someone. "I upset you. That was not my intention."

Arik looked back at Fenrir, gave him a small smile. "It's grand. It's actually refreshing not to have someone tip toe around me like I'm delicate. I don't know how I'll feel if I ever do want to be with someone like that. I know my family loves me and my friends but there have been too many times when I've not been in full control and another person gets obsessed by me. But if it happens, and I find out, I can let you know."

Fenrir inclined his head, thinking that Arik would leave him now that he had gotten what he wanted from Fenrir. The other man stayed where he was though, then he asked softly. "Are you having trouble understanding how Ash feels about you?"

"No. I know all too well that she despises me."

Arik chuckled, then stopped when Fenrir glared at him. "I meant no offense, but since I am the son of the goddess of love, then maybe I can help."

That sounded reasonable to Fenrir.

Fenrir tilted his head and watched the other man as he smiled. "Ash is an open book with her affections. She loves hard and she isn't stingy with it."

"She is not like that with me. I know what it feels like for Ashlyn to love and she does not have that emotion with me."

Arik tapped his chin. "You know that there are different kinds of love, right?"

Fenrir just stared back at him blankly so that Arik would know that he didn't.

"Okay, let me see if I can explain this to you. If it doesn't make sense, tell me and I can try and word it another way." When Fenrir didn't respond, Arik continued. "There is a difference between the love you have for family and being in love with someone. So, like your dad, is in love with Erika, but he also loves you and your sisters. He loves Ever and Ash. But he will only feel the kind of love he does for Erika with Erika. Cause you only have that with one person."

Fenrir's head was starting to hurt. "Does it feel different?"

Arik nodded and Fenrir noted that he had come a little closer than he would any other stranger. "Yup, so when it comes to Ash and you thinking she doesn't love you, then it could be because you have felt the love she has for say me, and you've just not understood the feeling of her being in love with you."

"Because she will only feel that with me?"

Arik grinned and nodded. "Exactly. But when someone tells you that they love you, and when Ash says it to you, then when you feel her feelings, you'll get it."

"And if she does not tell me that?" Fenrir asked, the words falling from his mouth before he could stifle them.

Arik's expression looked confused. "She's your mate, of course she would."

Fenrir knew there was no point in discussing his situation further with the other man, who understood emotions more than Fenrir ever could. It did not make sense to him that there would be different types of one emotion, like different flavours of crisps. That was too much for him to not be sceptical about.

"Arik, your dad is looking for you."

Fenrir had felt his mate the moment that she had come to the station, then tracked him out here. She had not heard any of his conversation with Arik, but Fenrir could hear the strain in her tone. Protective of her uncle, especially when said uncle reached out and rested his hand on Fenrir's forearm.

"Thank you for your honesty. I appreciate it."

Arik slipped off the bench and then Fenrir turned to see Ashlyn embrace him. Arik kissed her cheek, and she ruffled his hair. Fenrir looked away when Ashlyn lifted her amber eyes to his, and he rested his elbows on his thighs, then rested his chin in his hands.

Ashlyn came over and sat down on the seat, and Fenrir almost sighed when she leaned against his legs and tilted her head, so it was on his knee. Unable to stop himself, he ran a hand over her hair, and she sighed, sounding almost content.

"You gave the team a lot to work from today. Dad was impressed."

Fenrir snorted, rolling his eyes as he played with her hair. "It is not your father I was aiming to impress."

Ashlyn snorted, then her hand cupped Fenrir's leg and she ran her hand up and down his calf. His pulse quickened and his chest tightened. For a moment he wondered if he were dreaming, though he knew he did not have the capacity to dream. His body never reacted to anyone but his mate, his Ashlyn, and Fenrir knew it was because of the mate bond that he could react to her.

"Well, if it wouldn't go to your head and stroke your ego, then I would say I was impressed too. It never occurred to me that emotions had a scent. You taught me something today."

Her hand was still running up and down his leg.

"I think I prefer you stroking my leg more than my ego."

Ashlyn burst out laughing, and he felt it, her joy, like when she had laughed at the pretty vampire, and he had done that. He had made her laugh and be filled with joy around him. A tremor ran though him, and it had Ashlyn lifting her head to look at him,

"Grey?"

The joy was fading along the bond, and he wanted to hold onto it, savour it before she went back to hating him again.

"Talk to me, Grey. What just happened?"

"You laughed and I felt your joy through the bond. You felt the same as you do when with the cat or laughing at the stupid pretty vampire I cannot kill because it would upset you. But this time it was for me, and it…it… pleased me. I made you joyful."

Ashlyn's expression turned from joyful to pitiful and Fenrir snarled, shoving off the bench to stalk over to the fence that kept them caged in. He could feel himself getting angry and he did not want to lose his temper with Ashlyn. Fenrir should have just kept his mouth shut.

"Grey, it's okay."

Her hand landed on his shoulder, and he whirled round. "It is not okay, Ashlyn. You hate me. I know that. I *feel* that. You have me following you like a puppy on a leash, and I hate myself for it. And yet, I cannot stay away. I need you to stay sane and you do not need me at all. I try and I try and I cannot bear to even look at myself in the mirror."

Ashlyn's expression told Fenrir that she was shocked by his outburst, as was he, but he could not put a lid on his anger. His eyes reddened and he snarled, shaking his head. When Ashlyn made to put her hand on his chest hoping to sooth him, to coddle him, Fenrir jerked backward out of her grasp.

"Grey, I don't hate you. Far from it. That's the problem here."

"Don't try and confuse me with subtext, Ashlyn."

Ashlyn placed a hand over the spot where her heart was. "I'm not trying to, Grey. I'm trying to tell you that I don't hate you. I'm trying to understand you, understand the bond."

"So you can sever it? So you can be free of me?" He snarled, saw it in her eyes.

Fenrir clenched his fists and pressed them to his temples. There was too much in there that he could not contain, and he longed to go back to the time when he was just him and he did not have parts of her inside of him. There was no going back though, and he would only ever be hers.

Her fingers wrapped around his wrists, and she gently pulled his fists down to look him in the face. He couldn't stand to have her look at him like he was weak. He rested his forehead against hers. "This is torture. This is killing me. I would prefer to be bound by Gleipnir once more then to live this never-ending cycle with you. I would be free of you if I could. I escaped one binding for another but at least with Gleipnir, I did not feel."

Ashlyn sucked in a breath, her amber eyes widening, and Fenrir could take no more. He crushed his lips to hers, stroking his tongue into her mouth, felt her soften against him. He kept on kissing her, pouring his anger, his pain into it, though he was not sure what outcome he wanted to achieve by unleashing himself on her.

Walking them backwards so that Ashlyn's back was against the fence he kissed her and kissed her, her hands clutching his tee as she tried to pull him closer, and it drove him insane for her. Fenrir wanted to strip her bare, bend her over the bench and mount her in the most primal of matings, have her moan his name as he took her like a mate should take their mate.

Her nails scrapped at his neck, her moan vibrating against his lips. Fenrir knew that he could get drunk from the taste of her, the feel of her, and he would use his body to persuade her because when he kissed her, Fenrir knew in that moment Ashlyn wanted him as much as he wanted her.

Though it would not last.

Fenrir broke the kiss, taking a step back and Ashlyn stumbled forward. Her lips were kiss swollen, her cheeks flushed, and her lips parted to form an O, like she was surprised that Fenrir had put a stop to what could have happened.

Already he could feel her regret kissing him back.

"I would have swallowed the sun for you, let it burn me from the inside out. But perhaps I do not need to...you are doing a great job of that yourself, Ashlyn. Your flame will burn me from the inside out until I am nothing but ash."

Fenrir flashed away before his mate had a chance to respond.

The Killer

THE RAT DIDN'T PUT UP ANY FIGHT WHEN THEY SLICED THEIR throat. He cried when he realized that he was about to die. This kill did not sit well with them. The rat was not part of the ring, and he did not deserve to be used as a decoy just to pin the blame on Fenrir. It was why they could not bring themselves to eat the heart and had tossed it to the side. Everything about this felt wrong.

Changing into their new wolf form, they clawed and shredded the rat who was already dead, then padded over to the bag and pulled out the t-shirt they had taken from the station laundry and ripped that to shreds too, scattering Fenrir's scent and clothing all over the crime scene.

Changing back, they picked up a piece of the t-shirt and pressed it into the rats clawed hand, to give the appearance of a struggle. They assessed the scene, knew that was all they could stomach, and tried to ignore the overwhelming sense of wrongness in this kill.

It was for the greater good...the endgame of their quest for justice.

The rat was collateral damage, that was all.

It would all be worth it in the end...

It had to be.

Chapter Ten

Ash

Ash still felt like shit two days after her blistering kiss with Fenrir. There had been pure torment in his eyes when he had broken the kiss to say the words Ash would never ever forget for as long as she lived, each word like a bullet to the chest.

"I would have swallowed the sun for you, let it burn me from the inside out. But perhaps I do not need to...you are doing a great job of that yourself, Ashlyn. Your flame will burn me from the inside out until I am nothing but ash."

It wasn't exactly a declaration of love, but damn if it hadn't ignited something in Ash that she had been denying for years. Two days had passed since their kiss, and two days since Fenrir had made an appearance. Ash knew that he was still working because her dad mentioned him in briefings, and that he was chasing down some leads, but Ash wondered if he was avoiding her.

Well, you avoiding him for five years so what do you expect?

Ash hadn't told anyone but Zach about what happened, and all Zach said was that having spent a little time with Fenrir on the case, that it was easy to see that some things went over his head, and it must be confusing for him.

She knew that even if her dad had had to kinda explain it all to her. Having him around again prior to the last couple of days had given her a sense of peace, of calm, her anger less triggered and her sadness less so. She had attested it to her wolf being around its mate, of being so near after the years apart, and that theory was sort of proven with the way her inner wolf sulked and mourned the distance of her mate now.

"Hey kiddo, what's going on?"

Ash looked up to see Donnie striding into the canteen. She'd had a crush on him when she was a teen, one that had fizzled out long before she had gone to Niflheim, and the bond had snapped into place. He was still handsome, and Ash could see why her aunt had been driven to make the former rugby player a vampire.

Donnie chuckled, rolling his eyes. "If I could blush right now, I totally would."

"Fuck right off." Ash replied with a half-hearted growl that made Donnie laugh even more. The vampire leaned against the counter, hands in his pockets as Ash finished making her coffee and then looked over at him. Donnie's knowing smile made her sigh and she walked over to the other counter and hoisted herself up.

"What's got you thinking too hard?"

Ash gave him a look, that had Donnie offering her a small smile. "A certain wolf god?"

"Yup. We kinda had some weird argument and then he's been MIA the last few days. I only know he's still around because he's working the case." *Without me....*

Donnie sighed and glanced toward the door, then back at Ash. "Listen, I'm not looking to betray any confidences or anything here, but I kinda feel bad for the guy. It's a completely different scenario, and yet, I was once the vampire who could tell that his mate wanted him, and maddingly couldn't admit it to herself. But I had the capacity to understand why Caitlyn was so opposed to our getting together. Fenrir might feel things through the bond, but not understand them."

Ash took a sip of her coffee, digesting what Donnie said and then he continued. "He came to Loki's the other night. I was there with Erika and Lyra, and he arrived and just stood there. I could hear his thoughts, knew what had happened, and then he growled and punched the wall. Then he sat down against the wall. Erika called Loki, and despite Erika trying to stop her, Lyra went over and sat beside him and just stayed there until Loki came."

Ash hated that she was causing him all this pain. Despised that her flip-flopping emotions had led to Fenrir having some sort of breakdown. The coffee tasted like dirt, so she set it aside.

"I didn't mean to hurt him. I know there are things he can't understand but is it so wrong for me to want a mate that fits in with my life? One that gets on with my family and friends and doesn't hang around with them just because he knows it will make me happy?"

Donnie shrugged. "I can't tell you whether it's right or wrong, Ash. I think your wolf realized that there would be no mate stronger than Fenrir that they would accept. You'd never have been happy with a weak mate. The power imbalance would have been too great, and it would have made you both miserable. Though it seems you are both miserable now. Hell, even Erika felt sorry for Fenrir."

"Did he say anything?"

"Ya but are you sure you wanna know? Will it change anything?" Donnie asked, and Ash had no words to form an answer for him, so she just nodded.

"When Loki arrived, Fenrir finally lifted his head and asked Loki if it was possible to kill something that would not or could not die. Loki said that all things could die once you found a way. And Fenrir just nodded, and replied that it was good to know, since Loki may have to kill him yet. Then he vanished and Loki went off to find him."

Ash opened her mouth to respond when Donnie's phone rang. The smile that curved his lips was instantly illuminating, and Ash knew that there was only one person who could make Donnie smile like that.

"Hey babe, I'm here with Ash. You miss me already?"

Whatever Caitlyn said back to her mate had him laughing. Thanks to one of Zach's little inventions, he had done something to their mobile phones that meant that supernatural hearing couldn't listen in on calls. It had taken a couple dozen mobile phones and setting of the sprinklers due to fire later before he had perfected it.

"Okay, got it. I'll grab Zach and bring him with me and Ash. I love you."

Donnie hung up and glanced over at Ash who was staring at him. "What?"

"See, that's what I want…banter and teasing and I love you. I want easy like everyone else seems to have."

Donnie barked out a laugh, shaking his head. "Ash, none of us had it easy in the beginning. It's easy now because we went through all kinds of shite to get to where we are now. Your parents kept finding one another and dying in a curse. Ricky and Melanie had to get through some though things too to get to being happy. Me and Cait, you know what happened to her, I was never sure she could allow herself to love me. Hell, even Loki and Erika didn't get together for millennia because neither of them wanted to admit their feelings."

Striding over to where Ash was sitting on the counter, Donnie reached out and put a hand on her shoulder. "You have to go through the hard stuff to appreciate the easy stuff. One day, it will be you talking to your kids or your friends' kids, and you'll get it. I promise. Right, we got a body, same MO but Caitlyn said they've deviated from wolves."

Having collected Zach from the control room, they headed off to the crime scene and Ash's brain hurt. She wondered if Fenrir would be at the crime scene or if he'd still stay away...she knew she needed to talk to him, but she really didn't know what she was going to say to him.

When they arrived at the crime scene, Ash recognised the place as where she usually met up with Twitch, his patch behind in the alleyway. Fuck, was one of Twitch's minions killed by the killer and why the hell would the killer switch up their victim types right in the middle of a spree?

Were the Paranormal Investigations Team getting close to finding the killer and this was a way to throw them off the scent, disrupt the hunt?

Jesus, she was starting to sound like Fenrir...

Her dad was crouched down over the body, pointing things out to a stoic looking Gideon, who must have been with him when the call came in. There was no denying that the two men were related, even if you looked past the amber eyes that Ash also shared. Her brother was tall, dark and didn't actually look anything like the troll she constantly called him.

As if he sensed her approach, Gideon lifted his gaze, gave her a nod, then went back to watching their dad point stuff out on the body. Ash walked toward them, the scent of blood, urine, and death lingering in the air. As she got closer to the body, Ash felt her stomach bottom out as she finally got a clear look at the victim's face.

The only part of the body that was not ripped apart in a frenzy, Twitch's eyes were wide in fear and his mouth was open in a silent scream. Fuck...had Twitch managed to get some information about the killer and the killer had struck so that Twitch could not pass on the information to Ash?

Or had Ash led the killer right to Twitch and it had gotten him killed?

"No ID on the body. Scent alone tells me he's a rat, so I sent a call to the rat alpha to see if she's missing any of her people."

Zach had come up behind her as Ash replied to her dad. "His real name is John Smith, aka Twitch. He was my CI."

Her dad got up and came over to her. "Don't let this unnerve you, Ash. Use it as fuel. Means we are getting too close, and the killer is running scared. Work the case. Can you do that?"

"Yes sir."

Ash stepped around her dad and went to examine the body. Twitch's body seemed like overkill. Yes, a lot of the crime scenes had violent murders, but something about Twitch's body seemed…off.

Each of the other wolf kills had seemed personal, like the killer had enjoyed the hunt and the kill. This one though, just didn't feel right to Ash. It was frenzied, yes, but no deliberate strikes apart from the throat, and then it was like the killer just wanted the killing to be over. The heart hadn't even been eaten, just ripped out and discarded.

Thinking back to the way Fenrir had assessed the scene, Ash closed her eyes and inhaled. She got the scent of fear, of anger, then what the hell was that…regret?

Ash inhaled deeper, then froze, leaning more toward the body. There was a faint scent that she recognised, and it made her stomach dip and she almost stumbled backward. She knew that it must be too faint for anyone else to pick up, the strongest coming from the piece of fabric clenched in Twitch's grasp.

Grey…the scent was Grey's.

Ash thought back to how Grey had changed forms and shrunk himself down to match the claw marks on the previous victim. Grey enjoyed the hunt; he enjoyed a kill. It was a quirk of being a wolf that meant he sometimes behaved in a manner outside of the atypical parameters of sociopathy. But Ash knew that if Fenrir was responsible for killing Twitch, she'd not have scented any regret. She knew this because regret was not something Grey was capable of.

Before she keeled over, Ash got to her feet and walked away, trying to make sense of things in her head. Ash knew that there were two possible outcomes here. One – Fenrir had been the killer all along and he was killing under their noses. Or two – someone knew that P.I.T. had brought in Fenrir and were closer than ever to catching them and had somehow managed to put Fenrir's scent on the body to make it look like Fenrir was the one behind the murders.

It wasn't that Ash believed that Fenrir wasn't capable of the murders, far from it, Ash just had a hard time believing that he would risk being back in her life by killing Twitch, plus it hadn't seemed like he had anticipated her dad would have asked him for help in the first place. She had read once that sociopaths acted so that circumstances benefitted them, however Ash couldn't see how any of the murders would benefit Fenrir.

It would give him an excuse to be around you...

The thought struck Ash like a bolt of lightning. That couldn't be it, could it? Had they all misjudged the situation that badly? Had Fenrir really killed all those wolves, including Arthur De Valera and his family, just to put himself in her orbit? Had he orchestrated all of this for a purely selfish reason?

No...it wasn't possible.

That's what Ash told herself as she tried to make sense of it all in her head. If this was Fenrir, then he would have been smarter to hide himself and wouldn't have let Ash pick up his scent on Twitch. There had to be an explanation that made more sense, because right now, this was a head fuck of epic proportions.

"Ash, you okay?"

Ash peered over her shoulder to see Zach looking at her with a worried expression. He was her best friend, she could tell him, right? She could tell him the conclusions that she was jumping to, and Zach would tell her that she was wrong, that Fenrir wouldn't do this. Zach would keep her secrets like she did his, but he would urge Ash to tell her dad and then her dad would try and lock Grey up while they investigated to see if he truly was behind all the killing.

She couldn't see him locked up again because of her. If she was wrong, if Grey was being set up, then Ash would just have to prove it herself and then give the team the heads up. Fenrir was her mate, and she would protect him until she was sure of the truth.

Plastering on a fake smile, Ash nodded to Zach. "Ya, all good. I can't believe Twitch is dead. He was a little dickhead but harmless most of the time."

"Your dad said that the MO didn't fit, so we could be looking at a copycat, someone who knows the ins and outs of the murders and was trying to replicate um."

That tracked with Ash's defence of Fenrir, though all it proved was that this murder was different to the others, and still kept Fenrir in the frame for killing Twitch. If there was a copycat, then it had to be someone with inside knowledge of the crimes, because it was almost picture perfect.

Did they have a mole inside P.I.T.?

Her dad came over then, and repeated what Zach had just said, then he asked Zach and Ash to go back to the station and scour CCTV footage to see when Twitch entered the area and if by some miracle the killer's frequency hadn't messed with the CCTV in the area. Of course, if it was a copycat then the fact that the CCTV footage was OK would also help support that.

Donnie tossed Zach the keys to his car, told them to take it to go back to the station and then he walked over to where Caitlyn was standing with a woman in skyscraper heels and a stern expression. The rat alpha had made an appearance herself and Ash was relieved that she had already been sent to sit down and watch hours of footage. That was far preferable than dealing with shifter politics right now.

Plus, she was hoping she would catch something that exonerated Grey.

Her dad called out to Ash as her and Zach were leaving, asking her to take Gideon to the station as well. There was no way Ash was going to divulge any findings to Zach while Gideon was in the car, so as they headed away from the crime scene, the three of them sat in a stony silence.

Zach tapped the steering wheel along with the music, and Ash leaned back in her seat and closed her eyes, trying to put all the pieces of the puzzle together, but just couldn't get them to all fit. Her head was starting to pound, then it suddenly subsided, like it was sucked into a drain.

Grey?

The mating bond crackled with static, and Ash huffed out a frustrated breath. Had Fenrir been able to decipher her thoughts through the bond? As much as Ash didn't want to be mated, she knew that it would be easier if the bond was working as it should so that she could know for certain that Grey wasn't the killer.

"Wolves in Cork are getting angsty." Gideon said as Ash glanced into the mirror to see her brother looking out the window, his dark hair falling into his face. "A couple of friends from secondary school have already dropped out of college to travel. No one is believing dad when he says that the killer is targeting wolves who are the scum of society. Arthur wasn't scum. Everyone is scared."

Ash flashed Gideon a wolfish grin. "It's okay little bro. I'll protect you from the scary killer."

Gideon barked out a laugh, shaking his head, Ash's remark having the desired effect. "Fuck off, Ash. I can look after myself."

"Sure, baby bro. If you say so."

Gideon growled and leaned forward to flick Ash in the ear, and she turned to slap him upside the head. Zach yelled at them to behave, or he was pulling the car over and that had Ash and Gideon laughing so hard because Zach had sounded so much like his dad, that they were crying.

"This is why I'm glad to be an only child. The moment you two are in a small space you resort to being kids again."

Ash punched him in the shoulder. "Hey, you used to torment him as much as I did, and you were older. You were the one who suggested we dressed him up in a gown when he got drunk at fourteen and told him that he had told dad that he wanted to be a drag artist."

Zach snorted as he drove into the station and parked the car. "It was better than you suggesting we do a makeshift pumping of his stomach. The science didn't make sense. You could have killed him."

"I fucking hate you both, you know that?" Gideon mumbled as he slipped out of the car, slammed the door and headed into the station.

Ash chuckled, then closed her eyes again, feeling guilty for enjoying just a sliver of normality in the horrible situation she found herself in.

"You sure you're okay, Ash? You can talk to me."

Her chest constricted. Zach knew her better than anyone, knew something was bugging her, but all Ash could do was lie and tell him that she was okay, and just a little tired. Ash would tell Zach, she would...she just needed to speak to Fenrir first...

Chapter Eleven

Ash

AFTER MINDLESS HOURS OF SCANNING CCTV, ASH FELT LIKE her head was fit to burst. Zach had figured out the path the killer had taken by piecing together the CCTV footage where the cameras went on the fritz. He tracked the killer the moment they stepped from one area to another, missing a couple of streets simply because there was no CCTV.

Ash had been the one to see the moment right before Twitch was killed, the exact moment the killer entered the alleyway and when they left, and Twitch was dead. The entire attack took less than half an hour, and it screamed with wrongness.

She still hadn't been able to bring up Fenrir's possible involvement to Zach, and her best friend was suspicious. He didn't ask her again, but Ash could feel the weight of his eyes on her as they worked in relative silence.

Ash gave up around two in the morning, and got up to stretch her legs, leaving Zach to his toys. She was going to go home and try and get some sleep, but instead Ash found herself walking toward the training centre on instinct.

Pushing open the double doors, Ash ground to a halt. Fenrir was standing to the side, his sister, Lyra watching him with an eagerness that had Ash wondering what they were doing. Fenrir's back was to her, and yet, she saw him tense as he sensed her arrival.

She hated that she had done this to him. That because of Ash, Fenrir would tense like that when she entered a room. Ash knew it was her fault, and that it must be hell for Fenrir to feel how conflicted Ash was about her feelings for Fenrir, but she couldn't help how she felt about everything. It wasn't like she was being awkward for the sake of it.

Lyra glanced over at Ash, then back at Grey, the young woman not offering Ash her usually sunny greeting and instead, there was a fierceness in her eyes that Ash approved of. They might all be this weird fucked up family, but Lyra was not happy that Ash had upset her brother.

Fenrir was showing Lyra an arm throw, where if you used your strength in the right way, you could flip an opponent and gain the upper hand. Lyra moved to do it, and Ash knew she would be no match for Fenrir's strength and agility, though Ash was surprised when Fenrir allowed himself to be flipped, or helped Lyra along, Ash couldn't be sure, then landed sure footed and nodded his head in approval.

Lyra beamed at that slight nod, as Fenrir shifted his gaze to the right, then back at his sister. Ash looked in the direction of where Fenrir had been looking to see her aunt sitting on the bench, and Ash had been so focused on Grey that she hadn't noticed her mom sitting on the bench beside her.

Ever Chace, now Doyle, gave her a knowing smile and then rose with then grace of a queen, which was not that surprising considering her mom was just that, Queen of the Valkyrie. Her mom looked like any other twenty something woman with shoulder length blonde hair, blue eyes, and a warm smile. You'd never know that Ever was the daughter of Odin, her power coiled inside her for when she needed it.

Growing up, Ash had never once wished to have more of her mother's Valkyrie genes, because she had the power of Thor running in her veins so she could fly like her mom, just in a different way since she had no wings. Since losing

Mjolnir though, there had been times when Ash had longed to fly again, and she may have secretly hoped some dormant gene might be triggered.

Her mom came over and pulled her in for a hug. For a time after Ash had returned from the past, and the knowledge of the change affected the future, her mom had tried to overcompensate for what she might have done, even though Ash had explained numerous times that they were good. She'd had to leave her mom to deal with her own feelings, as Ash tried to deal with hers and there had been a little distance between them.

But then it had one day just all been okay...

"I missed you, Ash."

"I missed you too, mom. How was Valhalla?"

Her mom let her go, and grinned. "As beautiful as always. Lots of Asgardians landing to be trained. Danae is in her element. Your grandmother scolded her for being too hard on some of the younger ones, according to Kenzie."

Ash snorted, knowing that Freya had once been closed off and sometimes cruel to the Valkyrie she had under her tutelage. Not that Ash blamed the goddess after what Odin had put her through. Seeing her with Killian and Arik now, you'd never have known she once was so closed off that no one thought she could ever be capable of loving anyone.

"Have you seen dad yet?" Ash asked as her mom linked her arm and they walked over to the benches to sit down beside Erika, the Valkyrie general's eyes not moving from where her daughter trained with Fenrir.

Her mom shook her head. "No, he was out when I arrived. He'll come find me when he gets the time. He always does."

Her mom's love for her dad had transcended multiple lives, and obstacles, but they were still going strong and had a romance worthy of a romcom. Ash wasn't sure if she wanted that kind of bond with a mate, but she wanted to know that she was loved and understood.

Erika muttered a cruse and jerked like she was going to get up, as Ash turned her attention to where the siblings sparring, where Lyra had managed to land a punch to Grey's face. She stepped back, her eyes wide as she looked at her brother, waiting for him to react.

A burst of connection through the bond had Ash sucking in a breath.

Tell the general I will not harm the child. She is following what I tell her so no need to harm her.

The static came roaring back and the loss of the bond almost brought tears to her eyes. Erika went to get up, but Ash put a hand on her leg. "It's okay. Grey won't hurt her. He said to tell you that he won't harm Lyra for simply doing what she was told to by him."

That seemed to relax Erika just a little bit as Fenrir took step toward Lyra and motioned for her to give him her hand. He folded her fingers into a fist, making sure to tuck in her thumb. Then Ash watched with curiosity as Fenrir began to speak.

"You do not have the benefit of claws, or balance, so you must make it so that if you are attacked that you strike and give yourself the opportunity to run."

Lyra pressed her lips together in a pout. "But I don't want to be a coward and run away. My mom would never run away, Ash would never run away, and they are both bad asses. You would never run away."

Fenrir lifted his free hand and his fingers morphed into claws. "I have claws and teeth, as does Ashlyn. Your mother has the song of war in her blood. That is enough to halt her from having the sense to run when she is outmatched."

"That's fucking rude. Not totally untrue but still fucking rude." Erika mumbled and Lyra laughed.

Lyra's face went serious, a look of sheer determination on her face. "Okay, show me what to do."

Ash watched as Fenrir showed her the old reliable of nose, throat, and groin, the last part making Lyra blush in a way that had Fenrir tilting his head like he was unsure what he had said that had embarrassed Lyra. There was no doubt that Lyra had already gotten this training before, like she had when she was younger, but she kept her face interested and then it dawned on Ash.

Lyra just wanted to spend time with Fenrir, and this was probably one of the only ways she could get him to spend time with her. Ash thought back to the messing about she and Gideon had in the car, and how Lyra must be smart enough to consider that she wouldn't have that kind of relationship with her brother.

So Lyra was adapting to accommodate Fenrir, to have him in her life.

Why was Ash so reluctant to do that as well?

Should she be adapting to make sure that Grey fit in her world?

It seemed like the sparring session was coming to an end, and Ash could almost feel the disappointment coming off of Lyra. She stood in front of Grey, an expectant look on her face and she knew that Grey just didn't get that his sister was standing there, awaiting his approval.

She wants you to tell her that she's done good, Grey. Lyra wants your approval. Just tell her she did a good job. Trust me.

Ash hoped that what her dad said about the mating bond was true and Grey could get stuff from her, and the theory was proven when Fenrir hesitated, then rested a hand on Lyra's shoulder in a way he must have seen others do.

"You did good. Practice some more and we will see if you can improve."

Lyra beamed and threw her arms around Grey. "Thanks bro."

"I've told her to stop doing that," Erika muttered, shaking her head. "Kid just doesn't fucking listen."

"Just like her mom then." Ever teased and Erika flipped her off, and they all laughed.

Ash watched as Lyra stepped back from the embrace, smiling and then her smile began to fade.

"Erika, spar with Fenrir." Her mom said to her own best friend.

"Do I look like I have a fucking death wish?"

"No but you love a challenge. Go on. It will make Lyra's day."

Erika rolled her eyes, mumbling about what parents did for their kids, as she pushed off the bench and strode over to where her daughter and her stepson still stood. Fenrir stepped beside Lyra and Ash could now see his face as he arched a brow at his stepmother.

"Fancy giving me something to get my blood pumping, Fenrir?"

"Is my father not looking after your needs, General?"

Ash barked out a laugh, Grey shifting his gaze to her for a moment before Lyra scrunched up her nose.

"Ew, Fen, that's not an image I wanted in my head."

"How else do you think you were conceived, Lyra?"

Ash knew Fenrir wasn't actively trying to be funny, but it was hilarious all the same.

"You laughed and I felt your joy through the bond. You felt the same as you do when with the cat or laughing at the stupid pretty vampire I cannot kill because it would upset you. But this time it was for me, and it...it... pleased me. I made you joyful."

Her chest suddenly ached in a way that had Fenrir looking at her with a fierce expression. "I should go."

Shit, he was gonna leave because he thought Ash didn't want him here.

"Stay, I wanna see you two spar." Ash said with a smile, then in her head she said. *I wasn't sad because you were hanging round, Grey. I just thought of something that made me sad. Stay, please.*

Fenrir inclined his head to Ash, then gave Erika a wolfish grin. "Do you need to fetch a weapon, mother, in order to make it even?"

Erika snorted, rolling her eyes as she took off her jumper and handed it to Lyra. "I am a weapon, Fen. Come on then, hit me with your best shot."

Fenrir slowly blinked and Ash could almost hear him working things out in his head. "Father would be upset if I hurt you."

Erika rolled her eyes again. "I can handle your father."

"Obviously not if you are looking to fight me to relieve some tension."

Both Ash and Ever burst out laughing at Fenrir trash talking Erika. It was not something Ash ever expected him to be good at, but it was brilliant to watch. Ash watched then as Fenrir kicked off his boots, then stripped off his black tee and tossed it aside.

Ash's mouth went dry, and her laughter died. She and Grey had been mated for years and she had never seen him like this. She leaned forward, admiring the finely sculpted chest, and abdomen, the strong muscular arms and that delicious V of the hips that seemed to drive any woman crazy.

She wanted to stroke him, pet him, and the shock of it was so visceral that a small growl rumbled in her throat. Fenrir shifted his gaze toward her, and then his lips curved into a smug smile as if he knew that Ash was admiring his body.

That cocky smile let her know that he approved.

Attraction had never been their issue. It was this red-hot flame that was so hot that it was almost combustible whenever they gave in to their desire. Ash had always been honest with him that she was attracted to him...it was everything else that terrified her.

Fenrir turned his attention back to Erika, then he lifted his hand and motioned her forward. "Come, then, daughter of Tyr. Let us see if you keep your hand."

Ash knew that Fenrir was trying to needle Erika, get her to lose her composure but Erika flashed Fenrir this almost sadistic grin. "Stop trash talking, puppy, let's go."

Fenrir chuckled and then neither of them moved, each assessing the other and waiting for them to strike first. And while Erika was one of the best warriors that Ash knew, Fenrir was the bigger predator, the one with the most patience when it came to a hunt, and he would wait for Erika to succumb to the thrill of a fight.

Careful Ashlyn, that almost sounded like a compliment.

It was meant to be, Grey.

Erika must have sensed that Fenrir was distracted because she lunged forward, hoping to catch him by surprise, though Fenrir side stepped her advancement, then swatted her with his hand to use her momentum against her so that she stumbled forward.

Catching herself before she tumbled, Erika spun, and then the fight was on. Fenrir grinned as he dodged Erika's strikes with an almost lazy precision. Erika, on the other hand, threw her attacks in rapid succession, fists and feet flying as she sought to find an opening. Her eyes blazed with determination, a fierce grin playing at the corners of her mouth as she revelled in the challenge before her, and Ash could see the moment Erika realized what she needed to do.

Fenrir on the other hand somehow missed the subtle shift and looked almost bewildered as he went to block a punch only to have Erika perform some ridiculous acrobatic flip bringing her foot cleanly up under his chin with such a crack that even Ash winced.

With only a quick shake of shake of his head, Fenrir swung out his hand across his body and backhanded the Valkyrie general across her face, but it barely even gave her pause. Moving with speeds that no mortals could track Fenrir and Erika seemed to be attacking and blocking in such a way that it seemed neither was making any progress.

Ash had never seen anyone move like Erika and Fenrir did and there was something poetic or some shit about the way they fought. Almost as soon as that thought had occurred to her, her eyes widened as suddenly Fenrir hooked Erika under the arm and swept her legs out from under her. Ash couldn't help but wonder if Fenrir had picked up on her thoughts as Erika landed on her back with an oomph, and Fenrir was on his knees beside her, his hand on her throat, a satisfied grin creeping across his face.

The fighters were both breathing hard from the exertion, as Erika tapped the floor and conceded the fight. Fenrir removed his hand and got to his feet, then held his arm out to help her up, still smiling as he did so.

"Fucking hell, Fen. I haven't enjoyed a sparring like that in ages. Don't tell Boyband, but he might be getting replaced."

Fenrir chuckled. "I would not be opposed to a rematch. You do not pull your punches like some do. You are not afraid to hurt me."

Erika snorted, grinning. "Hell no. You are stronger and bigger than me, and hella fast. If you decided to kill me, I'd have to be prepared to hurt you."

"Then let us hope that neither of us are in that position. It would be a shame to lose a good sparring partner."

Erika brushed the hair from her face, then winced as she

touched her cheek. "Shit, I think that might be broken. Should be healed by the morning though."

Fenrir blinked slowly and took a step back. "I did not mean to do that."

Ash felt his panic along the bond and was about to go to him, try, and explain, but Erika laughed. "I did it when I walked into your elbow. Don't worry about it, Fenrir, I've come home with worse things broken than a cheekbone. Your father mated a warrior, he gets suspicious when I don't come home with bruises. He'll be going mad he missed it though. He would have loved to watch it. Next time, we'll have to invite him."

Fenrir didn't say anything, just vanished, leaving his boots and t-shirt laying where he'd discarded them. Ash sighed, fighting the urge to go find him as her mom reached out and placed a hand on Ash's shoulder, gave it a reassuring squeeze before leaving Ash to her thoughts.

The Killer

THEY HAD NOT FELT LIKE THEMSELVES SINCE KILLING THE RAT.

Each kill they had planned since then did not motivate them, like they were not deserving of the power of the gods in their veins. They still could not stomach the ritual of eating the hearts, which Odin confirmed to them that was needed to sustain the power that was not meant for mere mortals. They might be a werewolf, but the god considered everyone who had no Asgardian blood a mortal.

Reaching out to the cold mirror, the connection between this world and Niflheim burned in their veins as Odin came into view. He looked like he always did, the white-haired legend from Norse mythology.

"You disappoint me, child. You sully the blood of gods that I bestowed upon you."

They were used to disappointing others. Their whole life had been a mistake.

Weak little wolf.

Strange little wolf.

"I can't believe you wet the bed again."

"Come here, little wolf."

"Take off your clothes, little wolf."

"Scream little wolf, I like it when you scream."

They tried to push the memories from their head and focus on the god in front of them.

"You will retrieve the blood of Tyr and bring him to me. I will not be made a fool of by someone like you. My patience is not infinite. Do what you promise, or I will take away the power. And hand you on a platter to my daughter and her meddling family and friends."

They laughed, reminded of a cartoon they used to watch as a child, before that childhood was stolen, about a crime solving group of friends and their dog. A snarl rippled through the connection, and they jerked back from the mirror to clutch a hand to their face, and almost covered the angry handprint on the right side of their face.

Odin was getting more powerful through their connection...

They needed to get Donnie alone and to Niflheim.

Chapter Twelve

Torin

WHEN TORIN MCNAMARA HAD JOINED P.I.T. OVER SIX months ago, he had been delighted to be part of something that he had not been part of in a long time. Torin hated being by himself, for that gave his mind time to replay memories he wished he could forget and took him to a dark place that he would rather not visit.

It was not easy though, being an outsider looking to gain access to the agents and their families. They had been through so much that it did not surprise Torin as to why they kept him on the edges. Ash tried to keep him involved but Torin had not yet earned their trust.

He was adamant that he would though.

It would take time to get them to trust him and Torin knew this because it had taken him a long time to trust that Derek Doyle's offer had been a legitimate one. Torin had once been foolish enough to trust the words of good-looking men, and it had led to nothing but agony.

He was a member of the team, but not quite a member of the family like Derek had offered him. Torin thought back to all the times Derek had shown up, asking him to join P.I.T., and Torin had turned him down, until the last time that Derek had tracked him down to a pub on the very coast of Ireland and Cork, where he had been looking out for a place that he could no longer visit.

Torin was a couple of pints and a few chasers in when he felt someone sit down beside him. Without so much as a glance at the other man, Torin lifted his glass and ordered Derek a whiskey like the one he was now knocking back. A fog had settled outside, and Torin could almost scent the air of the place he had been born, now cast out forever for the abomination he had become at the hands of a monster.

"I'm not sure how you always end up finding me." Torin admitted as he swapped his empty chaser glass for a pint.

"I put a tracker on you."

Torin spat out his drink and turned to look at Derek. "You did not."

Derek grinned running a hand through his hair. "Nope, but I had ya guessing there for a moment."

Torin chuckled, shaking his head. He liked Derek, he really did, but his constant offering him a job was starting to grate on him. The first few times, Torin had politely said no. Then he hadn't been so polite, yet still the werewolf kept coming back and asking him.

The last twenty odd years Torin had been telling the persistent wolf that he was not a law-abiding citizen and was the wrong choice to join his Paranormal Investigations Team.

"I need someone with your skill set, Torin. I heard what you did in Spain. You delivered the kidnapped girl to her parents and the vampire who took her to Marcel in France. You tracked him like no one else could have and saved that girl. You keep telling me that there is no goodness left in you and then you go and prove yourself wrong."

Torin should have known that Marcel would have shared the information with Derek. Marcel had become the European liaison for P.I.T., and his little side kick Mateo had been hunting the kidnapper, though it was Torin who had found him.

With a nonchalant shrug of his shoulders, Torin simply said. "I was in the right place, right time. It is quite fortunate that I had a desire for some authentic sangria, is it not?"

Derek looked into the fog outside. "I'm sorry that you can't go home. But if my life has though me anything, it's you can make your own family. Come join my team, and we can be the family you so desperately want, Torin."

"The team will never accept me, Derek. They will never accept who and what I am."

Derek clasped him on the shoulder. "You'll never know unless you give them the chance. Give us a chance, Torin. And if it doesn't work out you can go on your way again. What have you really got to lose?"

Derek drank his whiskey, then rose, reaching into his pocket and then he placed something next to Torin's pint glass. Torin waited until Derek had left before he glanced down to see the P.I.T. badge with his name on it.

Cocky fucking wolf.

Torin had shown up at the station the very next night and told Derek he would join if the details of his past stayed between them until he was ready for the others on the team to know. He hadn't been ready for others to know the full truth, and Torin wasn't sure he ever would be.

The murderer they had been chasing had suddenly gone dormant. There had been no fresh kills in a couple of days and Derek was close to sending them all home to get some rest. Everyone looked exhausted, even the immortals. They were all good people who just wanted to catch the killer.

Torin found his gaze wandering to where Arik was sat in the corner. He tended to do that. It had been a long time since Torin had been attracted to another person, and yet the moment he was in the same room as the young god, his body had felt things it had not in centuries.

Blondish brown hair that was always slicked back and off his face, Arik had full lips that begged to be kissed. High cheekbones and blue eyes that were so dark, they seemed navy in colour added to the appeal. Arik tended to keep his sun kissed skin covered in those delicious suits that clung to his frame and cupped his ass to give Torin something to think of when he couldn't sleep during the day.

Arik was the toughest nut to crack in their peer group because no matter how many times Torin told Arik that his power didn't affect him, Arik didn't believe Torin. And while Torin might push the other man a little, he would never force the issue if he considered that Arik didn't actually fancy him too. Torin would never do that to someone…not when…

Torin shook those thoughts from his mind as he concentrated on the conversation going on around him.

"I think this unsub is right up there with some of the most fucked up bastards that we've dealt with." Ricky said as his wife leaned against his shoulder.

"Please don't tell me you've made a list of top ten?" Derek said with an amused look.

"Nope. But we all have a number one and if you say you don't, you're all lying."

Torin watched as Derek lifted his hand to the scars on his throat, his mate taking his hand and giving him a comforting squeeze.

"I bet I know yours." Donnie said with a grin and Ricky threw a crisp at him.

"Nope, you won't get it."

"It was Mel's ex, the drug dealer who got you killed."

Ricky shook his head. "That dope. Hell no."

Everyone laughed and then Melanie said. "Well, since I was killed by Donnelly, I guess he'd be my number one, Chrissy's too, right?"

Chrissy nodded, then looked away. Torin knew that the human who had killed Melanie had also tried to kidnap Chrissy when she was a kid and that's why she became a cop.

"Come on, Ricky spill. Who still gets your knickers in a

twist?" Donnie pushed, earning a chastising look from his mate.

"That bitch succubus. I hated having someone control me like that. Succubus, sirens, all that category I have no impartiality on."

Torin felt like he'd been kicked in the gut. He felt Derek look at him, but he didn't say anything. Of course, Ricky had no clue about his parentage, but it still gave him another reason to not say a goddamn thing about his past, and who and what he was. As the team continued to trade war stories, Torin slipped from the room, not bothering to use his own power. He walked out of the station and just went to one of the picnic tables and sat down on the table.

It was an unusually clear night, the moon shining bright in the sky and Torin basked in its glory. For a long time after he had been made a vampire, Torin had mourned the loss of the sun, for it had always been part of the creature that he had been prior to being remade, along with the water.

Torin heard the door open behind him, half expecting Ash or Derek to have come looking for him. He blinked in surprise when it was Caitlyn Hardi who came to sit beside him.

He cursed Derek for trying to push Torin to reveal himself to them before he was ready.

"Derek Doyle can be extremely infuriating when he wants you to do something you'd rather not."

A husky chuckle slipped from Caitlyn's lips. "Oui, he has always possessed an innate ability to direct you to his way of thinking."

Torin snorted and rested his elbows on his knees. "I had not expected him to send you. Though he must think this conversation is long overdue."

"I am sorry that we have not had much time to speak since you joined the team."

Torin tilted his head to peer at Caitlyn, then he said in perfect French. "It is me who is sorry. I have been avoiding you since I joined the team and perhaps that influenced your actions."

Caitlyn's eyes narrowed as she replied in English. "Your French is almost perfect."

Torin sighed, scrubbed a hand down his face. "I'm terrified to tell you who I am. What I am. It has been a long time since I have called a place home, and I would rather not have to leave."

Caitlyn gave him this look of understanding. "I was once lost in a sea of grief and pain, and Cork became my home, my anchor. Tell me what it is that you have been hiding from us, from me, and I swear that I will not chastise you for it."

"You might not say that when we get to the end."

Caitlyn didn't say anything in response, just gave Torin a few minutes to gather his nerve. There would be no better opportunity than now, so he decided to take the risk and maybe get some of his baggage off his chest. Something in the way Caitlyn had spoken rang with truth. Perhaps there was still a chance for him, he so desperately hoped that was the case.

"I have to start from the beginning, so that you understand my power." Torin sighed, then sat back, resting his hands in his lap, then closed his eyes. "I was born in Cork, just off the coast. My mother was royalty to our clan, and when she decided she wanted to sire an heir, she lured a ship from the coast and took one of the Viking raiders to bed. I never knew him, but I think like most bedfellows of sirens, he died on the rocks."

Torin cleared his throat, before he continued, "I was the only male siren ever born. That I know of anyway. I was treated like a gift from the gods, my siren magic so unique it could not be disproven. My mother tried to find me a match, a mate, but I wasn't attracted to females."

"That must have been quite difficult."

"And the reason why I never wanted the team to know what my powers were. Ricky especially hates my kind, and I don't blame him."

Torin felt Caitlyn shift beside him, felt her touch his arm before she responded. "He would understand, Torin, they all would."

Torin let loose a strangled laugh. "Believe it or not, this is not the worst of the story." Opening his eyes, he looked Caitlyn dead in the eyes. "You don't remember me at all do you?"

Caitlyn's gaze narrowed and Torin prayed for a sliver of recognition, found none.

"It's grand. I get it. But now I've started, I will need to tell you the rest. Please don't hate me."

Looking away from Caitlyn, Torin went on, not knowing if he could get through it all, or if he would still have a place on the team with the truth being out there. Once this door was open, there was no turning back.

"My mother knew I was unhappy, so she sent me out to find my happiness. I had not seen a man other than the ones who crashed on our island but I knew then that I was attracted to men. I travelled the world and left lovers heartbroken in every shore in search of my one true love and then I thought I had found him."

This was it…this was where his story darkened and became uncomfortable.

"I fell in love with a man who promised me everything I had been searching for. He told me he loved me; he told me he needed me. He told me that we could not be lovers until I was like him, a vampire. I didn't know what that truly meant until I wound up with a hunger for blood and found out that the vampire had tricked me into thinking he loved me. All his promises were lies, but I had been so desperate for affection I either didn't see it, or just refused to admit it until it was too late."

It was clear that Caitlyn had not connected the dots yet, so Torin ran a hand through his hair. "I was a fool, right? But who doesn't go to Paris and hope they might be swept up in the romance of it all?"

Caitlyn let loose a shocked gasp. "You are of Cain."

Torin dropped his head. "Ya, I am. I'm older in vampire years than you, little sister, but I was twenty-three when I was reborn a vampire. Things changed for me, but I retained some persuasion powers and Cain was only too happy to use them even if they were unreliable. Then when he grew bored, he gave me to Markus to play with."

Caitlyn got up off the bench and walked over to the fence, like she couldn't stand to look at him. She was probably fuming that one of Cain's creations had slipped past their notice.

"I had been under Markus' care for about two years when Cain made you. He brought me in to try and compel you to love him, yano. He promised me a reprieve from Markus, from Esme, if I just did this one thing for him."

Caitlyn still couldn't look at him. "You obviously failed."

Torin snorted, rubbing the back of his head. "I lied. I told him that my power didn't work on you because the love you had for your husband and your children was so engrained in your being, that their deaths had cemented it. Cain didn't understand love outside of his obsession. He never thought I'd be strong enough to deceive him. The days blurred together for a while after that as Markus passed me around. Cain having lost interest when I had apparently failed. It was a while before I saw you again."

Caitlyn turned and Torin saw a sheen of wetness in her

eyes. Her voice was tight as she asked him. "When did you see me again?"

Torin offered her a weak smile. "It was just before you left and never came back. Esme had yanked out my fangs so I couldn't feed and had beaten me and you-"

"I dragged Esme from the room and gave you some blood from the unconscious human she had been taunting you with."

"Now, you remember." Torin said with a sigh. "I'm a little bit cleaner than I was during our last meeting, and my hair is shorter. When I found out you had escaped, I clung to it like a fucking life raft. You were strong enough to get out, and it let me believe that maybe one day I would be too."

Caitlyn's gaze narrowed. "And Derek knew whose line you were from?"

"He did," Torin replied. "But I asked him not to tell you. I asked him not to tell anybody. I guess he should have believed me when I told him you'd only hate me. Probably not as much as I hate myself but still …." Torin's words trailed off as the hope that he would still be accepted faded into the night.

Caitlyn didn't utter a word, just stared at him. Torin pushed off the table and made to leave.

"Torin."

He turned back toward Caitlyn, shoved his hands into his pockets and rocked back and forth. "I stayed. I was too afraid of the outside world. Call it Stockholm Syndrome. I only left when my path crossed with Kenzie, and I knew what Cain had done. I used his distraction to flee. For the last two decades I've been trying to deal with centuries of trauma that could make a therapist weep and never recover.

I went back home, and I was no longer considered a siren. I was a monster created by another monster. Then Derek convinced me to come here. Until then I'd been wandering the world, helping others like me without staying anywhere too long."

Torin kicked at the ground. "I know it's a lot to take in. I'm not expecting anything either. If my presence here makes you uncomfortable or brings back some painful shit, I can go. I would have never shared this with you if it meant adding to the burden."

There was one more secret that Torin had yet to unveil, and it was now or never. "The doubts that Kenzie started to have, that was me. I persuaded her that Cain wasn't the saviour she thought he was. I pushed her towards Cork, towards you. It was all I could think of to do to help."

Caitlyn stood very still for a moment, then she came toward him, and Torin prepared himself for the worst. Whatever pain Caitlyn wanted to inflict he deserved, that and more. But the pain didn't come. Instead, she did the opposite thing to what Torin expected as she wrapped her arms around him and pulled him into her. Torin wrapped his arms around her, almost clinging to her.

"What you did, saved Kenzie's life. Thank you. She would also thank you."

Torin didn't say anything to that, just stepped back. He was so grateful for her response, but he still had to ask one more thing. "Please don't tell the others."

"I have no secrets from my mate, but neither of us will divulge your secrets."

As he turned to leave again, Caitlyn cupped his cheek. "I will offer you no platitudes, Torin. What we went through, it should have broken us beyond repair and yet, as much as we would love to, the truth is that we can never return to being who we were before our lives turned upside down. But you can learn to embrace who you are now. This person you were meant to become after you survived."

Torin wasn't so sure of that...there were parts of him that

he really never wanted to embrace. In fact, if he was being honest, he didn't even want to acknowledge them, but now was not the time to dwell on that.

"Come back to my house with me and Donnie. I would get to know you more."

Torin nodded, not sure why he did, but one thing he knew for sure was that there was no way he wanted to be left alone with his demons for the day...because no matter how many times he tried to drown them, those fuckers knew how to swim.

Chapter Thirteen

Ash

ASH FLASHED HER AND ZACH TO THE PLACE THAT HAD BEEN *calling out to her for weeks, teasing her, taunting her, and luring her with an ache in her chest that would not subside. She would have come herself, had planned to do so, but Zach had caught her trying to sneak out, and demanded that she bring him with her.*

They stood in a clearing and Ash had to blink a few times to make sure she wasn't imagining her surroundings. The world was a mix of shades of grey, everything was devoid of colour, the grass and the trees. Even the mist that crept around them like it was scoping them out was grey. Ash wasn't sure in a world like this if the mist was just mist, or if it might be sentient.

"Well, this isn't creepy at all, A.K."

Ash turned to look at her best friend, who was scanning the area as if searching for threats. "It's like something out of a horror movie."

"Then you are fucked mate, being blonde and all."

Ash gave him the finger and Zach laughed, his laughter the only sound that Ash could hear. The lurch in her chest intensified and she rubbed at her sternum. As if she were in the midst of a hunt, Ash knew instinctively where to go and she started walking through the forest, hoping that once they got to where she had been pulled toward for weeks, it might stop the pain inside of her.

Because it honestly felt like she was grieving.

"Hey Ash, can you use your powers? I've got nothing."

Ash frowned as she tried to summon Mjolnir, her beloved hammer not appearing like it should have. She closed her eyes to try and summon her lightening and got nothing. Dammit.

"Shit."

That was all she said as she continued to trudge through the forest and when it seemed like she and Zach had been walking for hours, they emerged from the forest and in front of them was a cave. Zach leapt up and leaned into the cave.

"I don't scent anyone."

Her heart started to race, and her legs moved of their own accord. Ash only stopped her march forward when Zach grabbed her arm. "Ash, wait. Something doesn't feel right."

But Ash felt the tether yank at her, and she plunged into the darkened cave, Zach hot on her heels. She was thankful for her supernatural eyesight, the darkness growing thicker as she went further and further into the abyss. The pathway suddenly opened up and it was then Ash heard the growling.

Blood-red eyes watched them from the darkness and Ash felt the strangest urge to step toward the being that was shrouded in the darkness. The growl sounded again, and it was like every hair on Ash stood to attention. Her heart was in her throat as a massive paw emerged from the darkness.

Little wolf.

Ash heard the voice in her head and her wolf let out a keening sound. Another paw came out of the darkness and Ash saw a flash of dark grey fur and while the wolf side of her was ready to lay down and submit, the human part of her was ready to bolt.

Running from bigger predators didn't end well...

Ash stumbled back as a monstrous grey wolf the size of a bungalow stepped out of the darkness and gave her the equivalent of a wolfy grin. Her feet slipped out of her shoes, and she scrambled backward.

The wolf was solely focus on Ash, tilting its head as if studying her, then Zach moved and its head swung round to snarl at him.

Zach growled back, and then the wolf swiped out a massive paw and Zach went flying through the air to slam against the wall with an oomph.

"Zach!"

The wolf snapped its gaze back to hers as Zach yelled at her to run and then she was up off her ass and bolting back the way she came. Ash heard a howl ripple through the cave as she burst outside and ran as fast as she could to the forest, hoping to loose whatever monster was chasing her.

A branch snapped behind her as she ran as fast as she could, her bare feet stinging. Zach was hurt, and she needed to get him some help; the fact that she was being chased didn't erase that fact. The scent of her own blood filled her nose and made her easier to track, but with no powers, Ash was simply a human.

The woods were eerily quiet as if they knew of the monster that had been unleashed and now, despite the various creatures that roamed through this magical forest, they were afraid of the one that chased her. And rightly so.

Ash stumbled over a tree root and rolled, ignoring the pain that bloomed in her shoulder. With a hiss, she got to her feet again and held out her hand, urging, pleading for her trusty Mjölnir, but the hammer of the gods failed to come to her aid.

Ash let loose a growl of frustration as she came to a diverged path, one going to her right and one path leading to the left. The path to her left led only to darkness, but the path that was illuminated by moonlight meant she'd be easy to track and easily seen. If she wanted to get help for Zach, she needed to be brave.

She heard her name on the wind as the darkened forest beckoned her forward, and without another thought, Ash bolted down the pitch-black pathway as fast as she could. Her eyes scanned all around her, yet she could not see a single thing and had to trust herself not to stumble or to be able to stop herself before running into danger.

Well, more danger.

She ran and ran for what seemed like days, and she still had not been able to find her way out of the forest. Skipping to a stop, she blew out a shaky breath. A deep, masculine chuckle sent shivers up her spine, and her wolf tilted her head in interest.

Ash felt the hairs on her neck stand to attention as a firm hand cupped the back of her neck, and Ash froze. Even in the dark, she sensed him watching her, knew he stood beside her, felt every one of her nerve endings ignite as he leaned in and brushed his nose against the nape of her neck. His scent overwhelmed her, the smell of wolf and magic and the air after rain had fallen.

"Little wolf, little wolf. Little red hood. I do love a good chase."

Ash felt panic surge through her body, and the urge to fight coursed through her. Reaching down to the waistband of her cargo pants, Ash gripped a dagger, slowly edging it out of its sheath until she felt the kiss of the blade against her stomach.

"Do you know who I am, little wolf? Do you know what I am?"

"Don't know, don't care. You hurt my friend, and now I'm going to repay the favor."

Ash jerked the blade up and struck, driving the dagger into the monster's neck. He let out a hiss as Ash stumbled away, the darkness of the forest suddenly lifting. Ash had to blink her eyes at the sudden brightness that flooded them. Her eyes took a moment to refocus, her vision blurry as she stepped back and glanced over her shoulder for an escape before turning her attention back to the monster that had hunted her.

Her wolf howled so loud pain laced through her mind as Ash's mouth dropped open. Standing in front of her was a boy so gorgeous he could only be of the gods. His black, inky hair was cut raggedly as if he'd used a blade to cut the ends that had gotten too long, and his eyes were so dark they resembled the night sky. He watched her from behind hooded lids, with lashes so long and dark they brushed his cheeks. And gods, when he smirked, those high cheekbones and full, sinful lips made Ash want to crawl out of her skin for him.

He was broad in shoulders and muscular, his tee straining against his chest as he yanked the blade from his neck and tossed it back to her. Ash caught the blade at the hilt, then braced herself for a fight.

The monster smiled as he stepped closer, and for every step he advanced, Ash retreated one step. The boy's grin deepened, and Ash felt her wolf flex her powers. Ash was powerless to stop the inevitable.

Ash gasped as the wolf's mating bond snapped into place, connecting her mind to his. The magic of it was like someone had whipped her mind, and Ash growled, resenting her mind linking with the monster's.

"Mine," the boy growled.

Ash snorted. "I don't think so. I need to have a word with my wolf and convince her to make better choices. So, why don't you stay there, and I'll go straighten things out."

"What is your name, little wolf?"

Ash knew the mating bond would tell him all he needed to know, as it would Ash, but it would be a cold day in Hell before she messed with the magic of the bond and set the thing firmly into place. She needed to break it because she would rather die than be forced into this.

"What is your name, little wolf?"

Ash growled and readied herself to run, but a second later, the monster was in front of her, his hand wrapped tightly around her neck. For a second, the boy licked his lips as his eyes wandered down to her own lips. For a brief moment of madness, Ash wanted him to kiss her, needed him to kiss her. It was all-consuming and terrifying, but she didn't care.

"What is your name, little wolf? I will not ask you again."

Gritting her teeth against the command in his tone, Ash found herself saying, "Ashlyn. Ash. My friends call me Ash."

"Hello, my Ashlyn. My name is Fenrir, and I have been waiting for you for an eternity."

Ash awoke slowly from the dream with the awareness that there was someone in her bedroom. Slipping her hand under her pillow, she wrapped her fingers around the dagger and slowly began to move her body to fight off an attack.

"Go back to sleep, Ashlyn. It is yet early."

The dark tone sent a shiver coursing through her as she let go of the dagger and sat up in the bed to focus on the god in her room. Ash could see him in the dark, but it almost felt too intimate, so she reached out and turned on her bedside lamp. Light illuminated the room, and her eyes landed on Grey sitting in the chair by her window.

He wore a pair of black sweatpants and a black t-shirt and no shoes. He was reclined in the chair, his eyes focused on a leather-bound journal that he was currently writing in. Ash had seen him with it a number of times over the years, but since she was avoiding him, she never had a chance to ask him about it.

"What are you doing here, Grey?"

Lifting his black eyes to hers, Fenrir set the pen down in the centre of the journal. "I came to retrieve my boots. Your wolf was restless, and you needed to sleep. My presence eased the restlessness."

Ash narrowed her gaze. "How long have you been watching me sleep?"

"This night or before tonight?"

"Oh my god, have you been watching me sleep before tonight?"

The blank expression on his face told Ash all she needed to know. Jesus, even after she had been a colossal bitch to him, Fenrir had still sat with her to ease her wolf so she could function.

"You can't just sit in my room at night and watch me sleep, Grey."

"But then you would not sleep well and you are more

cranky with me when you do not sleep well. Obeying that does not seem to benefit me in any way. And had I not been so engrossed in my journal, then you would have woken and never known I was here at all.

She leaned against the wall with a sigh and the blanket slipped down.

His eyes latched on to the shirt that she was wearing. It was the one he had discarded the other night, and his gaze narrowed, though he didn't say anything, just picked up the pen and went back a couple of pages to write a note in the journal.

"Whatcha writing?" Ash heard herself ask, as Fenrir placed a hand over the pages possessively, and Ash wondered who had given him the journal for him to be so possessive of it.

"It was a gift from my father," Fenrir explained, having plucked the thoughts through the bond. "He gave it to me so that I could write down anything that I did not understand, things that were confusing for me. I write down interactions that may occur again, so I know a more appropriate means to react. I noted what you told me about Lyra looking for praise. I added it under the note that she likes to show her affection with hugs and she doesn't want to attack me."

Ash gave him a smile. "That was a thoughtful gift. Do you write about me in there?"

Fenrir closed the journal and slipped it into the pocket of his pants. "Of course. You are my mate and the person who confuses me the most."

Ash wanted to know more, because she did wonder what the hell Fenrir would write about her in his journal. "What kind of things do you write about me in your journal? Who do you ask questions to?"

Grey leaned back in the chair and his gaze held hers. "It is private. The things I write about you. The feelings you have that don't make sense to me and I want to understand them. Understand you. I ask my father, Donnie sometimes."

"You could ask me, Grey." Ash said softly, only to see Fenrir shake his head.

"And give you more ammunition to use to push me away. No. I could not ask you."

Fenrir was right. She used his difference to push him away and felt like a bitch for it. He couldn't help how his brain was wired, and Ash had taken that and used it as a weapon against him.

"Why do you block the bond? Why stop me from it?"

Fenrir folded his arms across his chest. "I have already answered that question, Ashlyn. As have you."

More ammunition she guessed.

Ash hugged her knees to her chest. "I guess I deserved that. I'm sorry. I would like to understand your reasons, Grey. Please."

There was a flicker of uncertainly in his fathomless eyes, then he lowered his lashes before speaking. "My mind does not work like yours, or the cats, or anyone that I know. It frightens you and you focus on that rather than other things. I could feel your fear, your horror and when you told me you hated me, I knew that I would have no chance to be your true mate if you could hear my thoughts."

"But my dad said that you probably get all of my feelings, my emotions, because you can only block the bond one way."

"Yes." That was all that Fenrir said, and it was enough, really.

"But then why do it when it means you get overloaded? I don't understand."

Fenrir ran a hand over the trimmed hair on his scalp and Ash remembered the gorgeous boy with the long strands of hair that she had run her fingers through. She really wanted to know how the bristles would feel now if she ran her palm over his scalp.

"You are my mate," Fenrir told Ash, his tone confident and Ash wished she could sound that confident when she thought of Grey as her mate. "I have never wavered in the knowing of this. I do not need to be convinced, but you do. Knowing the things in my head will not convince you. I do not like the confusion, the *feelings* I do not understand. However, I bear it because you are my mate."

Through the bond she felt a ripple of the intense devotion Fenrir felt for her, like he was trying to get her to understand that in his own way, he loved her. Ash didn't want to have feelings for Grey, but she did, even if she had convinced herself it was all because of the bond and nothing to do with how she actually felt.

"You should go back to sleep. I can leave, if you want."

There was no way she was going back to sleep with the way her mind was up in a heap. Her wolf paced inside her mind, growling at her like she hated that the human part was being foolish and chasing their mate away.

"Stay," Ash replied, her pulse quickening as she followed it with, "If you are gonna stay here for the rest of the night, you might as well be comfy. Come sleep in the bed."

Fenrir's gaze narrowed like he was trying to decipher what her motive was.

"Just to sleep, Grey."

Ash flicked off the light and lay down in the bed, her eyes fixed on the ceiling. Her heart was beating like a drum as she felt Grey get up, and stride to the bed. The mattress shifted as Fenrir climbed into the bed with her, then it was like he didn't know what to do, or how to react without pissing her off.

Turning over in the bed so that her back was to him, Ash reached behind her to pull one of Fenrir's muscular arms around her. She closed her eyes and sent him an image of what she wanted. Fenrir growled, then she was yanked against a hot, hard body. Fenrir moved his arms and placed his palm on her stomach. His face was buried in the curve of her neck, his breath warm on her skin.

Ash felt her lips curve into a smile as she closed her eyes, knowing that as much as the man curved around her body was terrifying, having him here felt right, and Ash felt more like herself than she had in years. Fenrir's arm tightening around her and Ash sighed, her wolf at peace as she tumbled into a dreamless sleep.

The Killer

THERE WAS A PRESSURE IN THEIR HEAD THAT WOULDN'T SUBSIDE. They knew that a vengeful god was the cause of it, pushing them to complete their end of the bargain struck between them. They hadn't eaten in days, hadn't slept, and the creature that they had now become was angsty to spill more blood. The control they needed was slipping away and only one thing would assuage it.

Walking into the staff room, they almost sighed in relief when the vampire they were looking for was alone. Luring Donnie O'Carroll to his eventual death was not an easy task, but a necessary one.

He lifted his head to look at them. "Hey, you okay? You're looking a little green."

Dismissing them with a soft chuckle, they replied. "Must have eaten some bad sushi last night. I'll be grand. Actually, I need a hand with something. I can't reach something. Short person problems, right?"

Donnie laughed out loud as he stood and grinned. "No hassle. Glad to be of help."

Anticipation flooded their veins, and they tried not to give away just how excited they were that once Donnie was in Odin's grasp then they would be a god forever. Donnie chatted away as they rounded the corner and headed to the back of this floor, and to the quietest part of the station so they could extract Donnie without alerting anyone.

They made it to the room, and they opened the door when they were stopped by Caitlyn calling to her mate. Donnie grinned, then asked them what they needed, and they blindly asked for something from the top shelf. Donnie grabbed it, handed them the item and then strode off toward their mate without a backward glance.

So damn close...so damn close.

Setting the item down and heading toward the bathroom, anger was a steady flowed in their veins. They looked at themselves in the mirror and despised what they saw. A pulse of pressure in their head as they coiled their fist and punched the mirror, shattering it.

They looked down at the cuts and the blood on their knuckles, healing almost immediately as a knock sounded on the door, a voice asking if they were okay. Washing away the blood, they took a deep breath, plastered on a fake smile, and opened the door.

"All good, Killian. Dodgy sushi."

The warlock and fellow agent groaned, then slung an arm around their shoulder. "We'll have to pick somewhere else for lunch then, partner. You good to go?"

They nodded their head.

So damn close...

Chapter Fourteen

Fenrir

SPENDING THE NIGHT CURLED UP AGAINST ASHLYN HAD BEEN the best night of his life. He had not pushed her, and still it pleased him that she slept so soundly in his arms, unafraid of him for the first time in what felt like forever. He had to control the primal urges in him and accept what Ashlyn had given him as a gift.

He had not wanted to leave her, however, the pleasure of sleeping beside his mate was something he did not want to ruin if she awoke, and he gleaned from the bond that she regretted asking him to stay. It might shatter any and all control he had left and succumb to the urge for violence.

There was a … shifting…yes, a shifting in Ashlyn's thinking and Fenrir was not going to do anything that might jeopardise that shift in thinking. He also had heard the unspoken question in her mind about whether or not he had killed the rat, and whilst she did not query him on it, Ashlyn had kept the knowledge of his scent at the scene from her father, and her fellow agents.

His mate was protecting him. He knew this because in her mind, she did not believe him to be the rat's killer, and instead thought he was being framed. She truly believed that, and yet, she still kept it from them on the off chance she was wrong.

Fenrir had not killed the rat but saw no need to offer a defence for it.

All that mattered was Ashlyn knew he had not killed the rat.

He had better taste after all, than to eat such a bland morsel.

Fenrir flashed to the outside of the home his father shared with his Valkyrie mate, and his sister still resided. Loki had explained to him a number of times that it was polite to knock and then be welcomed into a person's home. It was after he had flashed in and seen his father and the general in a rather naked position and Erika had thrown a dagger at him that he decided it might be worth following his father's advice with regard to this.

He had heard them talking after as he sat in the kitchen, and his stepmother had asked if her father, Tyr had been the cause of his sociopathy. Loki had replied, stating that perhaps they would never know, because Angrboða, his mother, had kept Fenrir from him until he had become too much to handle.

Then Angrboða had given him to Tyr, and then Tyr, who had built his trust and treated him like a son, had betrayed him for Odin, when the Allfather had become obsessed with a prophecy that Fenrir would be the one to kill him.

Fenrir did not measure his life in years or regard time much. He did not know how old he was when Tyr had betrayed him, only that he was a child, merely a boy who wanted to please the man who he looked upon like a father.

Fenrir was curled up aside on the balcony overlooking Asgard, just outside the throne room and basked in the warmth of the sun as it heated his skin. He much preferred being in his wolf skin, though Tyr reminded him that his human skin was the skin he would have to wear most to fit in with the other Asgardians and was less frightening to those around him. Fenrir did not care if others were frightened of him. His brother Jormungand was content as a serpent, though Fenrir knew his younger sister, Hel, constantly wanted others to like her.

She cried when other children were mean to her, and that made Fenrir want to bite them. That was what Tyr had told him, that brothers should want to stand up for their younger siblings when others were unkind, but while Fenrir would deem that as sufficient enough reason to bite them, Tyr had told him that it was not appropriate to go around just biting people Fenrir did not like.

The sound of Odin's booming voice roused him from his thoughts and Fenrir stretched, changing from wolf to human skin in the blink of an eye. Odin did not like Fenrir when he was in wolf skin, and he smelled of fear when he was. Fenrir did not like Odin. The god was one that he felt the urge to bite, though Tyr worshiped the Allfather, so Fenrir knew it was in his best interests for Tyr not to know just how much Fenrir wanted to bite him.

When Fenrir had changed to his human skin, he'd made sure to put on clothing, even if he would have been more comfortable with the air on his bare skin. He did not like things on his feet, though, and while he wore black pants and a vest, his feet were bare. Tyr told him that nudity was not something Asgardians did on a daily basis, and while Fenrir did not care, he did as asked by Tyr.

Sitting on the balcony railing, swinging his legs, and looking down at the massive drop, Fenrir waited until Tyr and Odin were done arguing, trying not to listen in because it was apparently rude. People should not talk loud enough if they did not want him to hear.

Tyr stepped out onto the balcony; his lips turned downward.

"Come Fenrir."

Fenrir twisted to plant his feet on the railing, and balanced. "Where are we going?"

"It's a surprise. Let us go."

The last time Tyr had gotten him a surprise, it was the rump from a large bore, and it had made Fenrir feel stuffed and he had slept for a long time. He padded after Tyr, but where the god of war was usually very talkative, he was quiet.

Perhaps he did not want to ruin the surprise he had for Fenrir.

Tyr rested a hand on Fenrir's shoulder and flashed them to a place that made Fenrir's fur stand on edge. Tyr urged him forward, toward a cave and Fenrir went with him. They went further and further inside the cave, and when they reached a massive cavern, Tyr nudged him forward and Fenrir turned round to look at the man who he wished had been his father.

Fenrir could not read the emotion that flashed on Tyr's face as he simply said. "I'm sorry, Fenrir."

His gaze narrowed as he sensed the change in the air and Tyr suddenly had a chain in his hand that reeked of magic. Fenrir lunged, teeth bared, and Tyr wound the chain around his neck and yanked. Fenrir slammed into the ground with a whimper of pain.

He shifted forms as the chains bit into him, using his wolf strength to try and break the chain that bound him. They did not so much as groan as Fenrir tried and failed to break free. Lifting his gaze, he saw Tyr with a sheen of wetness in his eyes, as if it hurt him to do this to Fenrir.

"Fenrir, I'm sorry. But Odin believes that the prophecies of you ushering in Ragnarök are the truth and you are too dangerous to be left to roam free. He had Gleipnir made to bind you. I wish it did not have to be this way, but if I had not done it, then it would have been someone else."

Fenrir understood that Tyr could not or would not disobey Odin, for if he had, then it might have been Tyr who was bound to these chains, or dead. But Fenrir would never be able to understand why Tyr had chosen to deceive him rather than speak the truth to him.

Fenrir growled as fury wove its way into his marrow, into the very fibre of his being. He bared his teeth at Tyr, who had now busied himself with latching the chain to hooks that must have been added to the cavern walls in preparation for his imprisonment.

Red hot anger flashed in his mind, his eyes bleeding to red as Fenrir lunged for the man who had betrayed him, snapping his massive jaws, and clamping his teeth down once they latched onto flesh. With one swift bite, Fenrir bit off Tyr's right hand, amputating it from the wrist to fingers. His saliva dripped down onto Tyr's flesh, and the god of war screamed in agony.

Fenrir thrashed against the chains as he swallowed down the hand of Tyr, his former teacher running from the cave as Fenrir tasted blood on his tongue and howled and howled until his throat was too sore to howl any longer.

The front door to Loki and Erika's home opened and his stepmother was standing on the other side. She gave him a welcoming smile, one that she had not given him before, and Fenrir dropped his eyes to the cheek he had broken.

"It is healed?" He said to her, and Erika nodded.

"Ya, overnight. I told you not to worry. I think your dad was happy that you and me were spending quality time together, even if we were sparring." The Valkyrie general grinned. "I was waiting for you to knock, but you were standing there for a while. You coming in?"

"I would speak with my father."

Erika stepped back, letting Fenrir walk in and then she closed the door, walked to the fridge, and took out a beer. Handing it to Fenrir, she motioned toward the living area for him to sit. Fenrir went and sat down because he understood it was the polite thing to do.

"Your dad's on his way back from Asgard. He'll be back soon."

Fenrir took a sip of the beer, then looked at Erika. "I can go and return once he is back."

"Nah, stay. I'm sure once your sister takes off her headphones and realizes that you're here she will come running out. If her hugging you or that makes you uncomfortable, you need to tell Lyra. She will appreciate you setting boundaries."

Fenrir tilted his head and stared at the Valkyrie, searching her to see if she was like her father. It was what had worried him about seeing Lyra as she grew, that she would remind him of Tyr, and it might trigger his fury. He had not forgiven Tyr for his actions, as much as he understood it, and perhaps if Erika had not been mated to his father, then he may have killed her as an outlet for his rage.

"I will if I need to. I understand that Lyra is open with her affections, and it is because it was how she was raised. I see no need to upset her and upset Loki by making an issue of it." Fenrir tried to remember what he was supposed to do and say when someone showed concern. "I appreciate your concern, though I do suspect that it is solely to protect your child."

Erika leaned back in her seat. "You might not believe me considering what my father did to you, but I was concerned for you. Just so you know."

Footsteps came down the hall and Lyra stopped when she saw him, her smile widening. "Hey Fen."

"Hello Lyra." It was then that Fenrir recalled what Ashlyn had said to him. *She wants you to tell her that she's done good, Grey. Lyra wants your approval. Just tell her she did a good job. Trust me.* "Have you been practising?"

Lyra swept her dark braid off her shoulder. "I have! Gideon wants me to meet him later to do some more train-ing. We have a test coming up and he's gonna help me. I'm gonna use what you told me."

Fenrir shifted his gaze to Erika at the excitement in her tone. It was a tone Fenrir recognised when females were interested in males. Erika shrugged her shoulders, like she was unconcerned. Fenrir must have growled a little, because

Lyra laughed, and he could tell she was delighted at his growl, even as she blushed.

"You can't eat Gideon for helping me. Besides, he's your mate's brother. That will make family dinners uncomfortable. I gotta go."

Lyra surprised Fenrir by kissing him on the cheek, then her mother before she flashed away. Erika was watching him, but all Fenrir did was take another drink of his beer. They sat there in a comfortable silence and then the air around them changed.

Loki appeared behind his wife, and she lifted her hand for him to take. His father squeezed her hand, then gave him a grin. "Fenrir, it's good of you to come by. What can I do for you?"

Fenrir didn't respond, and Erika rose, walking round to kiss his father and Fenrir watched as Loki seemed to soften. When they broke apart, Fenrir thought that he noticed the look of love that Arik had tried to explain to him that was different from the love of family and friends. He could not feel his father's emotions, like he could with his Ashlyn, but Fenrir had seen how Loki looked at Lyra and how he looked at Erika.

Arik had been honest with him in his explanation.

"I gotta go. I told Ever I'd meet her for a coffee." Erika glanced over her shoulder. "Maybe we could spar again next week?"

"I see my father is still not meeting your needs, General. I would be happy to spar."

Erika barked out a laugh and flashed away, leaving him alone with his father.

Loki took the seat his mate had vacated and summoned a beer into his hand. "If I did not know any better, son, I'd think you were flirting with my mate."

Fenrir shrugged. "I have a mate. I was merely stating facts."

His father grinned, tipped his beer bottle. "Of course. What can I do for you?"

Fenrir leaned forward and set his beer down, then took out his journal. He saw a flicker of what he thought was happiness in his father's eyes as Fenrir opened it to the section that he had reserved for Ashlyn. "I slept in Ashlyn's bed last night. With her."

Loki arched a brow. "Just slept? Or *slept*?"

"There was no sex. She wanted me to hold her so I did."

"Okay," Loki said, tapped a finger on his chin as if he were contemplating what to say next. "Did you want to sleep in the bed with her?"

"Of course. She is my mate and she wanted me to."

Loki looked at him for a long time. "That's good then. Do you have some questions?"

Fenrir inclined his head. "I know that mates sleep in the same bed. They hold one another. They do more than that. Ashlyn wants romance. She wants me to do things that I do not understand the need for. She is already my mate; I do not understand the need to convince her of this."

"So, you want me to give you romantic advice?"

"Yes." Fenrir confirmed. "Before the general, you are infamous for whoring around and there are woman who still speak of your romantic escapades. I do not wish to cut off Ashlyn's hair though. I like it."

Loki barked out a laugh, shaking his head. "First, I cut off Lady Sif's hair to force Thor to come to her aid and force the two of them to stop dancing round one another and two, yes, until Erika, I did have sex with a lot of people."

Nothing Loki said was new or useful to Fenrir, so he stayed quiet. Loki watched him, and he could almost see his father thinking. He frowned, his gaze narrowed, and Fenrir waited for him to speak.

"You said Ash wanted romance. But you didn't deem it necessary because ye were already mated?"

"Yes."

"Okay," Loki said, draining his beer and then it was gone, as his father linked his fingers together on his knees. "Ash might be your mate, but the bond snapped into place when you two didn't even know each other's names. When Ash says that she wants romance, how about getting her a gift, something that she might want or like?"

Fenrir did not think that any gift he would get for Ashlyn would be something his mate might appreciate, and it must have shown on his face because Loki continued. "You know Ash better than anyone because she is your mate. You have watched other people give her gifts. Maybe start with flowers. Then think of a gift that no one else would think of for her."

"Like my journal."

"Exactly like your journal."

Fenrir considered what his father had said. He had not seen Ashlyn with flowers in the time he had known her. He wanted to get his mate something that no one else would ever be able to gift her. He would have to think hard about what Ashlyn wanted most in the world and give it to her.

It struck him suddenly, and Fenrir growled low in his throat when he realized that he could follow Loki's advice and bring her flowers, and anything else that he considered that his mate might enjoy, and yet, there was only one thing that Ashlyn wanted that he could give her to make her feel happy.

Fenrir could give her the means to break the bond between them.

He could give her the artifact that she had been searching

for even if it meant it might be his destruction. Doing so went against everything Fenrir had in him, and yet, he was driven by the need to make his mate happy, even if that meant killing the bond that made her his mate.

"Fenrir, you okay?"

Fenrir closed his journal and slipped it into his pocket. "Thank you for your advice. I will bring her flowers. And I think I have an idea on what gift to give her that will mean as much to her as my journal does to me."

Loki grinned, obviously pleased that he had helped his son, and when he asked Fenrir if he wanted to tell him what he was going to get Ashlyn, Fenrir rose to his feet and held his father's gaze. "Ashlyn has only ever wanted to be free of me and I have lied to her that there was not a way to break the bond. However, there is, and in order to give my mate a gift that she will be pleased with, it will sever the mating bond, and no doubt destroy me."

His father's eyes widened. "No, Fenrir, just wait a moment. That's not what I meant."

"I know. But it is what she wants, and I would go to my death with her happy with me for once. Thank you for the advice."

Fenrir flashed away to the sound of his name on his father's lips, and it sounded an awful lot like the keen of a wolf in pain.

Chapter Fifteen

Fenrir

FENRIR HAD RETRIEVED ALL THE THINGS HE WANTED TO GIVE to Ashlyn this evening and had flashed to the courtyard outside the apartment complex she shared with the cat. Loki had tried to convince him not to go ahead with his plan, but Fenrir was resolved. There was a part of him that wanted to use this as means to manipulate Ashlyn into accepting him as her mate fully, though he knew the odds were not entirely in his favour.

It was a risk, a calculated risk that could backfire on him, but Fenrir was left without many options. He would have to do something, for if the killer was apprehended then Fenrir had no reason to stick around, and Ashlyn would go back to pushing him away.

Fenrir had one of his gifts in one hand as he made his way up the stairs, not wanting to be stuck inside the metal box that brought residence up and down the floors, then strode down the hallway before pausing at the door. Fenrir lifted his free hand and rapped his knuckles against the door.

He heard the whir of the camera as he lifted and eye to look into it, then focused back on the door as he heard footsteps beyond the door and his mate's scent called out to him. Ashlyn opened the door and he wanted to lunge forward, inhale her scent and bath in it. Her scent reminded him of the Asgardian sun from a time when he had been free and could lay for hours in his wolf form.

Her hair hung loose around her shoulders, her amber eyes darkening when she saw him, and he knew she was feeling the affects of the mating bond, the attraction, the lust. Fenrir did not need the mating bond to want his Ashlyn.

"Hi." She said, her tongue darting out to outline her lips. "You just took off this morning."

"I did not want you to wake and regret us sleeping together."

Ashlyn starred at him for a moment, and then Fenrir did not know what to do or say, so he thrust his gift into Ashlyn's hands. "I brought you a gift."

Her gaze narrowed at the object in her hands. "Why?"

"I asked my father, and he said that mates who wanted to be romantic gave their mates gifts. He suggested flowers."

Her amber eyes shifted downward, and Fenrir felt a ripple of confusion along the bond. "Okay, thank you. But Grey, this is a cactus. It's a plant not a flower."

"I know. But flowers are inconvenient. They need to be looked after. You work long hours, and the flowers would wither and die and that might make you sad. The cactus does not require much care and will live longer and when you look at it, you will think of me..."

Fenrir let his voice trail off as he noted the shaking of Ashlyn's shoulders as she tried to hold back her laughter. She was laughing at him, mocking him...

With a growl, he snatched the plant back from Ashlyn and spun round. He had done everything Loki had told him to do. He had considered the flowers, had even asked for advice from the florist and then settled on the cactus because he had thought it more considerate.

And Ashlyn has laughed at him.

He stomped down the hall, too angry to flash away when

he heard Ashlyn call his name and come after him. Fenrir ignored her, and yanked open the door to the stairs, his anger pushing him to throw the damn plant on the ground and shatter it to assuage some of his anger.

Ashlyn slid in front of him, ignoring his growl and reached for the plant. He let her take it, his fists clenched by his sides as he looked down so Ashlyn couldn't see just how close he was to letting his fury loose, and with her free hand placed it on his chest.

"I'm sorry I laughed. It's very thoughtful. I don't like flowers anyway and this is a great gift. Please, Grey, just come inside."

He detected no lies from the bond, so he followed Ashlyn as she walked back to her apartment, stepped inside, and watched as she took out her phone, then nodded as she walked over to the windowsill and placed the plant on it.

"So, according to Google, it's best to place cacti in a bright place. A south facing position will provide good sunlight so it will thrive up there. Thank you, Grey. Come in and sit down."

Ashlyn went back to the couch and curled her legs underneath her.

"Where is the cat?" Fenrir asked as he came to sit down beside her.

"It's his gran's birthday. They are having a family dinner."

"Were you not invited?"

Ashlyn glanced at him and smiled. "I was. Just wasn't in the mood. So I'm comfort watching."

He liked the way her lips curved into that kind of lopsided smile, and it made him want to kiss her. Fenrir looked away before Ashlyn could see the need in his eyes. The ghost of her touch, fingers on his jaw made him shiver.

"You wanna tell me what just went through that brain of yours?"

"No."

Ashlyn chucked and he felt her joy along the bond. "Come on, Grey. Just tell me."

He turned his head to hold her gaze so that he could see her reaction. "You smiled and it made me want to kiss you. I always want to kiss you."

"Me too. I mean, I want to kiss you too."

Fenrir wasn't sure if Ashlyn was being serious, then she shifted to her knees, leaned in and pressed her lips against his. His hands snapped out to grip her hips, holding her in place. He felt the first tentative flicker of her tongue against the seam of his lips, then she nipped at his bottom lip.

Fenrir growled, his fingers digging into Ashlyn's hips as he fought against the urge to drag her onto his lap. Instead, Fenrir slid a hand up from her hip, placed it loosely around her throat and tilted Ashlyn's chin up so he could deepen the kiss.

It started out slow, lips and tongue, then Ashlyn cupped the back of his neck, scraped her nails against his flesh. The kiss became more then, with Fenrir devouring her mouth, his tongue tasting his mate, her lust, her arousal, and he was almost drunk on it.

He knew that he could lay her down and sink into her right now and she would let him, though it would solidify the bond, make it harder to break. Fenrir pulled back from the kiss, his lips curving when she chased them, then flashed him a sheepish grin. "Damn, Grey, I do like how you kiss me."

Fenrir sat back, pressed his lips together before he said to Ashlyn. "I have another gift for you."

"You don't have to bring me gifts, Grey. The plant was enough."

Fenrir shook his head, his eyes on her kiss swollen lips for a heartbeat before he looked at her again. "The journal my father gave me is the gift I wanted but never knew I did.

He told me to get you a gift that you wanted, and I can only offer this to you, knowing that it has been what you wanted as long as I have known you."

Closing his eyes, he summoned the dagger, holding it out to Ashlyn. It was a small, ornate looking dagger, the thrum of magic off it made her hiss through her teeth. "What the hell is this?" He watched for a moment as Ashlyn turned the dagger over in her hands, then looked at Fenrir. "This isn't an ordinary dagger."

"No, it is not. It is a gift to you, what you want most. The dagger is old, fashioned by the same dwarfs that made Odin's staff, and your hammer. It has been locked away for eons, and I give it to you, as a gift."

Ashlyn looked at the dagger with confusion, so Fenrir continued. "It has a name but speaking it may just nullify the magic in it. Translated to the Midgardian tongue, it roughly means bond breaker. It only works once, and it is final. Once it is used, it cannot be undone, nor can the bond ever be restored."

Ashlyn dropped the dagger and jerked backward. "Why the hell would you give this to me?"

Fenrir was confused at her reaction. "This is what you wanted, a means to break the bond. As your mate, I am driven to give you what you want and now you have it. The dwarfs tell me that to use it, you must drive it into the heart of the one you wish to break the bond of."

Ashlyn's eyes dropped to the dagger, then Fenrir heard her whisper. "Will it hurt?"

Ah, so she had already decided to use it. He had gambled and lost.

For once he was glad that Ashlyn could not hear his thoughts through the block on the bond, so that he could lie to her. "It will not hurt you. I will ensure it."

Ashlyn didn't look convinced. "But what happens after the bond is broken?"

Fenrir shrugged, picked up the dagger and put it in Ashlyn's hand, then angled it against his chest. "Once you pierce my heart, the bond with shatter. It will be as if it had never been. You will go back to who you were prior to the bond snapping into place."

Her fingers trembled. "And what about you?"

"It matters not. The bond will be broken." What Fenrir didn't state was that because he had spent years getting the feedback from Ashlyn, his mind would not be able to function, and he would fracture too, mindless in the moments before the dagger might actually kill him.

"I don't want to hurt you."

Fenrir could sense how much she meant it, and perhaps she might mourn him if he were to die, but it would be too late then. He just wanted to give her what she truly desired and get it over with.

"One full thrust, Ashlyn. I am ready."

Closing his eyes, Fenrir exhaled, bracing for the slice of the blade through his flesh and into his heart, the one that beat now only for her. He wondered if he would understand the pain or understand what Ashlyn had meant to him if he survived. The future that Ashlyn wanted so much was within her grasp and yet, she did not dole out the killing blow.

"Ashlyn." Fenrir said her name softly, not wanting to spook her, however he did not want to draw this out any longer than it had to be.

The magic of the blade meant that he could not simply lean forward and force her hand. It was the will alone of the wielder than brought the magic. If Ashlyn wanted to break the bond, then she would have to do it by her own hand. Fenrir had no desire to break the bond, only to make Ashlyn happy.

"Ashlyn."

"No. Just...just wait a minute." Ashlyn mumbled, then the blade was away from his chest and so was Ashlyn. "This is madness. You bring me a goddamn plant, then kiss me, then ask me to hurt you? I know your brain doesn't work like everyone else's, but this is all kinds of fucked up."

Fenrir didn't respond to Ashlyn, just watched her as she paced back and forth in front of the window, the dagger still in her hand, and then she stopped before the plant and just starred at it. She looked over her shoulder at him, and down the bond he felt her confusion, her sadness, and it made him want to embrace her.

"If you will the dagger away, it will do your bidding until you are ready to break the bond."

Ashlyn glanced at the dagger in her hand, her gaze narrowing until the dagger vanished. Her shoulders sagged, and Fenrir was almost certain that he saw relief in her eyes. Fenrir rose, and his movement snared her attention.

"Where are you going?"

"I assume you will come find me when you decide it is the right time."

Fenrir walked to the door. His finger was on the handle, ready to leave Ashlyn to her thoughts.

"Grey?"

He turned round and leaned against the door. Ashlyn came forward and stopped inches away from him. They held each other's gaze. Fenrir wanted to stride over and capture her mouth and convince Ashlyn with the only thing that he knew she liked about him, his body.

"Will you stay?"

Fenrir tilted his head, not sure why she would want him to stay.

"Please. Can you stay with me? I don't want to be alone. I want you to stay." Fenrir inclined his head, and he saw

Ashlyn sigh with relief. "Okay, you want something to eat, or drink? I don't think I've ever seen you eat...what do you like? Zach did a shop, so we have stuff in. I'm not very domesticated but I cook good nuggets."

It stirred something inside him, primal, at the thought of his mate feeding him and he wasn't sure if Ashlyn knew how significant it was to have your mate feed you. But she was a wolf herself, so surely she knew, and yet she still offered to feed him.

Perhaps his plan might work. Perhaps Ashlyn when presented with the thing that could get her out of this mating, was the very thing that might help her decide if she could be mated to him or not.

"Grey? Food?"

Fenrir shook his head, then strode over to Ashlyn and cupped her cheek. "I will stay. You do not have to feed me. Come, show me what it is that you are comfort watching. I would like to know what it is you are watching."

Ashlyn grinned and grabbed his hand pulling him toward the couch. "Okay, so this might seem weird, and Zach tells me it's weird, but I love watching it and when I'm feeling sad or confused I kinda like to watch it to make myself feel better. We could watch from the start, sometime, if you enjoy it, but I can catch you up, like give you a summary."

He stood and let Ashlyn take off his coat, and he grinned as she leaned in and inhaled, then her cheeks flushed. Fenrir didn't comment because he was always fighting the compulsion to bury his nose in the crook of her neck and take as much of her scent into his system as possible.

Lowering himself onto the couch, Fenrir peered over at Ashlyn, and chuckled. "Stop fretting, Ashlyn and come sit down. Or else I might be tempted to bite you."

From the flush of her cheeks, Ashlyn did not seem to be offended by his statement. Far from it, in fact. She came over and flopped down beside him, curled her legs up on the couch and leaned into him. Fenrir lifted his arm and pulled her in even closer.

He sat and listened as Ashlyn gave him a full rundown of the TV show that she claimed was a comfort watch, amused at how animated she got at certain points, memorizing the little inflection of her voice when she described the main characters.

She grabbed some sweets from the table and offered him some, and he took the popcorn, and when it made her smile, Fenrir took some more. Then Ashlyn pressed play and sighed as she rested her head against his chest. She then reached for his hand when the episode started in earnest and intertwined her fingers with his.

Fenrir was surprised when Ashlyn didn't stop after one episode, but lett them play over and over, only stopping to go to the bathroom, or to grab them both a drink. They spent hours watching Ashlyn's comfort show about a cult of serial killers and Fenrir found that it amused him that she enjoyed it with such vigour.

And to think the obstinate she-wolf thought she was not meant to be his mate.

Though he did become rather confused when he heard said she-wolf sniffle at a scene and realized that she was crying. Taking the remote in his hand that was not held by Ashlyn, he pressed pause.

"Why are you upset?"

Ashlyn sniffled. "You'll think I'm weird."

"You are a she-wolf who has a Valkyrie queen for a mother and a demented god for a grandfather. And a sociopath for a mate. You are already weird."

Ashlyn laughed, her joy a blaze through the bond as she smacked him. "That's rude."

His lips curved into a smile. "Can you explain why you were crying?"

Ashlyn sighed, shifting so that she was looking up at him. "Okay, but you asked so this is on you if it turns you off me completely."

Fenrir did not think that would ever be possible.

"Charlie failed. He had a mission and he failed. He had a task given to him by Joe, and he couldn't do it. Charlie just wanted to make Joe happy, he wanted more than anything for Joe to be proud of him. It's kinda like Charlie was looking for a father's approval. And as mad as Joe is about the failed mission, he knew how badly Charlie was trying to make amends, so he grants him that, like a blessing. The death itself is probably the most intimate moment in all the seasons. That's what makes it beautiful."

Fenrir angled his head. He understood that Charlie had failed his task and could understand this Joe wanting to kill him as retribution. But he could not see it as Ashlyn saw it, as beautiful or intimate.

"You do not think it's beautiful when I kill. When I am a monster like your Joe, it frightens you."

Ashlyn shrugged and gave him a sad smile. "I know, and I'm sorry. My mind is a weird place, but you probably already know that with the..." Ashlyn pointed to him, then her, and went back to watching the episode.

It gave him a strange sense of hope that a show about serial killers might just be the thing that meant that his Ashlyn might just understand him, even if she did not know it. And when she yawned and asked him to stay over, Fenrir crawled into bed with his mate, wrapped his arms around her and he almost felt normal.

The Killer

PAIN...
All that they were made up of was pain...
The borrowed power inside of them wanted out.
They wanted to use their claws and shred flesh...
They wanted to cement the power inside of them as theirs...
And no one would stop them...
If they tried, they would die too...

Chapter Sixteen

Ash

ASH HADN'T KNOWN WHAT TO DO WHEN FENRIR HAD GIVEN her the dagger. She should be thrilled, right? This was what she had wanted since the bond had snapped into place all those years ago. Ash had desired nothing more than the means to be free of the shackles that bound her to Fenrir and now that she had it. So when he had just sat there, the dagger pointed at his heart, why the hell did she find herself unable to use it?

Then she'd given in to the urge to spend time with Fenrir, had actually enjoyed herself and then had the second-best sleep of her life, his body curled protectively around hers. And the plant...that stupid plant that Ash had laughed at because she had thought it was funny, though when Fenrir had explained why he'd chosen a cactus, Ash had realized just how considerate he'd been.

He had been gone when Ash woke and since the killer had been quiet, they didn't have to go to the station until later, and Ash had spent the morning summoning the dagger and sending it away to see if seeing it again would give her more of a sense of clarity.

Growing frustrated at her conflicting feelings, Ash had gone to the station, seeking out Caitlyn, who had taken her on a lot of walks when she was younger, talked to her, listened, and was one of her favourite people. Caitlyn was never anything but honest with Ash, even when she was younger, and Ash had always appreciated that.

Tonight, they sat in a corner of the underground bunkroom, coffees in hand. Caitlyn looked just as beautiful now as she did when Ash had gone back to the past and having understood Zach's assessment that Caitlyn used to smell sad all the time, Ash valued Caitlyn even more so.

Caitlyn sat and listened as Ash unloaded everything, her mind spinning. The vampire listened with a soft expression on her face, and when Ash finished, then said her life was all kinds of complicated, and that was it so wrong to want the kind of relationship with her mate that Caitlyn had with Donnie, or her parents had, Caitlyn gave her a warm smile.

"Ash, you cannot find your own love with Fenrir if you constantly compare it to others around you." Caitlyn told her, and Ash listened. "There are many kinds of love, it's one of the things that makes it so special, no? Sometimes you love despite what everyone else sees as problems. Sometimes people looking in can't understand the reasons, but they don't have to as long as the people involved know. And sometimes even the people themselves don't know - they just love."

"But how do I know if it's love or the bond?"

"I am not a mind reader like my mate, so that is something you need to discover for yourself. The love I have for Sebastian, it is different from the love I have for Donnie. I had time to fall in love with my husband, but my mate, I think I fell the moment I saw him bleeding in that alleyway, compelled as I was to make him a vampire. I thought myself selfish, and pushed him away, and it took me a while to realize that by doing so, I was giving Cain more power over me, to still feel broken."

Ash had hugged Caitlyn then, the vampire's soft chuckle making Ash smile as they went back upstairs, and Zach was leaning against the wall. He almost purred when Caitlyn grazed her knuckles along his jaw, and Ash rolled her eyes with a smile tugging at the corners of her mouth.

When Ash was alone with her best friend, Zach glanced her way. "You've been avoiding me."

Ash sighed before falling into step with Zach. "I haven't meant to. There's just a few things going on in my head I need to sort out."

"This have anything to do with Fenrir's scent being at the scene of Twitch's murder?"

Ash stumbled over her feet, and Zach grabbed the back of her hoodie to stop her from falling. She looked at him dead in the eye, and Zach shrugged. "You forget that I've been around Fenrir a couple of times too. I figured you would tell me once you figured out there was no way that your mate killed Twitch."

"What makes you so sure?" Ash asked Zach.

"Fenrir would have either just eaten him or made sure no one found the body. Killing Twitch would have made you angry and Fenrir doesn't want you angry with him. And considering he's spent a couple nights in your bed, then you must have believed he was being set up too."

Ash put her hands over her face. "I'm an idiot."

"Nah, you were protecting your mate. The team knows that. Fenrir told them that he knew you suspected him. He went to your dad and told him he did not kill the rat, and if you were to be punished for protecting her mate, then he would take the punishment."

Ash's heart skipped a beat. "Why the hell did no one tell me?"

"Fenrir asked them not to."

Ash wasn't sure how to processes all that information, so she walked into the kitchen and grabbed a bottle of fizzy lemon and a bar of chocolate. She devoured the bar as Zach watched in amusement, then hopped up on the counter opposite her.

"Okay, I know you talked to Caitlyn, but talk to me now."

"Listen, if you laugh at what I'm about to say to you, I swear I will deck you."

Zach grinned. "Hey, I can only promise to try."

Rolling her eyes, Ash took a slug from her bottle, then set it down after corking it. "So, Grey came over yesterday. He gave me a cactus, because they don't need much looking after and I work long hours…"

"That's actually a thoughtful thing, right?" Zach swung his legs, his heels tipping the cupboard. "He was being considerate."

"Ya and then we kissed a bit, and then he stopped."

"Did you want to stop?"

Ash shook her head. "That's the thing, Zach. The attraction had never been mine and Fenrir's problem. He kisses me and I forget everything else. But he put the brakes on and then told me that he had another gift for me. He gave me this."

Willing the dagger into her hand, Zach leaned in to get a better look. "That reeks of old magic. Like Loki and Fenrir old magic."

"Grey said its roughly called bond breaker. That all I have to do is stab him in the heart and the mating bond will die. He gave me the one thing I've been searching for."

Zach's eyes widened and he sat back. "Fuck. He found it."

"Ya, he did."

They sat in relative silence for a good while, and Ash knew that her best friend was trying to come to terms with the fact that the god who didn't want the bond to be broken, was the one who had given Ash the artifact that she had been searching for.

"I take it from the way that you still carry his scent that you didn't do it yet?"

Ash shook her head. "He gave it to me, then moved my hand and put the tip of the blade right at his chest. Closed his eyes and told me he was ready. The fucker had kissed me five minutes before that and then he wanted me to hurt him. I couldn't do it...I couldn't."

Zach's emerald-coloured eyes were laser focused on Ash. "You still want to break the bond, right? Or has something changed?"

Ash just shrugged her shoulders. "I mean, I should still want to, right? It's why I haven't let myself be near him, until like now, because it would only confuse me if I ever had the chance to break it. And then he gave the dagger to me, and I feel so confused. Maybe it's the bond making me feel this confused. I don't know, Zach. I don't know what I want anymore."

Zach hopped off the counter and came over and she leaned into him, rested her forehead against his broad shoulder as he said. "You think too much, A.K. You head will tell you one thing, but I think you gotta listen to your heart. Fenrir might not be what you pictured in your head but maybe your heart knows exactly what kind of mate you need."

Ash straightened and looked at Zach. "How'd you end up so damn smart, Z?"

Zach grinned, running a hand through his hair. "I'm older and wiser. And handsome...we can't forget handsome."

Ash laughed and snacked him on the shoulder at the exact moment shouts sounded in the hallway and boots pounded down the hall. They exchanged a look, then they too were racing out of the kitchen to see what the hell was going on.

People were standing with their weapons drawn, pointing down the hall to the main squad room. Zach was taller than Ash, so he was able to see over the heads of some of the people and then he looked at Ash and just said. "It's Fenrir."

Ash shoved through the crowd, growling, and they moved out of her way. She managed to get through the crowd, Zach behind her. Her dad was trying to talk to Fenrir, who had one of the shifter agents drafted in to help on the case by the throat, his legs dangling off the ground. Fenrir's eyes were molten-red, his claws out, and his fangs elongated but he hadn't shifted and that was good.

The shifter would be dead if Fenrir had changed forms.

Ash caught her dad's eye, and he looked to the ground where Arik was staring at Fenrir with a mixture of fear and awe. Zach must have seen Arik too, made to go to him, even as Arik shook his head and Fenrir snarled.

"Do not touch him, cat."

What in the actual fuck?

The shifter tried to move as if he thought Fenrir might be distracted. The growl that came out of Fenrir made Ash's wolf lay down inside her, as her mate dug his claws into the flesh at the man's throat, the copper scent of blood filling the air.

Ash turned around to face the other agents and growled herself. "Put down the fucking weapons and get gone. Now!"

Maybe they actually listened to her, or maybe her dad had given them a nod, because they all holstered their weapons and retreated. Ash turned and looked at her uncle, who was paler than usual.

"You okay, Arik?"

"I think so. Fenrir stopped him."

Zach and Ash exchanged a look. This wasn't something

that they would expect Fenrir to do, but Ash had to get to the bottom of it all. Her dad had seen Ash calm Fenrir down before and when he leaned against one of the desks, she knew he trusted her to defuse the situation.

"Grey, you wanna tell me what's going on here?"

"No."

Ash chuckled, rolling her eyes as she took a step closer. His lips twitched around his canines, like he wanted to snarl at her, but reigned it in. "Okay, but it looks like you protected Arik and I'm not gonna be mad at you for that. Quite the opposite in fact."

"Do not try and treat me like a child, Ashlyn."

"Wasn't trying to. If this prick intended to hurt Arik, then I'd have clawed off his balls without a second thought. You have more control than I would have. It's very attractive."

Fenrir didn't say anything, but his grip on the shifter's neck eased a little.

"Either you can tell me, or Arik can tell me what happened, but someone's got to do it."

"I fell asleep." Arik said sheepishly, ducking his head. "I haven't been sleeping well and I was, eh, dreaming, and I must have loosened the control on my power. I woke up and he was touching me. I tried to push him away and leave, but he followed me and then Fenrir showed up."

Ash felt her own anger surge inside her. She hated this for Arik, hated how he had to keep himself on guard all the time. He'd retreat into himself again now, as he tended to do when such incidents happened, and it would take a while for him to trust himself with others again.

"I want him. I love him. He's mine."

The shifter decided to offer up an explanation at the most inappropriate time and power rippled through Fenrir's body. Ash strode forward and put her hand on Fenrir's shoulder. He shuddered but did not take his laser focus off the shifter.

"I do not understand why I have this urge to protect the little god. I want to tear out this shifter's throat and harm your cat if he takes another step toward Arik. I cannot stop myself and I cannot let him go. What is happening to me, Ashlyn?"

Ash had no idea what the hell was going on because Fenrir shouldn't react in this way to anyone but her, the mating bond allowing him to care about her, but...

"I think I did it. I didn't mean to, but we were talking, and I think I touched him and maybe because he doesn't understand emotions, it triggered the wolf protectiveness. I'm sorry, I'm so fucking sorry."

Arik let loose a sob and that seemed to trigger Fenrir. The shifter howled in pain as Fenrir clasped his hand and shattered the bones. "You cannot touch without invitation if you have no hands. It has been a while since I have tasted shifter flesh."

Ash slid her hand up to his neck and dug her nails into his flesh and his head snapped around to hold her gaze. He looked fierce and very much the god that he was. He inhaled, then looked at her confused. "You are not afraid of me. Is this one of your weird things where you would find beauty in my killing him?"

Ash laughed despite the situation. "Maybe. But not today. Let him go and we can get him help. Please, Grey."

It took a few minutes, but Fenrir eventually let the shifter go and Zach had helped Arik into a standing position. Fenrir let Ash clasp her hand on the nape of his neck, supporting him as her dad came forward to get the lovestruck shifter the help he needed. The danger had passed.

Or so Ash thought.

The shifter shoved her dad away, then shouted. "If I can't have him, no one will."

Ash saw the glint of a knife and let out a shout of her

own. She lunged to get between Arik and the knife wielding shifter, but Fenrir was faster, stronger. The knife went into his shoulder, however that didn't stop him.

Fenrir grabbed the shifter and all Ash heard was the snap of bones as he broke the shifter's neck and then tossed him aside. Her dad had his weapon drawn, though Ash was unsure if he had been aiming for the shifter, or for Fenrir.

"Arik!"

Killian came running up the corridor, and Arik went to him, letting his dad embrace him. "What the hell happened?" Killian asked, and it was her dad who explained. When he was done, Killian looked at Fenrir. "Thank you for protecting him."

Fenrir just looked confused, like he still couldn't understand what he had done, or why he had done it. Ash stepped into him, wrapped her arms around his waist and rested her head against his chest.

"You did good, Grey. Really good."

There was a slip, through the bond, and Ash felt his confusion, the panic, the anger at not being able to understand his actions and Ash just held him tighter as the block in the bond slammed back into place with such a ferocity that Ash hissed in pain.

Ash stepped back, hoping to see something in Fenrir's eyes. He was looking at Arik, and to be fair, Arik was looking at him too. Arik swallowed, like he was afraid that Fenrir might hurt him because of whatever exchange had happened between them.

Fenrir frowned, then leaned down to bury his face in Ash's neck. He inhaled and Ash trembled. Donnie and Ricky came rushing in, took stock of the scene and it was Zach's dad who whistled through his teeth.

"Looks like we missed the party."

Her dad explained again what had happened, and that

Fenrir had killed the shifter cleanly because he hadn't a shot to shoot him. Killian took Arik into one of the rooms, leaving them standing outside. Fenrir had lifted his head and stepped back, leaning against the wall, his eyes closed.

Her dad called her over, and Ash went to him. "You and me need to have a talk."

Ash winced and gave her dad an innocent look. "About what?"

Rolling his eyes, her dad then looked to where Donnie and Ricky had gone to Fenrir. "You know what. But it can wait."

Ash didn't know what made her pay attention to the conversations going on between Fenrir, Donnie, and Ricky, but she did, and she heard the tail end of the conversation as Ricky said. "- it's times like these that I'm almost glad that we released you from those chains."

"I beg your fucking pardon?" Ash snarled as she stormed over and pinned Ricky with her stare. Fenrir reached out and gripped the back of her neck, and she glowered at him.

"What do you mean that you released him? Loki did it."

"Ash, kiddo," Donnie started, holding up his hands. "Loki took the blame for us. It was me and Ricky who found him. To defeat Odin, we needed the chains. And to use the chains…"

"You had to let him out? I get that. I understand that but how the fuck do you let Loki take the blame for letting him out when it was you two all along? You've both lied to me my entire life and I can't stand to look at either of you right now."

"Ash, please, just let us-"

"Fuck off, Ricky. Fuck right off," Ash turned to Zach. "Did you know?"

"No, I didn't." Zach said cooly, and that was enough for Ash.

She turned on her heels and out of Fenrir's grasp, then stormed out of the station with Zach hot on her heels. She planned to get blind ass drunk and come to terms with the fact that two of the people she loved and trusted most in her life had lied to her.

Maybe everyone had.

The Killer

"YOU STUPID GIRL. YOU HAVE THE POWER OF GODS AT YOUR *fingertips, and you still cannot do the one thing that is required of you to make the power your own!"*

Anger crawled through her veins as she lifted her eyes and growled at Odin. "I can't just drag him out with the whole team watching. He's a mind reader. He will hear my thoughts."

"I. Don't. Care!" Odin roared and the mirror connecting them shook. "Do what needs to be done or I will rip the power from you and leave you nothing more than the pathetic wolf whose mere existence screams for her to be abused."

Chrissy snarled and slammed her fist into the glass. It cracked, and Odin laughed at her.

She was not pathetic.

She would not be a victim again.

She was so consumed with her thoughts that Chrissy did not hear the bathroom door opening.

Not until she heard her partner speak. "What the fuck is this?"

Chrissy spun round as Odin chuckled. "Ah, the warlock who fucks my cast offs."

Killian snarled and Chrissy felt him pull his magic to him.

She was so close to achieving her goals.

One more death...

One more...

Chrissy let the change ripple through her body and then she lunged...

Chapter Seventeen

Ash

Ash sent out a group text to tell everyone on the team to join her at one of their favourite bars right in the middle of the supernatural quarter. She didn't care that the place was almost empty since it was the middle of the week, the alcohol was good, and the music even better.

Zach had nursed his beer, his own expression dark as Ash tried her best to drain the bar of all of its vodka and tequila. Torin arrived with Chrissy, and a very stern looking Fenrir. Ash didn't even bother to look at Fenrir, since it was obvious he had lied to her too, as he took a seat next to Zach.

Ash downed another shot, the burn in her throat making her head spin, then she was out on the dance floor. Having taken off her jacket, Ash knew her white string top was almost see through in the cheap fluorescent lighting, but she just wanted to have some fun and forget all the fucking bull-shit. Her dad had tried to call her, as had her mam, hell, even Caitlyn had called her, but Ash had ignored them all.

Loki reached out and rested his hand on Ash's shoulder, giving it a sharp squeeze. "So, this is why you hate me?"

Leaning in, Ash whispered in his ear. "No, I hate you for letting him out."

Loki blinked in surprise. "I do not know where Odin hid him away."

"You will."

Lies… all bloody lies that meant that she had blamed Loki for something he hadn't even fucking done, and everyone had let her. Her anger with him had killed any relationship they could have had, hurt her mom, even though she had to have known, and now, it had ruined her relationship with both Donnie and Ricky. Sometimes, when trust is broken, it can never be rebuilt.

Nope, Ash didn't want to talk to anyone, she just wanted to drink and dance and forget that nearly everyone she cared about had lied to her for her entire life. Waving her hands over her head, she moved to the Fallout Boy track, her shoulders moving and her feet bouncing off the floor.

Ash was surprised when Arik showed up out of the blue. She would have guessed that her uncle would have not wanted to be out and about, but he immediately went and sat next to Fenrir, as if he knew that her mate would protect him.

Her phone rang again, and Ash pulled it out of her pocket and turned it off, before sliding it back into her pocket. As if word of agents of P.IT partying at the bar got round, the bar cleared out quickly and Ash saw Torin give the barman a wad of cash before he took a sip of his whiskey.

Torin then walked to where the others were sitting, flashed Arik a grin and asked him if he wanted to dance. Arik went a furious shade of pink and shook his head. Torin grinned, shrugged, and slipped off his grey coat, leaving him in just a charcoal long sleeved top.

"Torin! Come dance with me!"

Torin laughed, shook his head, but Ash was having none of it. She bounced over to him, yanked him forward until he had no choice but to join her on the dance floor. The music changed to something more seductive, and Ash put her back against Torin's front.

She knew she was safe with him, since he had no interest

in her as a lover, and she placed a hand on the side of his neck and rolled her hips in time with the music. Torin clamped his hands down on Ash's hips to stop her from moving but she just wriggled a little more, then Torin swore, retreated a step and Ash turned to face him.

"What's up with you?" she said as she tried to link her arms around his neck and Torin ducked and raised his brows.

"Using me to taunt your mate is a shitty idea, Ash darling. Using me to make him jealous is a shitty thing to do to both of us."

Ash pursed her lips. "I'm not trying to make him jealous. I'm having fun. Don't be such a buzzkill. Just cause Arik doesn't want to dance with you doesn't mean you can be rude."

Torin gave her a haughty look and tapped her nose. "You are a mean drunk, Ash Doyle."

"I'm a fun drunk and you are killing my vibe. I don't want to dance with you anymore."

Torin grinned, winked at her before he said. "Thank the gods because your mate looks like he wants to snap my neck. Maybe your bestie can talk some sense into you."

Zach made to pull her to him, but Ash pushed him away and finally linked her arms around Torin's neck. "I wanna dance with you. You're very pretty."

"So you don't care that your mate is about to leave?"

Ash looked around Torin to see Fenrir knock back his drink, his eyes a little glassy from what Ash could see, then he said something to Arik before he headed out of the seating area and headed down the back hall to the back exit.

Where was he going?

Ash moved before she could stop herself. "Grey! Wait up."

His long strides ate up the narrow corridor and Ash had to hurry to catch up with him.

The alcohol had already burned through her system, and she was starting to lose the haziness she had craved to forget all the hurt and pain. Fenrir moved, a little slower than he normally did, and Ash assumed that he was waiting for her to catch up to him.

"Hey, why are you leaving?"

They faced each other now, his eyes ringed with red. Fenrir didn't respond, just leaned against the wall, and continued to glare at her. Ash glared back at him, jutting her jaw as she raised an eyebrow. "You just not gonna talk to me. I'm mad at you for not telling me the truth."

"And I am furious at you for using a vampire to make me jealous. It is childish, Ashlyn."

His voice was pure animalistic when he growled. And Ash hated being chastised by him. Like she cared if she was being childish. Maybe she had wanted to elicit a reaction from him. Maybe she still did.

Keeping her eyes locked with his, Ash knew she should drop her gaze, because Fenrir was an alpha wolf and she had learned a long time ago that you shouldn't hold the gaze of an alpha wolf and

certainly not one who was already pissed off.

And it certainly wasn't the best idea to push his restraint even more.

"Maybe I should go back to dancing with the vampire."

"Do not test me, Ashlyn." The growl was feral, threatening and Ash felt like she was tethering on the edge of danger. It thrilled her, sent a rush of blood to her brain. She kept her gaze locked with Grey and then a muscle ticked in his jaw a second before Fenrir moved.

His hand wrapped around her throat, tight but not enough that she couldn't breathe. Fenrir wedged a muscular thigh between her legs, and Ash couldn't stop herself from arching her hips, rubbing her core against his thigh.

Fenrir's free hand reached out to grip her hip, to stop her from moving and his eyes were blood-red as his body shook.

"Ash." Her name came out in a rough groan, like he was having trouble controlling his base instincts. Especially if he was using the shortened version of her name. He never called her Ash. "He was touching you and you let him."

Ash sighed, then reached her palm out and rested it on Grey's chest, felt the rapid beating inside his chest. "I'm pretty sure you're more of Torin's type than I am. Besides, Zach touches me all the time and it doesn't bother you."

Fire in her mate's eyes as he replied. "The cat knows where I stand."

Huh, that was news to Ash...when did Grey and Zach have that conversation and why the hell had Zach not told her?

"And you should know where I stand, Grey." Even as Ash said it, she knew that there was no way Fenrir could have known that because she had been giving him completely mixed signals. When he finally spoke, Ash knew that to be true.

"You let the cat touch you. You let the vampire touch you. You offer affection to your team freely. And yet, every time that I so much as look in your direction, you flinch. You offer me crumbs, when it suits you and have no care of how much pain it may cause me. I cannot help that we are mates, Ashlyn. But I will not allow you to belittle me in front of others by having you flirt with vampires."

There was nothing Ash could do when Fenrir lunged for her throat and bit down hard enough to break the skin. Heat flooded through her body at the sharp pain, and she threw her head back, exposing her throat more to him. Fenrir kept his mouth latched to her throat; his human teeth embedded in her flesh. He was marking her as his. She knew that, and if she was being honest with herself, she didn't care.

Mate.

Mate.

Mate.

Fenrir finally lifted his head, a trickle of her blood on his lips. He blinked, like a haze was lifting. "I hurt you."

Ash cupped the sides of his neck. "It's all good. I provoked you. You acted more rationally than I would have expected you to. I'm sorry."

Fenrir starred at her, then Ash leaned forward and nipped at his lower lip. Fenrir growled, nipped her jaw and Ash sighed. She was starting to understand what everyone had been trying to tell her for the longest time. Everyone loved differently. Not everyone's relationship was the same, and maybe, in his own unique way, Fenrir did love her.

And maybe she really loved him too.

Leaning her forehead against his, Ash sighed. "I'm sorry. I think I've been blaming you for the bond, for losing my goddess powers, and it's unfair. I feel like who I was, who I am had been stolen from me. Every time I hear thunder, or see a flash of lighting, it's like losing it all over again."

Fenrir cupped her face, held her gaze. "No one can steal your thunder because you are the fucking storm, Ashlyn."

His eyes were back to black and filled with a devotion to her that she had overlooked. Fenrir stepped in close and pressed a kiss to her lips, a hard, possessive kiss before he stepped back, and let Ash stand on her own two feet.

"I cannot dance; however, we should rejoin your friends. It makes you happy to be with them."

Fenrir took her hand and led her back to the bar. Chrissy was calling a round and she brought the tray over to the table where Torin was trying to charm Arik. Chrissy handed Ash a drink, and she sipped it slowly, happy that her friends were including Fenrir as Chrissy handed him a tumbler with whiskey in it.

Zach caught her eye, and she flashed him a five by five, Fenrir's hand still in hers. Her best friend grinned, then stepped in front of them and asked Fenrir if Ash could dance with him. Zach waited patiently as Fenrir mulled things over in his mind.

"I'll allow it. No kissing on the lips. I am only allowed to do that."

"Okay, hooker rules it is then." Zach replied with a grin as Fenrir looked confused, but Zach just gripped his shoulder and said, "I'll explain it to ya later, Fen. Don't stress about it."

Ash squeezed Fenrir's hand, put her drink down because that hadn't helped matters, then pulled Arik out to the dance floor. Torin hesitated, his feet tapping to the music and then Fenrir perched next to him, leaned in, and said something that made Torin's eyes widen. Then the fear was gone, and the vampire smiled, and replied to Fenrir.

Then Torin came out to dance with them, though Ash noted that the vampire stayed a good few inches from her. She kept an eye on Fenrir, who Chrissy stayed with and kept topping him up, and Ash appreciated the other wolf looking out for her mate.

It didn't slip Ash's notice that saying that Fenrir was her mate had become easier and easier.

Happiness bloomed in her chest and for a few hours, Ash forgot that they had a murderer on the loose, her family had lied to her, and she had within her grasp the means to kill a mating bond that she wasn't sure she wanted to kill anymore. So, she danced and laughed and enjoyed the reprieve with her friends.

Ashlyn, there is something wrong...

Fenrir's voice in her head alerted her and she glanced over to see him get to his feet, stagger, and knock over his glass in the process. The static in the bond fizzled. She caught a glimpse inside his mind in that moment, felt the haziness and Ash swayed, like she was drunk.

"I didn't know he could get drunk? He didn't drink that much, right?" Zach asked her as Fenrir growled, his eyes flickering red like he was vying for control.

"I don't think so."

Ash started to head over to Fenrir, but he had already staggered away from Chrissy and was now headed into the bathroom. The door slammed shut behind him, and she heard him wretch from outside the door. There was no one in the bar but them, so Ash knocked and pushed the door open.

"Grey, what's wrong?"

Fenrir vomited into the toilet again, then he leaned against the wall. He was breathing hard and Ash had seen him spar with Erika and barely showed an exertion from it. But now? Now he looked the most mortal Ash had ever seen him look and it bloody terrified her.

His skin looked grey in colour so suddenly that Ash was worried, and when she touched his forehead, it was clammy and boiling. "Fuck, you're burning up."

He slumped against the wall and growled. "Poison."

By the gods, what could have poisoned Grey and left him in such a state? Ash had spent a lot of time researching and searching for a means to break the bond or take Fenrir out of the equation and she hadn't found any way to do it. Even Zach's sleeping beauty potion only lasted a couple of hours at most on Fenrir, and any of the other gods he had tested it on.

But this wasn't Zach's sleeping potion...

This was something else entirely and Ash felt her blood ice over. Could this kill Grey?

The god in question snarled, his eyes fluttered closed, his chest rising and falling as Ash shouted for someone to help, yanking her phone out of her pocket so fast it clattered across the floor and landed right in front of someone's booted foot.

Ash lifted her eyes as she tried to rouse Fenrir. "Come on, Grey. Wake up for me. You're okay. You're okay."

Chrissy bent down to pick up Ash's phone and Ash held out her hand. "Hey, gimmie that. I'll call his dad and find out what the problem is."

Her teammate didn't hand her the phone. Instead, she crushed it in her hand and tossed the pieces aside. Ash snarled and narrowed her gaze. "What the fuck?"

Chrissy snarled, and it was as if she lifted a veil, revealed her madness. "You're not gonna call anyone. I poisoned him. I don't think it will kill him, but who knows."

Ash got to her feet and snarled. "I don't know what the fuck you think you are doing but you will get out of my way, or I will rip you to shreds."

Chrissy smirked. "You cannot kill a god, Ash. Only a god can kill a god and you are not a god anymore."

Then Chrissy lashed out, her hand morphing into claws as she swiped at Ash. Ash jerked backward, slamming into the bathroom stall door and it swung open, and Ash regained her footing. The bond blazed again, making Ash stagger, whatever poison Chrissy had used filtering through the bond now that Fenrir wasn't able to consciously block the feedback.

Ash blinked away the dizziness, and leapt, grabbing onto the doorframe, and kicking out, sending Chrissy flying back into the door. The other werewolf was on her feet a second later, like the blow hadn't phased her, and she hissed as Ash dropped down and landed in a crouch.

Her mind swam and she couldn't stop from dropping to one knee, letting out a moan. Fenrir's head lolled to the side, his breathing shallow and Ash crawled to him, putting her hand in his as she tried to push through whatever Chrissy had poisoned him with.

"You almost look romantic." Chrissy said as she crouched down in front of them. "At least you'll both die together. But if I was you, Ash, I woulda fucked him sooner. Now, you'll never get to do that."

Panic flared inside her chest as she prayed that Zach would realize that they were missing and come searching for them. Chrissy couldn't get them both out of the bar without drawing attention to herself. What the hell was going on?

As if she sensed Ash's thoughts, Chrissy reached out and grabbed Ash's chin, and Fenrir snarled, not as out of it as Chrissy or Ash thought. "I told you I was a god now. I have god powers. I think we need to move this party to somewhere more private."

Chrissy grabbed her hand, then Fenrir's and the last conscious thought Ash had before darkness consumed her was how the fuck did Chrissy gain the ability to flash.

Chapter Eighteen

Zach

ASH AND FENRIR HAD BEEN MISSING FOR A WHILE.

Zach had a feeling that the two of them weren't off cementing the mating bond, a sense of unease prickling his senses. Chrissy had also disappeared to check on their friends, and she had yet to come back. Zach walked off the dance floor and made his way to the toilets and pushed open the door to the men's room.

His heart sank as he saw signs of a struggle then spotted Ash's crumbled phone in the sink. Zach tuned on his heels and rushed out to the dance floor to see Arik holding his phone up to his ear. Zach motioned for the barman to kill the music, and the moment he did, Arik put his phone on loudspeaker.

"The killer is Chrissy. She attacked Killian. He's alive but in pretty bad shape, Arik. We've got him. Your mom is ready to spill blood."

Derek's voice was reassuring as Torin placed his hand on Arik's shoulder.

"Sir, Ash, Fenrir, and Chrissy are all missing. Signs of a struggle in the bathroom and Ash's phone was in pieces. Fenrir was ill and Ash went to check on him."

Derek swore, his tone feral as he said. "We will find her. We will find them all. Arik, you okay to flash Zach and Torin back to the station?"

"Ya, I can do that."

Derek hung up then and Arik stashed his phone. Zach had been flashed a lot of times by Ash, but Arik turned to Torin. "Have you been flashed before?"

Torin grinned, his fangs on display. "No. It's my first time. Be gentle with me, won't you?"

Zach shook his head as Arik frowned at the blatant sexual innuendo. That didn't stop Arik from reaching for them both and then they were standing in the ops room at the station. Zach shook himself as Torin staggered and placed a hand on the wall to steady himself.

"Well, that's a mind fuck. Is the room spinning or it just me?"

Arik rolled his eyes as he went over to his computer and Zach did the same. His mind raced with all the scenarios that could be happening right now and he had to stop, and take a deep breath to stop himself from thinking the worst was going to happen.

Ash might be a badass, but she was still like a sister to him and ever since she had been born, Zach had known that he was meant to be there for her, to protect her. Zach had seen enough of fate and destiny to know that Ash and he were meant to share this bond and he couldn't stand the thought of losing her.

Closing his eyes, Zach replayed the earliest memory he had of Ash, of when she had gone to the past and he was just a child, but he had felt the love he had for the girl who called him brother.

Zach knew that he should stay inside like he was told and not come outside but the girl who stood outside, he knew her, even if he had never seen her before. In his cat form, Zach darted out from behind his dad's legs, and rushed toward the girl, this Ash who made his heart feel happy.

She sank to the ground, a smile curving her lips as she set her hammer down and he changed his form to stand in front of her.

The adults were calling him back, but Ash held up her hand to halt them. Zach didn't want to go back. He wanted to protect her from those who might want to hurt her. She bent her head down, grinned at him and then spoke loud enough for all the adults to hear her.

"Hello, Big Brother. This is the only time I've ever been taller than you. You mind if your dad gets you a T-shirt? I've seen enough of your naked butt over the years that I am going to totally tease you about this when I go home."

That made Zach return her grin as he climbed into Ash's lap and rested his head in the crook of her arm. She petted his hair, and it made him happy, so he purred. Then she said. "The last time we did this, when you had your head in my lap and I stroked your hair, you had the galaxy's worst hangover after we raided your dad and Uncle Donnie's homebrew."

Zach didn't understand what it was that Ash was talking about, but it sounded like they had many adventures in the future. He knew from how she spoke that Ash loved him, because it was how his mom used to talk to him, how his dad did, and his vampire mom Melanie did.

Ash tapped his nose and ruffled his hair. "You and me, Z, we take on the world together. You are my best friend in the whole world, you know that kid? You and I are family. Now, before they all pounce on me, go back to your dad. We can play later."

She lifted him up then, nipping his nose in a playful way and Zach swiped at her with his human hands. She rose, setting him down on the ground and Zach stayed where he was for a moment, not wanting to leave Ash by herself.

He went back to his dad, his heart now full because she was his person.

A hand landed on Zach's shoulder, jerking him from the

memory. His dad looked down at him with a fierceness, an understanding in his eyes. "We will find her."

"We'll find them both. Can Loki track Fenrir?"

His dad shook his head. "He tried when you told us that they'd been taken. He said it was hard before unless Fenrir wanted to be tracked but whatever was done to him, or wherever they are, it's blocking any magical means to track them."

"Could Chrissy of made Fenrir flash them somewhere?"

"Who the hell knows? Why the fuck did none of us see it? That she was behind it?"

Derek came into the room, gave his old partner a quick pat on the shoulder. "Because we didn't know the full extent of her background. She managed to hide it from us, but we just managed to get more details."

Zach turned in his chair, waiting as the rest of the team, including Ash's mom, and Fenrir's father came in and Zach watched as the entire team, minus Killian, old and new, all agents of the Paranormal Investigation Team gathered to find their missing people.

His mom came over and perched on the end of his desk, and he took her hand when she reached for him, listening as Derek began to speak.

"Everyone here knows that Chrissy was one of the victims of Stephen Donnelly who survived and that was her reason for wanting to join the guards. What we didn't know was that Chrissy had a hard time adjusting after the attack. She acted out, had violent outbursts, and her parents sent her away."

"They sent her to a boarding school up the country for shifters who had behavioural problems. It was also a front for the sex trafficking ring that most of the victims were a part of." Donnie said, anger in his eyes. "It would appear from recounts from other shifters who had been placed there that Chrissy and many others were passed around to monsters who liked kids."

Caitlyn took a step closer to Torin, who looked like he wanted to kill someone. "The boarding school was reported, and the children sent home. Chrissy's parents had left Ireland at that stage, and Arthur De Valera had fostered Chrissy with a well-known werewolf couple, not knowing that the male had been involved in the trafficking ring."

"How are you only getting this information now?" Torin snarled, stopping when Caitlyn put a hand on his arm.

"Due to her age when all the abuse took place, her name was redacted and once she had access to the system, she tried to delete anything that could link her as the victim of all the abuse." Derek told Torin and that seemed to douse some of his rage.

"When we upgraded the computer systems when P.I.T. moved to this building, I made sure to have back-ups of back-ups, and with Derek's high clearance we were able to make sure we had un-redacted files." His mom said, and Zach squeezed her hand.

His mom might be one of the strongest people she knew but when the case you're working brought up memories of the man who killed you, Zach knew it must be hard.

"We think that while on a case six months ago, Chrissy came face to face with one of her abusers and stalked him and killed him. She blamed Arthur for putting her back in the grasp of her abusers. The rest of the men she took from our records for with potential players in the trafficking ring. She matched the men with those she had seen and killed them all."

Zach let go of his mom's hand to look at his computer screen. He brought up the rosters and the logbooks and noted Chrissy's absences or time off the night of the murders, or the fact that Killian was working with others any time a murder took place.

"The timelines add up. She was off rotation, or sick, or swapped shifts any night a murder took place."

"So, motive and means." His dad said running a hand through his hair. "She passed the psych test. She passed all the fucking markers we put in place to make sure we didn't end up here. How the hell did she do that?"

"She studied and watched." Torin answered his dad quietly. "She was smart enough to take the time to think that her first answer might not be the right answer and went with what sounded the most like a police officer would say. She gauged reactions and then pulled back when she seemed to cross a line."

"What makes you think that?" Derek asked.

"She asked me not long after I had joined P.I.T. how many people I'd killed. It was one of the first interactions I had with her, and it struck me as strange. Everyone else, like Ash, tried to pry personal information from me and all she wanted to know was how many people I'd killed."

"You were an unknown to the team. She was assessing you to see if you were a threat."

"And I was too busy trying to fit in that I didn't flag it as weird. I'm fuming with myself."

Zach's dad placed a hand on Torin's back. "Join the club. We're all fuming that we didn't see it. But we have all the information now and we need to figure out where Chrissy would take them."

They worked all through the night to try and figure out a location, with Zach even trying to see if there were any live feeds that had the same static screen that happened to the CCTV when Chrissy was in the vicinity. Nothing was showing up, even as Zach widened his search to Europe. He wasn't sure if Fenrir could have flashed them far in the state he was in, so Zach assumed they would be closer rather than on the other side of the world.

He had the shard of the Bifrost locked in the bottom drawer of his desk. He could take it out, go into the past and warn Ash and Fenrir about Chrissy, the Fates be damned. He had nothing of value of his that they could take, he could survive his life without his magic or his ability to shift to his cat form, but there was no way he could survive without Ash.

"You know the consequences of meddling with the past, child."

Zach lifted his head and glanced round the room. Everyone was frozen, time standing still as Zach saw the Fates, Urðr, Verðandi, and Skuld standing like apparitions. The last time Zach had seen the three sisters, was when they had sent his ass back to the future, no DeLorean needed.

He leaned back in his seat and gave them a grin. "Ladies, it's been a minute. A vision as always."

The Fates seemed unimpressed by his flirting, so he waited for them to give him the heads up as to why they had shown up when they had been MIA for five years.

"The past has come calling for the present, Zachary."

Zach nodded, assuming that they were referring to the fact that Chrissy and her past was what had brought them to this moment. Then Verðandi said. "The present lingers on the verge of change."

Skuld chimed in then "The future is unclear."

"But if I use the Bifrost and go back, then the future will not be unclear. Ash will still be here, and Fenrir, and Chrissy will safely be in custody. Everything will be right again."

Skuld narrowed her gaze. "The path to destiny cannot be tampered with. Venturing into the past, even as minuscule as you believe, could impact course of the future. One ripple in time to undo all that the warriors in this room have sacrificed to have peace in the nine realms. You must not interfere."

Zach's hands curled into fists. "She is my sister. I'm meant to protect her."

"Yes, that is a part of your destiny. As she is determined to protect you. but the bond you share is only a small fraction of what fate had in store for you all. Forget the Bifrost shard and do not meddle with the past, or we shall visit you again under less cordial circumstances."

As Verðandi finished her sentence, the three sisters vanished, and time started up again.

Loki glanced around the room and frowned. "The three sisters of doom and gloom were here. Who did they visit?"

Everyone looked around and Zach cleared his throat. "Ya, that was me."

His dad came over and ran his hands over Zach which made him laugh. "Dad, I'm good. I still have some shards of the Bifrost and was gonna use them to go back and warn Ash and Fenrir. I was advised against it."

His dad's eyes narrowed. "You said you got rid of all of those."

"I lied. I'm not going to apologise when you all lied to Ash and me for years. Ash wouldn't have been pissed off and dragged us to the bar if you guys had been straight with her. So don't look at me with all your judgement when your lies put us in this fucking predicament!"

Zach pulled his gaze away and stared at his computer screen, then closed his eyes, taking in a sharp breath to try and sate his anger. Jesus, Ash was normally the hot head, with a quick trigger temper and he was the calmer, more reasonable partner.

He would give anything now to have Ash here, taking the piss out of him for losing his cool.

Zach hoped she got the chance to tease him.

"Why would Chrissy take Ash and Fenrir? Ash wasn't even born when Donnelly tried to kidnap her, and Fenrir isn't involved in the trafficking ring."

"She has been digesting the hearts, much like Donnelly tried to do with his victims. Perhaps she thinks by consuming Fenrir's heart that it will give her his power?"

"She must be batshit crazy if she thinks that she can fuck up Fenrir like she did the other wolf." His dad said, and Zach had to agree with him.

They were missing something, something major that could lead them all to where Ash and Fenrir had been taken and Zach tried to think, to focus on the little things they might have missed. The door to the comms room opened and Freya came in, her expression fierce as she helped Killian in. His face was clawed, a gash across his throat where Chrissy must have tried to slash it.

"Dad!" Arik exclaimed as he got to his feet and went to his dad, his mom urging him to be careful.

"My idiot of a mate demanded to be brought here as soon as he woke, despite the fact that he had multiple broken ribs, and his throat was almost ripped out."

Killian grinned. "I love you too, babe. I'm grand."

"You look half dead, bro."

Killian laughed and then coughed, and it rattled in his chest. "Fuck off, Ricky. I have info."

Freya helped Killian sit down on a chair and Arik got him a glass of water. "I'm not sure how much I'll get out before I pass out again so shut up and listen. I heard Chrissy talking in the bathroom, arguing with someone. I tried to listen, but I didn't recognise the other person's voice."

Killian coughed again, then took another drink of water. "I went in, and she was talking to the mirror. There was a man in the mirror. He smirked at me when I went in and said - "Ah, the warlock who fucks my cast offs.""

That made Zach sit up a little straighter. Odin? How the hell was Odin involved in all of this?

Freya had gone still beside her mate, and Ever looked at Killian. "Odin is locked up in a place only a handful of people know. Are you sure it was him?"

"Without a doubt. I tried to fight her off but she obviously got in some good licks. She was about to kill me, and I asked her if her vigilante shit made her feel like a bitch knowing a deranged god was pulling her strings?"

"Nice Taylor Swift nod there, bro."

Killian grinned. "I try."

His mom shook her head. "You two are insane."

The brothers grinned, and the mechanics in Zach's brain started to work again. If Chrissy was working with Odin, then there would be only one reason that Odin would use Chrissy and it would be to his own advantage. And Ever was right, there were only a few people who knew where Odin was being kept, and only one place that no one would think to look for them.

Zach stood up so fast that his chair fell backward with a slam, and everyone turned to look at him. He tried to get the words out and they came out all jumbled.

His dad gripped his arms. "Zach, take a beat. What have you figured out?"

Zach did what his dad told him, took a beat and then he said. "They are in Niflheim. Chrissy took them to Niflheim. She means to free Odin from Gleipnir."

Chapter Nineteen

Ash

ASHLYN WAKE UP. WAKE UP, LITTLE RED.

The sound of Fenrir's voice inside Ash's mind stirred her from the darkness, her eyes fluttering open to see her mate slumped against a stone wall, his eyes closed and his body utterly still. His skin was soaked in sweat, beading on his forehead and slipping down his face. Ash had never seen him look so damn mortal and it terrified her.

The static that kept her hidden from his mind was nothing more than a flimsy shield. She could feel him now, weakened from whatever poison Chrissy had used and Ash could hear some thoughts that filtered through to her.

I must protect my mate.

I must protect Ashlyn...she is mine, I am hers and she is mine.

As much as Ash had always been conflicted when Fenrir claimed her as his, she somehow felt comforted to hear it through his mind. It meant he would fight whatever shite was in his veins to get to her, to protect her, even if she didn't need any protection.

Grey, do you know what she poisoned you with?

A muscle ticked in his tightly clenched jaw and Ash heard him growl through the bond, try to erect the block again because there was a sudden burst of static and then it crumpled again. Ash pushed up off the ground and looked around for Chrissy as she said to Fenrir in her mind.

Stop wasting your strength trying to block me. I need you strong enough to kill. Come on, Grey. Do as you are told for once!

The last time I did as you asked you sent me away...

Ash heard the pain in his tone, and part of her wanted to pretend that it was from the poison and had nothing to do with her telling him to leave her alone. Though, she knew that it was.

Sitting back on her haunches, Ash scanned the space they were in. It was then that Ash realized that it was vaguely familiar. Her ears twitched as she heard shouting coming from the darkened part of the cavern and then Chrissy stormed out, red in her eyes and she stopped dead when she saw Ash sitting there.

The stupid bitch hadn't even bothered to bind her or Fenrir. She was so deluded in her thinking that she was a God. Fenrir was a god too, and if he was able to push the poison out of his system, he would rip Chrissy apart piece by piece.

Ash would enjoy watching it.

Blood thirsty. My mate is blood thirsty.

She felt a strange sense of approval down the bond, and she sucked in a breath. Holding her hand to her head, she faked that it was a reaction to the poison and not the realization that Fenrir liking her blood thirsty nature pleased her.

"You're awake."

Ash snorted, rolled her eyes. "No shit, Sherlock. How the fuck did you get away with the murders for so long? You can't be that smart, right? You obviously had a puppet up your ass working your strings."

Chrissy snarled, took a step closer to Ash as Ash readied herself to defend if needed.

"None of you saw it. I've been killing for months. Months! Bodies you'll never find. The power I have should be mine and mine alone. One last task and I will be strong. I will never be weak again."

Ash shook her head. "Betraying all the people who cared about you, that's weakness, Chrissy. Loyalty to others is the strongest power you can wield."

"Loyalty? Fuck off, Ash." Chrissy laughed as she paced back and forth. "You were never loyal to me. I didn't fit into your little fucking click. Your family. I was an outsider looking in. Even the fucking vampire got more of a welcome than me. Even the fucking monster you call a mate was included."

Ash could hear the bitterness in Chrissy's tone and wondered when her mind had become so twisted. She needed to keep her talking, and give the others time to figure out where and who was behind all the murders.

"We never excluded you, Chrissy. You got it all wrong there."

"Shut up!" Chrissy shrieked and moved, faster than any ability she should have possessed as a wolf and slapped Ash across the face.

Ash's face stung as she growled, and Chrissy retreated just a little and tugged at her own hair. The power inside her was never meant to be hers and it was slowly, painfully, driving her insane. As much as Chrissy's eyes were red, they were also filled with madness.

Getting to her feet and using the wall of the cavern as a pretend prop to pretend that she was still kinda woozy, Ash wondered why she wasn't feeling as bad as she had back in the bathrooms.

Grey, are you stopping the poison from affecting me? Is it hurting you more that way?

Fenrir didn't respond, but Ash felt a short burst of pain through the bond. Shit, it really was affecting him. She hated the thought of him hurting, and she didn't even want to contemplate how she would feel if the poison could kill him.

"Explain it to me, Chrissy. Explain why you decided to kill all those wolves, and how you ended up with borrowed power."

"The power is mine! It belongs to me now!" Chrissy snarled; her fists clenched at her sides.

"Whatever you say," Ash replied with a shrug. "Come on, just tell me. You are gonna kill me anyways, right? So what harm is there in telling me?"

"You wouldn't understand. No one would understand. That's what he said."

Ash narrowed her gaze. "Who told ya that Chrissy? Come on, we're friends."

The other werewolf laughed, and it was bitter sounding. "We're not friends, Ash. We were colleagues. All the family gatherings, all the times I wasn't invited, and you just forgot to, and I had to listen to all the stories about the fun times while I went back to my apartment alone and all the memories, all the things that were done to me came flooding back."

That couldn't be right. Ash was almost certain that Killian would have invited Chrissy to things, or someone would have sent her a text to come to any spur of the moment nights and that. Chrissy couldn't have killed all those wolves just because she was feeling left out, right?

Realization flooded Ash's mind. "The trafficking ring. You were one of its victims?"

The growl that rumbled inside the other woman's throat was pure animal. "Once a victim, always a victim. I stopped Donnelly from killing me and what did it get me? PTSD so bad my parents sent me away to a school that was a front for a trafficking ring. I was passed around like a fucking toy. Do you know what it's like to have men scare you so badly because they can only have sex when the other person is afraid?"

Fucking hell...no wonder Chrissy had killed all the sick assholes...Ash wanted to do it herself.

"Then the school was closed down and I was sent back to Munster. They knew what had been done to me and then Arthur De Valera gave me to one of his wolves, a man who made the sickos at the school seem tame. I snapped one night and pushed him down the stairs, snapped his neck."

All of this information must not have been in any of Chrissy's personnel file because her dad and the rest of the team would have put two and two together at the start of the case. There was no way any of them would have missed this.

"I was a new recruit during the longest night." Chrissy said, referencing the days leading up to the battle to save the world from Odin's plan to remake the world anew. "I went to fight off the berserkers. It was like they could smell that I had been raped before. It excited them. But I was just a werewolf. I couldn't fight them off."

Nausea rolled in Ash's stomach. Chrissy had been handed bad hand after bad hand and someone else had used that against her, but she was so drunk on the power that she didn't even realize that someone was using her to do their bidding.

"Your dad was the worst."

Ash snarled, took a step forward. "My dad never fucking touched you."

Chrissy's gaze narrowed. "No. But he was the first person to offer me any praise, to tell me that I would be okay. He fucking lied. You know, he came to see me after Donnelly was killed, to tell me and promised me that he would keep an eye on me. I never saw him again until the day I started my P.I.T. training."

Fucking hell. How close had her dad come to being one of

Chrissy's kills? The thought of it chilled Ash to the bone and she held back a shudder, the pain in her chest only a sliver of the grief Ash would feel if she ever lost her dad.

"I'm sure if you had told my dad that he would have helped you. He would have."

Chrissy paced the cavern again, as if she was mulling over what Ash had said. Then she spun round with a snarl. "Stop. Stop trying to say shit you think I want to hear. I know all the tricks too; I have the same training as you. But this time, I didn't just get where I was because my dad was the boss and I used to be powerful. I am a power. I am vengeance and I will still be vengeance when the power is mine to claim as my own."

Brushing aside the fact that Chrissy had basically called her a Nepo baby, Ash held up her hands, her eyes slipping to the still unconscious Fenrir before she held Chrissy's stare. "I can feel it, your power. It's borrowed. It's not meant to be yours. It's eating at you from the inside out and the only person who will gain anything from this is the person who loaned it to you in the first place. Let me help you."

Chrissy screamed and punched the wall, rock crumbling to the ground. Blood dripped from her knuckles as Chrissy looked at her hand, and Ash watched as the wound healed as fast as it did for a lot of the god blooded supernatural's in her family.

"Help me? Help me? You can't help me, Ash. There is only one immortal who can help me now and I will fulfil my end of the bargain to claim my power."

Ash braced herself for Chrissy's conspirator to make an appearance. There came a rattle and a low chortle of laughter from the darkness, the hairs on Ash's arms standing to attention as the last person she expected stepped into view.

And then she burst out laughing.

Her grandfather stood on the edge of the darkness, his

legs and hands bound by the very chain that had once bound her mate, and it dawned on her why this cavern looked so familiar. This was where she and Fenrir had first crossed paths. This was where her life had changed forever.

Odin looked as he had always looked. An older white-haired man, his handsome features marred by dirt and grime that came part and parcel with living in a cave, the place where he had once committed Fenrir to be hidden, and where she now knew Ricky and Donnie had freed him from, later binding her grandfather here.

"You made a deal with this prick?" Ash said as she wiped tears from her eyes. "By the gods, Chrissy. Odin isn't out to help you; he doesn't care about you. He just wants out and you were too stupid not to realize it."

Odin took another step, then snarled as Gleipnir went taut and prevented him from moving any closer. "Did your parents not raise you correctly, child? You should respect your betters."

Ash snorted. "I would if there were any in this cavern. How's the bindings, gramps? Chaffing yet?"

She felt Odin reach for his powers, felt them stir and Ash knew if she made it out of here alive, then she might have to tell Ricky that it was time for him to syphon off some of Odin's growing power. But Odin pulled back and nodded his head to Fenrir.

"Your mate doesn't look well. Looks like the mistletoe did its job. Fitting that it would be his father's discovery that could harm him."

Ash scanned through her Norse history, remembering how Loki had been the architect of the god Baldur's death, and something about a dart.

"I slipped it into his drinks. Took a while for it to start working." Chrissy seemed damn well pleased with herself, and Ash would bloody her up for it, but then Odin turned his attention to Chrissy.

"You were supposed to bring me the grandson of Tyr. What use is my daughter's bitch and her mate?"

Of course, Donnie was the target. He was the other person besides Erika who could open Gleipnir, though Ash supposed that Lyra had enough of Tyr's bloodline in her to open it too, and Ash was really fucking glad that neither Chrissy or Odin had figured that out. Odin had been locked away here for so long that Ash wasn't even certain that he knew that Loki, his once adopted son, had fathered another child, this time with Tyr's daughter.

Chrissy folded her arms across her chest. "You told me you needed the blood of Tyr. Fenrir once ate Tyr's hand so it might work and if it doesn't, I'll use them as a trade. Donnie will offer himself up to protect her. Maybe even him."

"You stupid girl." Odin snapped, chastising. "Once they realize what you intend to do, they will all come, and you are no match for all of them. You are undeserving of the power I loaned you. You won't keep it unless I am free."

"Come on, Chrissy. Odin's not going to honour his end. The moment he's free, he will call back the power and leave you with nothing. Then he will stab you in the back and leave you to die. Alone. Is the power boost really worth risking your life?"

Chrissy looked from Odin to Ash, then started to walk forward, halting before they were within striking distance from one another. "What would you do, Ash, to get the power you fucking threw away back? Would you kill for it? Would you betray those you claim to love for it? Would you kill the monster who is your mate for the chance to be what you were before? What would you do to reclaim what you lost?"

Ash opened her mouth, closed it, and Chrissy laughed at her.

"You are jealous. Jealous that I have what you want most in the world. You tried to be the hero and save the world and they ripped it from you. They took what made you special and left you with nothing but a mere werewolf. You don't even have wings, so can't call yourself a proper Valkyrie."

Ash jerked back at the insecurities Chrissy was expertly throwing back at her, like the other woman had seen inside Ash's head and seen the things that had crippled her these past five years.

No one can steal your thunder because you are the fucking storm, Ashlyn.

Ash heard Fenrir in her head, felt the resounding confidence that he had in her.

"You're wrong," She finally said, and as she spoke, Ash found that her words rang true. "You're dead wrong, Chrissy. Being a goddess wasn't what made me special. I went back to the past to save the future-"

"You going back changed my future!" Chrissy screamed. "You changed too much, and it changed my future."

The Fates had warned her about the ripples that her trip to the past might have caused, and if Chrissy was one of those who had been dealt a shittier hand because of what she had done, then Ash was truly sorry. But she knew, deep down, given the choice to go back and help, or stay and see, she would have chosen action over ignorance.

"I'm sorry if my going back to the past made things worse for you. I am. But I would do it all over again if it meant saving my family and friends. They are what makes me special, Chrissy, not being a goddess. I grew up loved and supported. I grew up surrounded by laughter and by acceptance. I was given a safe environment to be myself. I have a best friend who I would die for, a family who will come to my aid, if I need it, but let me save myself."

Ash glanced at Fenrir. "And I have a mate who loves me in his own way, even when I couldn't see it. Thor gave me a gift, thinking me worthy of the powers bestowed on me and I will only ever be grateful for that. I strive every day to be worthy once more, but if I never, ever gain back the powers I lost, then so be it. Being the goddess of thunder did not make me special, and I accept who I am, and whatever path destiny has set me on."

Pain seared Ash's arm as she grabbed it with a hiss, then she heard a whisper on the wind.

She is worthy.

Black inky tattoos spread from her hand all along her arm, to her shoulder, and Ash felt the burn as they cemented onto her flesh. Power flooded her veins, and it lifted her into the air, the wind whipping around her as the power she lost was reclaimed.

Landing on her feet, Ash heard the rumble of thunder in the distance and the blood in her veins fucking sang. She felt lightning crackle in her eyes, and Ash smiled, held up her hand and the moment Mjölnir was grasped in her hand, it felt like she was finally whole again.

Ash understood that the power had always been hers to reclaim, she just needed to accept that it did not define her, and it did not make her who she was deep inside.

"Only a god can kill another god, right Chrissy?" Ash said to the other woman, tossed Mjölnir in the air, caught it, and then she sighed. "Then let's dance bitch."

Chapter Twenty

Fenrir

HIS MATE WAS MAGNIFICENT.

Fenrir had been trying to keep the effects of the poison, the mistletoe, from leaking down the bond and it was making it harder for him to flush the toxin out of his bloodstream. He was not certain of how much of the plant might cause death, but Fenrir knew that Baldur had taken a dart to the heart, and it had killed him.

He had also been surprised when Ashlyn had not shied away from the thoughts she had evidently picked up through the bond while he was fighting the poison, and he was unable to keep up the shield that kept her from receiving the feedback.

Fenrir had not felt any disgust, or distain from his mate, and he knew what that felt like. Ash was angry that the other she-wolf had harmed him...did that mean that she cared for him? Of that Fenrir was unsure.

He had managed to open his eyes when Ashlyn had spoken of him, and he felt a burst of something along the bond when Ashlyn had said. "And I have a mate who loves me in his own way, even when I couldn't see it."

Was this what Arik had meant about knowing if Ashlyn loved him or not?

If she ever said the words to him, would it feel like this through the bond so that he would know for certain, and he could record it in his journal? The fire in his veins was subsiding and whilst he might not be at full strength, his mate was.

"Only a god can kill another god, right Chrissy? Then let's dance bitch."

Ash moved with a sureness that had been missing since she had lost her confidence when she had lost her hammer, kicking Chrissy in the stomach as the werewolf lunged, and Chrissy stumbled backward, almost crashing into Odin.

Odin shoved Chrissy back toward Ashlyn, and her hands were suddenly claws. Chrissy slashed with her claws, aiming for Ash's throat. Ash ducked and swung Mjölnir. The hammer caught Chrissy in the stomach, sent her careening into the cavern wall so hard, the prison that had once held him shuddered.

Fenrir saw it the moment Chrissy realized that she was not the biggest predator in the cavern any longer. Ashlyn could fight with claw and fang, but she did not need to. If Chrissy wanted any chance against Ashlyn, she would need to change to her wolf form and Chrissy did not have Fenrir's power to change the mass of her wolf. She would have little room to manoeuvre if she shifted, and Ashlyn was the better fighter in human skin.

Thunder rumbled all around them, the sound like a roar inside the cavern, and Ashlyn shifted her gaze to his, streaks of lightning flashing as his mate winked, grinned and started toward Chrissy. Fenrir watched as Odin closed his eyes and Chrissy screamed, the scent of borrowed power wafting from the woman. Odin was giving her more power, hoping that if he gave her enough power it would give her the edge in the fight.

It mattered nothing to the Allfather that the wolf was not built to contain that much power. It would eat away at her from the inside, stripping away who and what she was, and then leave her as nothing more than a shell. Some mortals were not meant to be immortal and carry such a power.

Chrissy shoved off the wall, her fury making her continue with her advancement, and Chrissy kicked out, connecting with Ashlyn's knee and it buckled, but his mate swung her hammer upward, connecting with Chrissy's chin and knocking her backward.

Ashlyn used Mjölnir as a crutch as she rose to her feet, grinned, her teeth stained with blood. "I could do this all day."

Fenrir snorted at her bravado, though he did not doubt that she could.

Ashlyn lashed out with Mjölnir once again, knocking Chrissy to the ground and she scurried backward, just out of Fenrir's grasp. Ashlyn turned to face Chrissy, and it was then that Odin acted.

Lunging forward, the God wrapped Gleipnir around Ash from behind, attempting to choke her. Ashlyn dropped Mjölnir as she grabbed at Gleipnir, trying to keep her grand-father from getting it fully around her throat. As weakened as Fenrir was from the effects of the mistletoe, now that there was no barrier between them now on through the mating bond, he gave what strength he had to her, his fierce mate, and her eyes went red the moment it transferred to her, using a leaf from Odin's book.

"Now, girl, kill her now and when the grandson of Tyr comes, I will be free and the power yours."

Fenrir growled, tried to get up but now that he had given Ashlyn some of his power, he had very little of himself to be of any use while there was still remnants of the toxin in his bloodstream. Chrissy stalked toward Ashlyn, her hands clawed and murder in her eyes, but his mate just smiled.

Pulling her legs up, Ashlyn kicked Chrissy square in her centre, and she stumbled back with a yelp. Fenrir stuck out his foot, causing her to stumble, fall backwards, and hit her head on the cavern floor hard.

It would not kill her, mores the pity, but it would stun her for a moment or two.

Ashlyn regained her footing, then kicked her leg backward, and Fenrir chortled when Ashlyn's booted foot caught Odin in between his legs. Odin let loose a moan, and his grip loosened, giving Ashlyn the chance to slip down and out of Gleipnir and Odin's grasp.

Have you been dialling down your power?

Fenrir lifted his head and gave his mate a wolfish grin. *Perhaps. I did not think it wise to remind you that I have never been human, Ashlyn. I did not need to advertise my power.*

Well, thanks for the assist but you can take it back now. I've got this.

Fenrir reached for the power that was his gently, not wishing to hurt Ashlyn but he did not need to worry. His mate just strode toward where Chrissy was staring up at her with panicked eyes.

"Get up you fool! Get up and stop being the victim. I should have chosen more wisely. I should have chosen someone with a little more spine! Once a victim, always a victim."

Chrissy looked defeated, utterly surprised that Odin had turned on her. Ashlyn called for her hammer, then she swung it round and round, building momentum before she flung it at her grandfather. The force of Mjölnir smacking into Odin sent him plunging into the darkness and out of view. Ashlyn lifted her hand and Mjölnir came right back to it.

"You have two choices, Chrissy," Ashlyn told the other woman as she glanced downward. "You can either surrender and I take you in peacefully, or you can keep fighting me and you end up making an even bigger ass of yourself. Your choice."

Chrissy closed her eyes, her lips curling into a snarl. "Stop talking to me, get out of my head."

Ah so Odin's hold on the she-wolf was embedded deeper than he had first believed.

As Fenrir came to that realization, Chrissy surged once more with power and she pounced, taking Ashlyn with her as she went. His mate landed on her back, her hammer slipping from her grasp. Chrissy slashed out her claws, catching Ashlyn on her arms as she tried to block her face and throat.

The scent of his mate's blood lit up his veins with fury. Fenrir dove for Chrissy, sinking his teeth into the back of her calf, and as Chrissy screamed, Fenrir sent his words along the mating bond.

Odin is still funnelling power into her. He will continue to do so as his power is infinite, always refilling. They must have struck a bargain through a blood bond. It is the only way that he could give her so much of his power and not kill her just yet.

Chrissy punched him in the face, causing him to let go, but Fenrir had held on long enough to give his mate a chance to defend herself. He did not need to be the one to save her, for any mate that he would choose as his would be one who was strong, capable, and vicious when needed. His Ashlyn was all of those things and so much more.

Ashlyn wrapped her legs around Chrissy and rolled them so that she was on top, then shifted slightly, pressing her weight down and Ashlyn swatted away Chrissy's feeble attempts to fight Ashlyn off. The murderer was trying to get free, and she aimed a clawed hand once again at Ashlyn's throat.

Fenrir saw something cross over Ashlyn's expression and then he watched in amazement as his mate willed the dagger, the one he had given her to break their mating bond, and for a moment, Fenrir could not breathe as Ashlyn smiled before she slammed the dagger right into her former teammate's heart.

Chrissy screamed, as the blade hit true, a glow illuminating the cavern as Fenrir heard Odin scream. Ashlyn yanked the dagger out, and as the power in Chrissy started to erupt, Ashlyn scrambled backwards toward him but he dare not reach for her, dare not listen on their own bond to hear her regret her actions.

The borrowed power cracked and then burst, dissipating as it went into the ether. Fenrir closed his eyes, leaning up against the wall, his knees bent and rested his hands on his knees.

He needed to be strong enough again to put the shield back up.

He did not think he could survive her rejection of him again.

"Grey, look at me. Are you okay?"

He didn't open his eyes, just said in a low tone. "You used the dagger to break their bond. It is useless now to you. I cannot break the bond and make you happy."

She did not respond for a time, then Fenrir felt Ashlyn punch him. "You were gonna die on me? You lied and told me that the dagger would only hurt, and it would have killed you. How could you think that I would be okay with that, Grey? What kind of monster do you think I am?"

Her voice broke at the end and Fenrir opened his eyes at the blaze of sadness along the bond. He tilted his head slightly, watching tears slip down her cheeks. Fascinated, Fenrir reached out and wiped one away with his thumb. "The thought of killing me upsets you. Why is that?"

Ashlyn looked at him, her eyes blazing as if she did not understand why he would ask that of her. He was confused too by the feelings that were coming through the bond, and it make him growl just a little and look away.

"Grey..." Ashlyn started to say but there was a commotion at the mouth of the cavern and the conversation that they had been about to have was halted.

Fenrir leaned his head forward, rested his forehead on his knees, and he felt Ashlyn's hand on the back of his head, and he released a sigh, hoping to commit the feel of her hand on him to memory. The case was over, and he would soon be of no more use to the team, or to Ashlyn, and she would send him away once more.

"Ash!"

Fenrir kept his head down as Ashlyn's hand left him, and he heard her rush forward. "Dad, I'm okay, we're okay. Keep Donnie out of here."

Fenrir wanted to flash away now that he knew Ashlyn was safe, but he did not have the energy to do so. He felt someone crouch down in front of him, and it was only then did he lift his gaze to look at his father.

"Are you okay, son?"

Fenrir knew that Loki's tone held concern in it, though he was not sure that he understood the expression on his father's face. Loki reached for him and rested a hand over his.

"Chrissy poisoned me with mistletoe. She was working with Odin. I have gotten rid of most of it, but the affects still linger. I cannot flash away. Can you flash me somewhere?"

Loki's hand was warm on his as he patted it. "Do you not want to wait for Ash? I'm sure she will want to make sure that you are well."

Fenrir glanced over at the blade Ashlyn had discarded on the ground next to him. Loki tracked where Fenrir's eyes had gone, and he sighed. "No. I do not think she will. I gave her a dagger that would sever the bond between us and did not tell her it would kill me. Ashlyn only realized when she killed Chrissy with it. She will be angry when she realizes that the mating bond can no longer be broken. I cannot stand to see her look at me with disdain once the adrenaline wears off. Please, father, take me anywhere but here."

Loki looked shocked, then nodded his head. "You can come home with me. Your sister was worried about you."

Loki got to his feet, then hooked an arm under Fenrir's, helping him to stand. Fenrir glanced over to see Ashlyn being embraced by her cat, then he lifted her arm to look at her newly gained tattoos and they bumped fists, the cat grinning at her before he lifted his gaze to Fenrir and inclined his head.

Fenrir returned the gesture and wished that Loki would just flash them away, so he did not have to endure any more of this pain in his chest. His vision blurred and he worried for a moment that he might have something wrong, then he noted the way Ashlyn had cried when she had felt sad.

Was he feeling sadness?

As if she had felt his unease, Ashlyn glanced over her shoulder and strode over, stopping only to pick up her beloved hammer. Fenrir closed his eyes, leaned more into Loki then he would like, a sudden need for comfort spearing him in the chest.

"Grey? What's wrong?"

He did not answer his mate, and he was …thankful when Loki answered for him. "I'm gonna take him back to our house so he can rest and get rid of the rest of the mistletoe. He can't flash just yet and I'd prefer if he wasn't alone. I'll look after him."

There was a moment of silence, and Fenrir could almost feel everyone in the cavern watching them, waiting to see what the outcome would be. He had noted in his journal everything that he had learned comfort watching with Ashlyn. He had been unable to put a halt to their mating, and in that he had failed her, the person who meant more to him than he could explain.

The dagger had been his means to make amends for that. To offer his life to Ashlyn, much like Charlie had done for Joe. And through no fault of his own, he had failed her again. His death would not be beautiful like on the TV show.

Fenrir would live and continue to disappoint Ashlyn.

He felt it even now.

"Don't you want to stay, Grey? You can stay with me."

Fenrir opened his eyes and looked at his mate in the eyes. He could feel her sadness, hear her thinking that she was confused and did not know what to do now. Fenrir was also confused, and her gaze narrowed as if she heard the thought and he tried to put up the wall between them.

The heel of her hand went to her head. "Don't, Grey. Don't shut me out."

"I find I do not have the energy to do so at the moment. As soon as I am well, I will initiate the block again. Loki will take me away and it will mute it like before."

Her gaze narrowed. "Is that what you want?"

No, it was not what he wanted. He wanted to gather his mate in his arms and bury his nose in the crook of her neck. He wanted to kiss her until he convinced her to keep him, and yet, he could not make himself say all of those things.

Derek had come to stand beside his daughter, and Fenrir shifted his gaze from Ashlyn to her father. "You need to find out who was meant to be guarding Odin while he gained enough power to manipulate Chrissy. There may be more who wish to lure the blood of Tyr here to free Odin." Fenrir glanced at his father. "He did not seem aware of Lyra's exis- tence. If she grows in power that might not remain the fact."

Ever strode over and rolled her eyes. "I think I need to have a chat with my father. I'll take Ricky with me. Might be enough of a deterrent for him if he thinks Ricky's hungry. Ash, I'll come check on you later."

Fenrir watched as the mother kissed her daughter on the cheek and then said. "You'll need to fill me in on what happened. I'm glad you and Mjölnir found each other again. Thor is no doubt raising a toast in the great hall that his niece is continuing with his legacy."

Ever and Ricky headed down into the darkness, and Fenrir glanced at Loki. "Can we leave?"

Loki looked from Ashlyn to Fenrir. "If that is what you want."

"It is."

Ashlyn reached for him, readying to place her hand on his chest and Fenrir knew that if she did, his resolve would falter, and he had already been weakened enough. When he stepped back, Ashlyn froze and then clutched her hand to her chest.

"Please, Grey. Please don't go."

It was ingrained in him to do all he could to please her, to give her what she wanted, and yet, he could not bring himself to do as she asked. Fenrir pulled his gaze from Ashlyn's, then his father flashed him away, and the moment they arrived in the garden of his father's home, Fenrir slipped into his true form, lifted his face toward the moon and howled out his pain.

He was aware of his father and his sister watching him, Loki with his arm around his youngest. Then Fenrir curled up on the deck and closed his eyes, the agonising feel of his mate at the other end of the bond, killing him slowly.

Chapter Twenty-one

Ash

ASH WANTED TO FEEL ECSTATIC THAT SHE AND HER HAMMER back and the case had been wrapped up, but she couldn't. It had killed her to watch Fenrir leave with Loki, to see him and feel him through the bond and know that she was responsible for him thinking that he had failed her by not being the one dead at the end of the dagger.

A couple of days had passed since then and when Fenrir had tried to put the block back in place, Ash had pushed back and told him not to dare doing that. He hadn't responded, but he hadn't tried to force the bond back in place either. She had tried to engage him in conversation through the bond, and he just didn't reply.

Ash had phoned Loki a couple of times to check in, and Loki had just said that Fenrir was still at his, and he was quiet, though that was not unusual for his son. When Ash asked if he was writing in his journal, Loki had sighed, and told Ash that he had been, then he had read all his entries from start to finish and then did it again.

"I fear he is hoping that by memorizing everything it will cure the part of him that is broken, and the part of him that his mate does not want."

Ash had cried when she had hung up the phone, Zach coming to comfort her. They had spoken after, when Zach had told her that he still had a shard of the Bifrost, and the

Fates had come to him to stop him from using it to go back and stop Ash from being taken.

"If I'd have done it, then you might not have gotten Mjölnir back. I almost fucked it up for you."

Ash had nudged his shoulder. "I would have done the same. Without a doubt and hey, it all worked out in the end, right?"

Except Ash felt like she was mourning the loss of someone she loved.

Ash glanced outside to where Fenrir was stood talking to Donnie, a beer in one hand and his eyes on where his sister danced with Zach. They had all been invited to Caitlyn and Donnie's to relax after the tough investigation, and Ash had been surprised when Erika told her that Loki and Lyra had convinced Fenrir to come.

Loki hadn't answered any of her calls after she had broken down and cried, and she knew that Fenrir must have felt it through the bond and ordered Loki not to talk to Ash about him any longer. She wanted to talk to him, to explain to him all that she had come to realize when they had been in that cavern and when she had seen him so ill.

Before they had come over to Caitlyn's, her dad had called her aside and told Ash of his intention to offer Fenrir a permanent place on the team, stating Fenrir had too much of a unique outlook to let go to waste and as Loki didn't want him to return to being isolated guarding Odin, having a purpose and a job might help him be around people more.

The only people missing today were Killian, Freya and Arik, who decided to stay home as Killian recovered from his injuries. Melanie and Ricky were around somewhere, and when Ash had joked to Zach that they might be in another compromising position, her best friend had told her to fuck off.

Ash heard Torin laugh and looked over to see Caitlyn

smiling at the other vampire, though she glanced up as if she felt Ash's eyes on her. Torin followed Caitlyn's gaze and tipped his whiskey glass at her. Ash raised her own bottle and turned back to catch Fenrir just moving his gaze from her.

"Are you going to go talk to him?"

Ash had felt Loki come to stand beside her and she shrugged. "I don't think he wants to talk to me."

"If you really think that, dearest Ashlyn, then you truly are blind."

Flashing him an annoyed glare, Loki laughed. "You forget I had centuries resisting a Valkyrie general who glared at me in a much worse fashion then you. I am immune to it after so long."

"Okay," Ash said with a snort. "Tell me then what I've been blind to because from my side, the moment I realized that I was in love with him, all of him, he was the one who ran off. Did the thrill of the chase end when I finally could admit my feelings?"

Loki was quiet for a moment as Lyra slipped and Fenrir moved to catch her, but Zach just grabbed her and twirled her like she had not lost her balance. Zach and Fenrir exchanged a look, then Fenrir went back to talking to Donnie.

"My son has always been resolute in his acceptance that you were his mate. That has never wavered, and I do not think it ever will. Fenrir does not know how to play games, Ash, he doesn't understand it. With the bond wide open, it was hard for him to separate the things that were his, and what was yours."

That made sense. Ash knew emotion and she could filter it, but Grey didn't have that, and he wouldn't let her help him.

"I asked him to come here tonight, and he refused at first,

because he didn't want you to feel uncomfortable. I could tell that the need to be near you was clawing him apart, and after his very persuasive sister convinced him, he came. His brain might work differently than yours, but Fenrir has never put his needs first over yours."

Ash took a drink from her beer. "I never apologised to you for how I treated you. Blaming you for letting him out. If I had known the truth, I would never have threated you so badly. I'm sorry, Loki."

Loki grinned at her, shaking his head. "It is okay, Ash. I offered to take the blame, and I'm not sorry that he mated with you. Doing so gave me the opportunity to know my son. If it meant taking the brunt of your anger so that it did not affect your relationship with Donnie or Ricky, I was happy to do it."

Loki nudged her shoulder and Ash smiled, catching Fenrir looking at her again.

"Your father offered him a job and he turned it down. He plans to go back to Niflheim. I don't think I can convince him otherwise."

Loki left her then, leaving her standing there. Was Fenrir really going to leave without speaking to her?

The patio door opened, and Lyra came in. Her dark eyes landed on Ash, and she glared. She opened her mouth to say something, then Ash heard a deep voice behind her.

"Leave her be, Lyra."

Lyra flushed and placed her hands on her hips. "You don't give me orders, Gideon Doyle."

Ash bit back a smile as her brother exhaled. "I'm not giving you orders. Just let it go for tonight."

Lyra and Gideon glared at each other, and then she stalked off. Ash glanced over her shoulder at Gideon. "Thanks, little brother."

Gideon just shrugged and went over to their dad. Gideon

was a tiny bit taller than their dad, and he rolled his eyes when their dad ruffled the hair that he liked to keep a little bit longer than needed. Ash felt a little sad for Loki, that the bond that her dad and Gideon had, would not be the same for Loki and Fenrir.

"You have to go through the hard stuff to appreciate the easy stuff. One day, it will be you talking to your kids or your friends' kids, and you'll get it. I promise."

Ash had spent the last couple of days mulling over all the advice that everyone had given her, but it was that advice from Donnie that had stuck with her. She had always considered that she would get to fall in love like in the movies. That her mate would romance her and dance with her until she was convinced, and they would fall in love and have as much of a great love story as her parents, as Caitlyn and Donnie, Erika and Loki, as much as Ricky and Melanie.

"I can't tell you whether it's right or wrong, Ash. I think your wolf realized that there would be no mate stronger than Fenrir that they would accept. You'd never have been happy with a weak mate. The power imbalance would have been too great, and it would have made you both miserable."

And she had been miserable. She was miserable and the thought of Fenrir going back to guard Odin made her feel even more miserable. Ash wasn't sure how they would work, but she wanted to try, she really wanted to try.

Ash looked up to see Fenrir watching her and when he handed Donnie his beer and started to walk away, she knew he had felt her misery down the bond and taken it as how she was feeling with him here.

Grey, wait...hang on a minute.

Ash had yanked the patio door open and was rushing toward Fenrir when Zach stepped in front of the god and stropped him from leaving. She loved her best friend even more in that moment.

Zach winked at Ash as he stepped out of the way and sauntered back the way Ash had come, and Ash stepped round Fenrir. He had a blank expression on his face; however, Ash could feel his trepidation along the bond.

"Hi."

"Ashlyn."

"Are you okay? After the mistletoe?"

Fenrir arched his brows. "I'm sure my father kept you up to date."

Ash shoved her hands into her pockets for something to do. "He did when he was answering my calls. But I want to hear it from you."

He tilted his head in that wolf way he did, regarding her with interest. Ash took a moment to run her gaze over him. His body was clad all in black, moulded to his muscular frame and hugged his body like a second skin. His sinful lips were pressed together, and Ash remembered what it felt to have this powerful man kiss her, to have those lips on her skin.

Ash shivered and then she heard Fenrir say through gritted teeth. "Careful, Ashlyn."

Ash grinned at him. "Can I not admire my mate?"

Fenrir's gaze narrowed. "I am not in the mood to play these games with you, Ashlyn."

Feeling brave and wanting to get her point across, Ash stepped into Fenrir, his hands automatically going to her hips, and she almost sighed at the contact. Fenrir sucked in a breath, like he was trying to inhale her scent and he leaned his forehead against hers.

"I realized something when we were in the cavern." Ash told him quietly, knowing that all of their nosy family would probably have an ear out. "I realized that I was being a fool, thinking that I wanted something other than you."

Fingers dug into her hips, but Fenrir refused to say anything.

"I told myself it was all physical, but that wasn't true. You never treated me like I was anything other than myself, Grey, and I didn't offer you the same. I'm sorry for that. I promise to make it up to you."

Ash leaned up and pressed a kiss to his mouth, felt the vibration of Fenrir's growl against her lips. Placing her hands on the side of Fenrir's neck, Ash held his gaze. "I told myself that I didn't want you, want this, but I was kidding myself. When you kiss me, nothing has ever felt so right I know that even if I had used the stupid dagger on you, there would never have been another mate for me."

"You cannot say all this and tell me that you want me as your mate, Ashlyn. Once this is done, it cannot be undone."

Ash grinned, digging her nails into the flesh at his neck like she knew he liked. "Good. I don't want it to be undone. You're mine, Fenrir. My mate and I love you."

Fenrir looked at her like she was insane, his eyes blinking, and the obsidian of his eyes seemed even darker still. "What did you say?"

"You're my mate and I love you."

Fenrir crushed his lips against hers and Ash felt the bond cement into place and she was powerless against the way he devoured her mouth, nipping at her bottom lip so she would part her lips, and then his tongue slid over hers and she moaned, her body tightening and she shivered against the immense pleasure at having her mate kissing her.

When they broke apart, Fenrir's lips curved into a smile that made her stomach do somersaults. "Your uncle was right."

"Arik?"

Fenrir nodded. "Yes. He told me that there were different types of love and that when you told me you love me, then I would feel it and understand. Or at least be able to tell the difference between how you love the cat and how you love me. Even when you didn't admit it, you loved me. It feels the same."

"Yup, I was just blinded by foolish stupid emotions. But I love you, Grey. With everything I have."

A hunger burned in Fenrir's eyes as he moved his hands from her hips to just under the curve of her ass and lifted her. Ash laughed as she wrapped her legs around him and he kissed her as he flashed them away, and then her back was against the wall and Fenrir kissed her some more, stealing her breath and her heart.

Fenrir was hard against her stomach and suddenly he had set her down and retreated a few steps, running his hand over his scalp. Ash gave him a moment because she knew all of this was new to him. It was new to her too, and while wasn't a virgin, having lost her virginity six months before she had met Fenrir with someone who hadn't been worth her time, Ash knew that Fenrir was a novice when it came to sex and even touch.

"I don't know how to touch you."

Ash chuckled and Fenrir glared at her. "Of course you do, Grey. Since the moment we met, your touch has set me on fire. I melt when you put your hands on me, your lips. We have time to work it all out. We have eternity to figure it out."

Fenrir didn't seem convinced, his thoughts all jumbled in his head, so Ash walked out of the cabin where they had flashed to, shivered at the sharp bite of cold as she leaned on the railing and looked over the picture-perfect landscape.

Snow blanketed the entire area, looking like a winter wonderland, and it was as if the entire place was made from peace and quiet and sheer beauty. Ash felt Fenrir come outside and he wrapped his arms around her from behind, rested his chin on her shoulder.

"Do you know where we are?" Ash shook her head, and Fenrir continued. "This is a cabin that Thor built for Loki. It cannot be reached by foot, and it is shielded from view by magic. We are on the Galdhøpiggen mountain. The cabin is in the Jotunheimen mountains within Jotunheimen National Park. My father suggested I bring you here, because it is where he feels closest to Thor, who built it for Loki so that he could be himself and at one with the cold."

"It's beautiful. I can just imagine Thor up here, putting it together. I'm glad your dad has this place to come to. He loved Thor."

Fenrir was quiet for a moment. "Will we live together? Like mates do?"

Ash leaned her head back against his chest. "I hope so. But only if you want. We can stay in the apartment with Zach, or we can look for a place of our own."

"It would make you sad to live away from the cat."

"Maybe, but I want to go to sleep with you beside me. I want to wake up without you leaving me and if we have to move out for you to feel comfortable, we can do that."

Ash turned in his arms and smiled up at her mate. "I can't believe that you're finally all mine."

"I have always been yours, Ashlyn. From the very first moment we met. I am unsure if what I feel for you is love, but everything in me, it has always been yours."

She felt this blaze along the bond, a possessive caress, and whether Fenrir understood it or not, Ash could tell that he loved her, was devoted to her, and she would try her best to love him in the way that he deserved.

Fenrir leaned down and nipped her jaw, her neck, and then he slipped off her jacket, the chilly air making her shiver as much as the god making her legs quiver. He sank his teeth into the curve of her neck, marking her, and she wanted to do the same to him, Fenrir, her mate.

His hand cupped her breast, squeezed, his lips on her skin and then they were walking back toward the cabin, losing clothes as they moved, Fenrir touching her with an expertise that she had not been expecting.

"I thought you didn't know how to touch me, Grey?"

Her mate grinned, wolfish as he picked her up and tossed her on the bed naked. "I made notes in my journal. I reread them when you went outside. Let me see if I'm a quick study."

Ash let loose a bark of laugher, as Fenrir prowled toward her, his powerful body all firm muscles and deliciousness. He ran his hands up and down her bare legs, parted her thighs and lowered his head between her legs. Then Ash stopped laughing as a moan slipped from her lips and her beautiful, fierce mate chuckled down the bond.

Epilogue

Ricky

RICKY STRODE OUT OF THE ELEVATOR AND HEADED DOWN THE hall to where Zach lived with Ash. He hadn't heard from Zach in two days, and it wasn't like his kid not to check in. With Ash away with Fenrir, Zach must be enjoying the peace and quiet, but Ricky hadn't been able to get rid of the unease in his stomach.

His wife and mate had sent him over to check in, and the unease only got worse when he saw the front door to Zach and Ash's apartment slightly opened. Taking out his gun, Ricky slowly pushed open the door and called out. "Zach, it's dad. You okay?"

The silence that greeted him sent a shiver along his spine. The moment Ricky stepped inside; it was obvious there had been a struggled. Furniture was broken, the entire apartment trashed with personal belongings thrown everywhere.

Ricky went down the hall, checked Zach's room and it was untouched, but someone had smashed up Zach's computer room, where he kept a lot of his inventions and ideas. Ricky's nose caught the scent of blood as he came back to the living room and crouched down to get a better look.

Fresh blood streaked the wooden floor, and he knew it was Zach's, his heart pounding as he pulled out his phone, and pressed to make the call.

"D, it's me. Something's happened to Zach. I think he's been taken."

His eyes were focused on the blood, and he snarled. "Get the team here right now, D. There's blood. Zach's blood. Some fucker took my kid and I need to find him. I really need to find him."

When he found whoever had harmed his kid, Ricky would kill them.

And make them rue the day they ever laid hands on his son.

The story will continue in
Hunt You Down, Paranormal Investigations Team Book 2.

Playlists

Ash

- UNSECRET ft Krigare - Heroes Never Die (Skrybe Remix)
- Moncrieff - Serial Killer
- AURORA - Running With The Wolves
- Dubkiller - Dynasty
- Izzy Bizu - Dumb
- Conquer Divide - Paralyzed
- Barns Courtney - Supernatural
- VUKOVI - QUENCH
- Royal & the Serpent - IM FINE
- Palaye Royale - Lifeless Stars
- AWOLNATION - Freaking Me Out
- Neoni - FANGS
- VUKOVI - XX
- Loveless - MIDDLE OF THE NIGHT
- MS MR - Bones
- Florence + The Machine - Howl
- Mumford & Sons - The Wolf
- David Guetta - She Wolf (Falling to Pieces) [feat. Sia]
- Taylor Swift - Vigilante Shit
- Dove Cameron - Breakfast
- Bella Poarch - Villain

- Neoni - DARKSIDE
- Halsey - I am not a woman, I'm a god
- Neoni - I'M NOT SORRY
- Allie X - Devil I Know
- K/DA - VILLAIN
- FJØRA - heaven is a place on earth
- The Weeknd - Nothing Is Lost (You Give Me Strength)
- Call Me Karizma - Kinda Scary
- Mimi Webb - 24/5
- Saint Mesa – Wolf
- PVRIS - GODDESS
- Leah Kate - Monster
- YONAKA - PANIC
- Paramore - Decode
- Thunderstorm Artis - Stronger (Grey's Anatomy Version)
- Ben Howard - Black Flies
- Nothing But Thieves - Gods
- Mammoth WVH - Another Celebration at the End of the World
- Bring Me The Horizon - Kingslayer (feat. BABYMETAL)
- League of Legends New Jeans - GODS
- Zayde Wølf Ft EDVN Sam Tinnesz- Maniac
- Bad Omens - ARTIFICIAL SUICIDE
- Sleep Token - Jaws
- Jake Bugg - Lightning Bolt
- Yenne - The Wolves
- Armin van Buuren ft Anne Gudrun- Love Is A Drug
- YONAKA - PREDATOR
- Rivals - Thunderstorm

- Merci Raines - Bite Before I Bark
- SKÁLD - Seven Nation Army
- Tommee Profitt ft William Joseph - Thunderstruck

Fenrir

- VUKOVI - TAINTED
- The Hunna - Trash
- The Hunna – Apologies
- Hidden Citizens - Hungry Like The Wolf - 2020 Remaster
- Godsmack - Surrender
- NOTHING MORE - TURN IT UP LIKE (Stand In The Fire)
- NOTHING MORE - DON'T LOOK BACK
- NOTHING MORE - DÉJÀ VU
- MISSIO - Villain
- PVRIS - ANIMAL
- Letdown. - Freak
- Call Me Karizma – Blood
- Dayseeker - Without Me
- Three Days Grace - I Am The Weapon
- Bad Omens - Just Pretend
- Highly Suspect - Wolf
- Ren Marabou - Fenrir
- Five Finger Death Punch - Times Like These
- Kat Leon ft Sam Tinnesz- I'll Make You Love Me
- merci, mercy - Why'd You Only Call Me When You're High?
- Circa Waves - Living in the Grey
- Sam Tinnesz ft Silverberg - Wolves
- Tribal Blood - Supernatural
- Godsmack - Cryin' Like A Bitch!!
- Fall Out Boy - Love From The Other Side
- Joey Valence & Brae – Startafight
- nothing,nowhere. - THIRST4VIOLENCE (feat. Freddie Dredd & Silverstein)
- The Sherlocks - Sirens

- Demob Happy - Voodoo Science
- Godsmack - You And I
- Bad Omens - The Grey
- Fall Out Boy - Hold Me Like a Grudge
- grandson - Drones
- nothing,nowhere. - VEN0M (feat. UNDEROATH)
- Wage War - Godspeed
- Bring Me The Horizon - Deathbeds
- SAINT PHNX - Bury a Friend
- KID BRUNSWICK - Stained
- Bad Omens - Like A Villain
- Nothing But Thieves - Do You Love Me Yet?
- Lil Uzi Vert - Werewolf (feat. Bring Me The Horizon)
- Sleep Token - Chokehold
- Sleep Token - Take Me Back To Eden
- Stitched Up Heart - Immortal
- Saint Asonia - Wolf (feat. John Cooper of Skillet)
- 2WEI Ft Marvin Brooks- Wolves
- Bad Omens - V.A.N
- Bohnes - You've Created a Monster
- Bohnes - Vicious
- Manafest - Learning How To Be Human

Zach

- The Used - Fuck You
- Sam Tinnesz - Sound off the Sirens
- Helmet - Unsung
- Seven Mary Three - Water's Edge
- Faces On Film – Sonnet
- Bea Miller - Playground (from the series Arcane League of Legends)
- FJØRA - you're so vain
- 2WEI - Bad to the Bone - Extended Version
- Godsmack - When Legends Rise
- G2 Jeris Johnson & Yonaka – Detonate
- Paramore - You First
- KID BRUNSWICK - Blow – Remix
- YONAKA - Welcome to My House
- Zayde Wølf - Jumping Into Danger
- Royal & the Serpent - ONE NATION UNDERDOGS
- Masked Wolf - Dark Matter
- KID BRUNSWICK - Dear Anonymous
- Tommee Profitt ft John Lindahl- Legends
- Manafest - I Run With Wolves
- League of Legends Mako, The Word Alive, The Glitch Mob - RISE
- UNSECRET Que Parks- Fierce
- Staind - Better Days (feat. Dorothy)

<u>Torin</u>

- Imagine Dragons - Bones - twocolors Remix
- Fred again.. - Clara (the night is dark)
- The Warning - CHOKE (with grandson & Zero 9:36)
- Aisha Badru - Bridges
- STARSET - Waiting On The Sky To Change
- Set It Off - Wolf in Sheep's Clothing
- I Prevail - Bad Things
- Disturbed - Hey You
- Gang of Youths - Achilles Come Down
- I DONT KNOW HOW BUT THEY FOUND ME - Choke
- Slush Puppy - EAT SPIT! (feat. Royal & the Serpent)
- Malia J - Smells Like Teen Spirit
- FJØRA – toxic
- Ely Eira - Never Say Die
- Demi Lovato - Still Alive - From the Original Motion Picture Scream VI
- PVRIS - GOOD ENEMY
- KID BRUNSWICK - The Fall
- Tommee Profitt ft Royal & Serpent - Wicked

Also By Susan Harris

THE MURDERING HOUR NOVELS

Own The Night, book 1

Dwell In Darkness, book 2

DEFY THE STARS

A Tale of Two Houses, book 1

Until Death Do Us Part, book 2

In Defiance of the Stars, book 3

Courting Darkness, a novella

THE SANGUINE CROWN

Chaos Theory, book 1

Butterfly Effect, book 2

Wicked Game, book 3

Burn Notice, book 4

Fight Song, book 5

THE SICARIUS SECURITY SERIES

Kiss Of Death, book 1

Leap Of Faith, book 2

Visions Of Destiny, book 3

War Of Hearts, book 4

Flames Of Conflict, book 5

ANTHOLOGY

A Lot Like Christmas

Acknowledgements

None of this would be possible without an amazing team supporting me! Many thanks to:

Publishing House: CTP Publishing
Cover design: Gem Promotions
Interior Formating: Gem Promotions

And as always:
Thank you to all the readers!
Whether this is your first book by me or you've been with me for years! I only get to do this because of you, and I am eternally grateful to each and every one of you who took a chance on this Irish author.

About The Author

Susan Harris is a writer from Cork, Ireland and when she's not torturing her readers with heart-wrenching plot twists or killer cliffhangers, she's probably getting some new book related ink, binging her latest TV or music obsession, or with her nose in a book.

Susan LOVES connecting with her fans!
www.susanharrisauthor.com

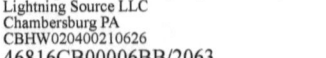